How to Excavate a Heart

How to Excavate a Heart

JAKE MAIA ARLOW

HARPER TEEN
An Imprint of HarperCollinsPublishers

Content warning: Contains a brief description of past sexual assault (survivor's experience is validated).

HarperTeen is an imprint of HarperCollins Publishers.

How to Excavate a Heart

For information address HarperCollins Children's Books, a division of HarperCollins Publishers, 195 Broadway, New York, NY 10007.
www.epicreads.com

Library of Congress Cataloging-in-Publication Data

Names: Arlow, Jake Maia, author.
Title: How to excavate a heart / Jake Maia Arlow.
Description: First edition. | New York, NY : HarperTeen, [2022] | Audience: Ages 14 up. | Audience: Grades 10-12. | Summary: Snowy weather and fish fossils help bring together two Jewish college freshmen spending winter break in Washington, D.C.
Identifiers: LCCN 2022008181 | ISBN 9780063078727 (hardcover)
Subjects: CYAC: Dating—Fiction. | Lesbians—Fiction. | Museums—Fiction. | Internship programs—Fiction. | Jews—Fiction. | Washington (D.C.)—Fiction. | LCGFT: Novels.
Classification: LCC PZ7.1.A7475 Ho 2022 | DDC [Fic]—dc23
LC record available at https://lccn.loc.gov/2022008181

Typography Michelle Gengaro-Kokmen
22 23 24 25 26 PC/LSCH 10 9 8 7 6 5 4 3 2 1
❖
First Edition

To my mom—I'm sorry for going through my teenage phase as an adult during a pandemic. I love you.

And to Lena, for the matzah brei. Спасибо (for everything).

Dead Fish Can't Break Your Heart

Four hours. That's how long I've been in the car with my mom.

We spent the first three arguing, but for this last one we mixed it up and sat in the most uncomfortable silence imaginable.

Even the windshield wipers are on edge. They're traveling through their arc at an alarming rate, but it's no use. The snow started when my mom and I gave up on talking, and it hasn't let up since.

So I almost jump out of my seat when she says, "What does that sign say?" in a panicked voice, leaning as far forward as her seat belt will allow.

"Uh, which one?" It's impossible to locate any identifiable shape through the whiteout.

"Never mind." She puts on a pointless turn signal and maneuvers off the highway.

"Mom, what are you doing?"

"I'm pulling off I-95," she snaps. "What does it look like I'm doing?"

That shuts me up. Well, that and the fact that I don't want to distract her, lest we die in a car wreck.

We're in a more residential area now, and the snow's coming down even harder than it was a minute ago. It streams toward the windshield in well-defined flakes illuminated by our Subaru's headlights.

And that's when I see her.

"Mom—"

She's crossing the street. A girl, wearing a red beanie and a puffy coat.

All of my muscles tense and I press my foot into the matted rug as if I could hit the brakes from the passenger side and stave off tragedy by sheer force of will.

My mom glances over at me. She clearly hasn't noticed the girl, and she picks the worst possible moment to rehash the argument we've spent most of the car ride having: "Are you sure this internship is what you want?"

She's not stopping.

"Mom!"

We're going to hit her.

"MOM, WATCH OUT!"

"FUCK!"

The girl must not have noticed us either, because she turns her head in shock and stares right at me.

Time stops.

We're going to kill her.

And it's all my fault. If I hadn't been terrible to my mom this whole car ride, she wouldn't be so angry and distracted. And if she wasn't so angry and distracted, we wouldn't be on a collision course with an actual, very-much-alive (for the moment) human being.

To be fair, I can't account for the blizzard, but at least 85 percent of this is my fault.

Because, of course, after all the shit I've been through this past week, I might as well add murder to the list too.

"Are you sure you'll be okay?" my mom had asked earlier in the trip, somewhere along the monotonous factories of the New Jersey highway. She looked at me for way too long before turning back to the road.

"I'll be fine."

"I don't like the idea of you spending Christmas away."

"I'll be fine," I said again, teeth clenched.

"You've never been away for Christmas. Do you realize that? Never."

"We don't even celebrate Christmas," I said to her, but

it felt pretty unnecessary considering the sheer quantity of Jewish guilt she'd been laying on me the entire car ride.

"All the same, Shani, it's the *holidays.*" She swerved a bit into the lane next to ours as she spoke, and a lime-green Mazda honked at us. She flipped them off.

"Is it, though? Like, is it *really* the holidays?" The brightly colored car sped past us. "Hanukkah's over, and it's complete bullshit anyway. It was invented by American capitalists so that Jewish kids could be included in the Christian hegemony."

I was proud of myself for using the word *hegemony.*

"Is that what they're teaching you at college?"

"No," I said, pouting a little. "I've always thought that."

"Yeah, you've always *hated* the eight days of thoughtful gifts I've given you." She swerved again, but into the lane on the *other* side of her, which was very egalitarian, I thought.

"Okay, jeez."

I sighed loudly and crossed my arms. I knew I was being childish and combative and all-around awful. But no matter what she said, she wasn't going to convince me to stay at home in Queens for the holidays. My mom and I had been snapping at each other from the moment she picked me up from my first semester of college, just three short (but at the same time incredibly, unendingly long) days ago.

Maybe she would've understood if I told her why I was feeling this way, but I couldn't do that.

If I was being honest, here's how I *wanted* to respond to

my mom's request: "Sure, yeah, I'd love to stay home for the holidays. But, now that you mention it, the thought of being in our apartment for winter break makes me want to rip all my teeth out, one by one."

For the three days I was home, all I did was avoid my mom's gaze and respond to her perfectly reasonable questions with one-word answers. I had reverted back to being a petulant child.

Because the thing no one tells you about going away to college is that even if your first semester beats you to a pulp and leaves you with no faith in humanity, it doesn't feel better to be at home. The couch no longer remembers your butt, the floor creaks in places it never used to, and your mom will switch the mug cabinet with the plate cabinet (which you'll fight about, of course, because you'll take any excuse you have to be shitty to her).

And all of my anger—all of it—is because of Sadie.

Sadie had told me she loved me on a Thursday. I'd been too anxious to tell her that I loved her before then, because I thought three months was too soon. We started dating two days into first-year orientation, and I knew I loved her, well, two days into first-year orientation.

All semester, we had a perfect routine: we'd sit in her dorm when her roommate wasn't there and watch Netflix. We mostly stuck to crafting-based competition shows, though we also watched all the movies in the "LGBTQ Movies" category.

Well, except the ones where women had sex. It would be too awkward to watch other people doing something we had thus far been too scared to do.

Or at least that *I'd* been too scared to do.

But even when I was just sitting with her, watching TV, my neck hurting from leaning against her shoulder, I felt a tug at my chest and I knew it was love.

I was all the lesbian stereotypes in one and I didn't care. They were stereotypes for a reason. I pictured our wedding, rustic and small. Neither of us would wear white, and all the guests would leave saying things like, "That challenged my conception of what a wedding is and, frankly, what it should be!"

"I don't really believe in this," Sadie had said to me on the Thursday in question, "but I just thought you should know."

"Know what?" I asked, looking up at her from my well-worn spot on her shoulder. I knew what she was going to say would be serious because she had paused *Jeopardy!*

She stared straight ahead as she said, "That I love you."

I immediately told her I loved her too

But after that I was stressed, because if we were in love, then the next logical step was sex. And seeing as I had never done *it* before, I felt like I needed to prepare.

So I Googled some unhinged key words on a very private

browser. I even cut my nails short because I knew that was something queer women were supposed to do. But when the time came for us to have sex, none of my preparation mattered. Because . . .

Oh god. This is so embarrassing.

Okay. We had sex for the first time a couple of days after we said "I love you," and, as it turned out, it was also the last time. That Sunday, she texted me that we needed to talk, and an hour later we had broken up. And two hours after that, I was heading home for winter break.

I can't think about this right now. I'm going to vomit.

The worst thing is, I'm not even mad at Sadie. If she were here in the car, I'd probably beg her to take me back. Because I'm pathetic, and she was the first girl I ever dated.

I didn't tell my mom about Sadie, so she must think I've been sad and angry for no reason. I had planned on telling my mom about our relationship over winter break, but now that we're broken up, there's no point.

I'd have to tell her that I was dating a girl, and that I like girls, and, oh yeah, now that you mention it, the aforementioned girl and I are no longer dating because something went horribly wrong seventy-two hours after we said "I love you."

"You can stay, you know," my mom had said yet again later in the car ride.

"What?"

"It's not too late. I'll turn the car around right now." She'd demonstrated her commitment to this statement by sharply turning the steering wheel to the left. She was met with a chorus of honks and had briefly removed both hands from the wheel for maximum flip-off ability.

"I really can't," I'd told her in a flat voice that I hated hearing coming out of my mouth. "I need to do this internship."

"You don't *need* to do anything."

"Well, I'm not going back to New York. This is an *amazing* opportunity for me. Do you know how many first-years have ever gotten into this lab?" When she didn't answer I said, "One. Just me. I get to study fish evolution with the best paleoichthyologist in the entire world. So, no, I'm not staying home."

She was silent for a moment, and I thought I'd won until she said, "If you're going to study dead animals, why not dinosaurs? Everyone loves dinosaurs."

"Oh my god, Mom. Literally stop."

She was never going to get how big of a deal it was that I got this Smithsonian internship. Dr. Charles Graham is the most famous paleoichthyologist—someone who studies extinct fish and their evolution—in the world, and I get to work with him for a month. Of course, being a paleoichthyologist makes him less of a celebrity than, like, a vaguely Instagram-famous cat, but still.

And, okay, fine. Doing this internship is about more than just working with Dr. Graham. I lost myself this past semester; the person I was for the first eighteen years of my life disappeared.

From the moment I started dating Sadie, she became my single focus.

But that's done now. I've decided that I won't be dating anyone ever again. Relatedly, I'm also never having sex again, because sex ruins everything. I will do neither. I'll be the Jewish version of a nun.

Working in the lab will be perfect. I can focus on dead fish. Dead fish can't break your heart. They can only teach you about the world and what it means to exist in it. Also, they've been extinct for millions of years, and in that way they're extremely lucky.

And up until my mom pulled off the snow-covered highway, I was confident that my time in DC would be uneventful. The perfect follow-up to my semester with Sadie.

But now we're staring death in the face.

And death is staring back, wearing a red beanie.

I'm about to be a murderer.

The car barrels toward the girl, and her neutral expression flips in an instant to terror.

My mom finally sees her and frantically tries to slam on the brakes. She pumps them over and over, but between the snow and ice, the car won't stop.

Then there's the thud.

The bump.

Not a hard bump, but still. A bump.

We *bumped* a person with our car.

Beanie girl disappears from view and I hold my breath, certain she's dead. My mom and I are both frozen to our seats.

And then she stands up in front of the car, brushes herself off, and starts screaming.

I can't quite make out all of what she says through the sturdy Subaru walls, but it sounds a lot like, "What the fuck are you doing?" and "Are you shitting me?" and "I could've died," etc.

She slams her fists against the hood, yelling and yelling and yelling.

I'm transfixed.

She's probably around my age, with big eyes and semi-translucent white skin that seems to glow in the light of the high beams. The whole scene is oddly . . . beautiful?

I shake the thought out of my head as my mom opens her door to check on our victim.

But as she steps out, the person yells, "What the fuck?" and slams her fist against the hood again. "Stay in the fucking car!"

So my mom closes the door.

The girl stomps away, but before she gets too far, she turns back to us. Then she looks me directly in the eye and flips me off.

My mom and I are silent for a moment.

"Well," she says, clutching the wheel, "I hope not everyone in DC is like her."

Half-Century-Old Sex Ghosts

My mom and I don't talk for the rest of the short ride to our destination. I thought she might bring up the fact that we almost vehicularly manslaughtered someone, but so far, nothing.

She pulls over onto a quaint residential street and turns the car off, but my heart won't stop pounding. It's been trying to free itself from my chest ever since we bumped into the girl.

The thing is, I'm sort of happy about the palpitations. For the first time in days, I'm not angry or sad. I feel—and I know this sounds terrible—exhilarated. And maybe that exhilaration isn't so wrong, because the girl was fine.

Even so, I can't stop thinking about her. The look she had on her face right after we bumped into her is seared into my retinas, the way her expression transformed from shock to fear to anger. When I saw that familiar emotion on her face, I almost wanted to help her. To get out of the car and walk her home. Make sure she was okay.

And, because I'm my own worst enemy, I *also* can't stop thinking about how cute she was.

Which is horrible. I know.

Like, pull it together, Shani—you of all people should understand that we're *not* going there.

You can't go around thinking these things about every cute girl you bump into with your car. That would be anarchy. It's no way to live.

"I think it's that one," my mom says, pointing to a house across the street. It's square and ivy-covered, with three stories and a dark redbrick exterior dusted with snow like a holiday postcard.

For some reason, my mom's simple comment flips the anger switch in my brain back on. I wish I could tell it to stay off, but the response comes out of me before I can help it.

"You *think* it's that one?" I ask. "I thought you said you've been here before." I wince at the words coming out of my mouth.

I'm not a terrible person.

At least, I don't think I am. It's just that it's so much

easier to take my anger about Sadie out on Mom than it is to do anything else about it.

"I have," she says. "In the nineties." She leans closer to the car window, as if that will help her to better identify the house. "Yeah, it's definitely that one."

I roll my eyes, knowing that I look like a caricature of an angry teenager and not caring.

The whole DC living situation was taken care of without my input. When I was deep in my Sadie-based fugue state for all of first semester, I didn't worry about finding a place to live during the internship, because it no longer seemed important.

Even though my mom hasn't exactly been subtle about wanting me home for winter break, she still found me a place to stay. She texted me a few weeks ago saying, "ur gr8 gma's friend Beatrice lives in dc & said u could stay if u need 2." (My mom texts that way because she thinks it's cool. I don't even know where to start with that one.)

While my mom grabs her jacket from the back of the car, I jump out the passenger side and run to ring the doorbell. A few seconds later, the door creaks open.

"Hi, doll," an ancient-looking woman says.

I have to crane my neck almost all the way down just to meet her eyes. She couldn't have been that tall when she was young, but now she's absolutely minuscule, a product of gravity and time. "What are you doing out in the cold?" she asks, then grabs on to my arm with a veiny and very wrinkled hand. She drags me inside with unexpected force.

The house has low ceilings, like it was built in the 1800s, when the general population was half the height it is now due to scurvy or some other old-timey ailment. It's perfect for this woman, though, who beams at me from the base of an ornate wooden staircase. She's barely taller than the handrail.

"Now, who are you?" she asks with a bark-like laugh. "I'm thinking I probably don't know you, but if I do, you can slap me across the face and say, 'Beatrice, you old bag, we met thirty years ago.' Though by the looks of you you're no older than what? Twenty? Twenty-five? Still a kid, obviously. And before you say, 'Beatrice, I'm a grown woman,' let me tell you that anyone under fifty is a child and that's the truth!" She laughs again and takes a huge breath.

I'm not quite sure what to say to that, or whether she really *did* want me to slap her, so I say, "Uh, I'm Shani."

"Speak up, doll."

"I'M SHANI."

"Well, there's no use screaming."

"I'm Shani," I say again, trying to find some midpoint that this woman—Beatrice—won't find offensive.

"That's nice, doll," she says, and at this point I'm certain she'll never call me by my name and will simply refer to me as "doll," which is more than fine. "And why are you here, might I ask?"

I clear my throat. "I'm staying with you for a month?"

She reaches up to grab my shoulders in a motion so fast I'm worried she might be possessed. "You're Sandy's girl? I should've known with that hair!"

The hair she's referring to is black and thick, with loose curls flying any which way they please. Everyone in the Levine family shares this trait. Mine is cut short (a decision that happened, like, two days after I realized I was gay) and puffs out around my face like a lion's mane. "How is that old bag? Goodness, why didn't you say something sooner?"

I don't have the heart to tell her that Sandy, our one mutual connection and my great-grandmother, died more than a decade ago.

But luckily, I don't have to, because at that moment my mom stomps in, knocking snow off her boots.

Beatrice lets go of my shoulders and stops cold. "Is that little Rachie?"

"Auntie Bea!" my mom says, squeezing Beatrice so hard I'm worried she'll break her.

I'm surprised to hear my mom call her "auntie," considering I've never met this woman. It's always weird to confront the fact that my mom had a life before I was born.

"I have to get the others down here," Beatrice says. "Oh, they're going to be thrilled!" She takes a deep breath and shouts up the stairs, "Come meet the new doll who's staying with us for a while," as if she's running an off-brand

American Girl doll motel and I'm the lucky eighteen-inch newcomer.

My mom had told me other girls lived here, but I haven't had to fully process that fact until right now as they bounce down the stairs.

They're both around my age. One of them is wearing an American University T-shirt and has dark brown skin and long box braids put up into a bun on top of her head. She puts her arm around Beatrice, who beams up at her. The other girl sits on the bottom step and nods my way. She has freckled white skin and bushy blond hair pulled into a low ponytail.

"Angels, this is the new doll," Beatrice says, not using a single name to introduce me to my roommates.

The girl with her arm around Beatrice's waist must've been thinking the same thing because she says, "I'm Lauren."

"Tasha," the girl on the stairs says in an accent I can't quite place.

"Shani," I tell them.

"Are you here for school?" Lauren asks. "I know there's a ton of spring semester transfers to American, and lucky for you I run a transfer orientation that you'll *love*. In the fall we do a cookout, but no one wants to stand around a grill in January, you know? So I was thinking about a potluck. But the last time we had one no one brought a single vegetable."

When she's done, I wonder briefly if speaking in monologues is a prerequisite for living in this house, or if it's just something Beatrice and Lauren bond over.

"I'm not transferring," I tell her. And then add, "Sorry," because I feel bad for throwing a wrench in her potluck plans.

"Well, you can still come to the dinner if you want to bring a crudités platter."

"Doll, let her breathe!" Beatrice squeezes Lauren and then wraps her fingers around my arm with her viselike grip. "Breathe, doll!"

She seems serious, so I make a big show of gulping down a lung full of air and loudly exhaling.

"Ha! And she's funny. You'll fit in perfectly around here."

Tasha has her head in her hands, and Lauren looks over at her and snorts with laughter.

"Now that we're all acquainted, do you dolls want to tell her the rules?" Beatrice asks after she releases me.

I try to keep my face neutral, but I wasn't expecting this. I haven't had anyone tell me what to do or how to live since I left for college this past summer. Sure, there are rules in dorms, but those are more . . . light suggestions than actual requirements. Almost everyone drinks, smokes, burns candles, and has an illegal pet or two.

But when a woman as old as Beatrice has rules, you can't

not follow them. Disappointing her would be like disappointing my (great-) grandma. And honestly, I *want* rules. I want someone to tell me what to do, so I don't fuck up like I did for the past three months.

So I listen carefully as Lauren says, "We're quiet late at night, we take out the trash when it's full, we clean up our messes in the kitchen,"—all of this feels fair, expected, even—"and no boys allowed in your room, ever."

I almost laugh out loud at this last one. But instead of doing that, I adjust the rule in my head, changing it to "no girls allowed in your room, ever," and feel good about it. I *want* to be cloistered away for the next month, and now there's a mandate saying it must be so.

"That all makes sense."

"Fantastic, doll," Beatrice says. "Why don't I show you to your room?"

She climbs the stairs, taking them two at a time, and I hurry to catch up.

But I'm distracted by the art on the staircase walls. There are crosses and portraits of saints, along with some Christmas decorations—garlands, candy canes, a couple of wreaths. I start to worry that she's really religious and that, even though she was friends with my great-grandmother, she'll be disappointed that I'm Jewish.

But then I get to the top of the stairs, where there's a beige quote block with bold capital letters that says,

"ALCOHOL: BECAUSE NO GREAT STORY EVER STARTED WITH SOMEONE EATING A SALAD," and I feel significantly less uncomfortable.

When my mom and I get to the second-floor landing, Beatrice is waiting for us by an open door. "This is your room, doll."

It's much bigger than I thought it would be: there's a king bed, two dressers, two nightstands. Two of everything.

"It used to be my master bedroom, back when my husband was alive." Beatrice plops down on the edge of the bed.

I sit beside her. "I'm so sorry."

"Don't be, doll. He died fifty years ago." Beatrice gazes wistfully around the room. "We made so many good memories in here."

"I can tell," I say, because this seems like the kind of thing you say to a nostalgic old woman.

"All six of my children were conceived in this room."

I lurch off the bed and stare at my mom with wide, disbelieving eyes. She stares back at me with the same, our disagreement temporarily forgotten.

"Where do you sleep, Auntie Bea?" my mom asks quickly. "Since Shani's staying in here?"

"The attic," Beatrice says. "I haven't been able to fall asleep in this room since my husband died. But I'm glad it'll be put to good use."

My face gets hot. It certainly won't be "put to good use"

in the same way it was when Beatrice and her husband conceived their six children here. Remember: Jewish nun.

But, oh my god. I need to burn the sheets.

"Well, I think I'll help Shani get unpacked now," my mom says in a way nicer voice than she's used with me all day. I get the feeling we're both just waiting for Beatrice to leave so we can fight again. "Thank you for your help, Auntie Bea."

"Of course, doll. I'll be upstairs if you need me."

And with that, Beatrice ascends another flight of stairs to her attic bedroom.

My mom turns to examine the dresser and the family photos that definitely contain at least some of the kids who were conceived in here.

"Holy shit." My mom grabs a framed invitation and holds it close to her face.

"What?"

She turns it around to show me, and there's a photo of Beatrice when she was young. Her skin is smooth and her dark hair is pinned up in a fancy, old-fashioned way.

"Why 'holy shit'?" I ask. "Just Beatrice when she was young?"

"No, look at what it says on the bottom."

I lean in and read: *Please join us in celebrating Beatrice Mancini's 90th birthday!*

"She's ninety?" I ask, in awe.

I just watched this woman bound up a flight of stairs

two at a time. It seems impossible that she's nearly a century old.

"No, read the date of the party," my mom says.

I move closer to read the smaller text on the card.

The party happened more than six years ago.

"She's ninety-six?" I practically scream.

"Isn't that wild?"

I nod, then look around the room, now even more interested in Beatrice.

"She met your great-grandma at college," my mom adds. "Just goes to show that the people you meet in college can be friends for life."

My mom tries to hold my gaze, but after that last comment my anger comes streaming back in. My college experience has been less "friends for life" and more "ex-girlfriends who'll make going back to college for spring semester a waking nightmare."

My mom doesn't know that, though. She doesn't know anything. And I can't blame her for trying to get *something* out of me, even if that's not going to happen.

"Can we just unpack?" I ask.

"Sure," my mom says. "Fine."

After a few awkward minutes of hanging clothes my mom asks, "Do you want different sheets or something? I could buy you some."

"What? No. Don't do that," I say, even though I had

been thinking just moments before that I'd like to set the bed on fire.

And my mom says, "Just trying to help."

And I say, "You don't need to."

And then there's more silence.

It takes a little while, but once we're finished unpacking my mom sits down and sighs. "I need something to eat."

I shrug. "Fine."

"If you're not hungry that's okay, but I'm starving."

"I said it's fine."

She shakes her head, then puts on reading glasses and scrolls through her phone for a minute. "There's a café down the street that's open late. We can walk."

Even though it's still snowing, I don't fight her, and we trudge through the slush to a place called The Big Blue Dog.

When we get inside, I like it immediately. It's warm and bright and smells like coffee—the three most important features of a good café. I start to think that I might actually feel like eating something after all, but then I look into the baked-goods display window and spot a giant carrot cake.

My stomach turns and bile creeps into my mouth.

I know this is an odd reaction to a baked good, but as with most things these days, the bile has more to do with Sadie.

On our first dining hall "date," Sadie and I ate shitty pizza and then split a slice of carrot cake.

That was when I learned she snorted when she laughed, and that she was smart and gorgeous and—

My blood boils in my veins until all that's left is a concentrate of cells and rage. The once-cozy café is now a hellish nightmare, and I want to hurl my fist through the glass display and smash the carrot cake to bits.

"Shani," my mom says, getting my attention.

"What?"

"The young man asked what you want." She points to the kid standing behind the counter. He looks like he just finished puberty an hour ago—gangly, pimply, dead in the eyes.

"Nothing," I say to my mom. "I'm good," I tell the kid.

"Come on, you gotta have something," my mom says, and the kid nods a little too vigorously along with her.

"Stop it," I say through my teeth, as if my mom is the one embarrassing me in front of this poor kid who has to work in a snowstorm, and not the other way around.

"She'll have an apricot Danish," my mom tells the teen barista, and he puts on gloves and grabs the pastry.

"I won't," I mutter.

But once my mom pays and we're sitting at a small table by the window, I immediately take a bite of the Danish.

"Last chance," my mom says after a minute.

"What?"

"You can still come home." She takes a sip of coffee from a large mug with the titular Big Blue Dog on it.

"I already told you I can't," I say, but the restorative

Danish bite must've flipped the anger switch off, because it comes out sounding more defeated than anything else. "I'm doing the internship."

"If you change your mind—"

"I'm not gonna."

She holds up a palm. "I know, I know. But if you do, I'll come get you."

I don't know why she's being so good to me. I wish she'd be as mean as I've been to her so that I could feel okay about how I've been acting.

After a minute, my mom says quietly into her own Danish, "I'm not looking forward to being alone for the holidays, you know."

I stare down at my lap, full of guilt, and see that I have a text from Taylor—my best friend since diapers—giving me an excuse to continue avoiding my mom's gaze.

TAY: hows dc ?

ME: cold and snowy

also i'm staying in a 96 y/o woman's bedroom

TAY: with her? ;]]]

ME: lol ew no get your head out of the gutter

but i can't talk rn

w my mom

Texting Taylor can sometimes be an ordeal because I can't look away from my phone for even two seconds. She only likes to text people when she has their full attention, and in return she responds right away. We've been talking way more since Sadie and I broke up. I hate myself for ever letting my friendship with Taylor slide—someone I'm so close with, we've had simultaneous stomach flus on more than one occasion.

I love that messaging her demands my full attention. I've missed the drama of it all.

But I can't focus on that conversation right now, because my mom's still here, and she drove me all this way, and I've repaid her by being the worst daughter in the history of daughters.

"You'll have Mikey," I say finally, pretending that this is an adequate response to her saying she'll be alone for the holidays.

"He's going to Florida with his girlfriend."

"Mikey has a girlfriend?"

"I know," she says. "I was surprised, too."

Mikey is my mom's weird cousin, and the only family we have in New York City besides each other. And it appears that even *he* has somewhere else to be over winter break.

My mom sighs and stands up. We put our plates and mugs away and walk back to the car.

"Tell Beatrice it was nice seeing her," she says when we reach our snow-covered Subaru.

"You're not coming in?"

"I think I'm just gonna go."

"This late?"

"I'd rather get home tonight."

"Oh," I say. "Okay."

For the first time all day, I don't want my mom to leave. I want to throw myself onto the hard, snow-covered ground and grab her ankle so she can't drive away, like I did when she dropped me off for my first day of preschool.

But I don't tell her to stay or that I want to come home. All I say is, "Try not to hit someone this time," and my mom smiles weakly.

She gets in the car and turns on the engine, but before she leaves, I knock on the window, and she rolls it down.

"Love you," I say.

"I love you, Shani."

And she drives away.

When I'm back in my room, I text Taylor again.

ME: ok i'm here

reporting to u live from the ~bedroom~

TAY: cute

send pics

ME: absolutely not

TAY: just one???????

i wanna be able to picture where ur staying

ME: fine

I take a selfie of me flipping Taylor off and send it.

TAY: 😛

hot

ME: ur the worst

anyway

ok lol so this might be a weird q but can you check in on my mom this break?

i think she's super sad about me leaving

TAY: . . . yeah . . . she's the super sad one

ME: uhhhh what does that mean???

TAY: i'm just saying

u just went through a breakup

and now ur spending the holidays alone

maybe i should check up on YOU??

ME: first of all rude

and you literally don't need to bc i'm fine

i'm never gonna date anyone ever again

so i'll never be sad like this again

so everythings fine

TAY: love that healthy attitude

ME: it might not be healthy

but am i wrong?

TAY: yes??

there are so many hot and kind girls out there for u

u just gotta find them

ME: i don't wanna find them

i wanna shrivel up and die

TAY: :(

well don't do that

but also next time you have a gf don't disappear on me

My heart sinks when I read that text, because I know she's right.

We were in constant communication when we left

Queens late in the summer to go to our respective schools. She sent me pictures of the wall over her twin XL bed plastered with Polaroids of the two of us. I sent her photos of campus so she could imagine herself at school with me, and screenshots of my class schedule so we could plan our FaceTimes accordingly.

And then I met Sadie.

ME: i know im the worst
i'll never stop being sorry
i'm a trash person!

TAY: that was not the takeaway

ME: well it doesn't matter
i'll never disappear on you bc
i'll never date anyone again

TAY: never date anyone again
right of course
ok but like what if there's someone in dc

ME: there's 700,000 someones

TAY: not what i mean
and did you just google the population of dc

ME: yes obvs

anyway

can we not talk about this anymore

just check up on my mom maybe?

TAY: i'll get coffee with her or something

ME: love it

but make sure she gets oat milk

she's lactose intolerant lmao

TAY: aw you do care

ME: only about her poop!

TAY: gross

ME: ur gross

TAY: ily have fun sleeping in the sex dungeon

**i meant bedroom

ME: sure u did

Then Taylor sends a thumbs-up, which means she's done with the conversation.

I sleep on top of the covers of my new bed that night,

even though it's freezing. I curl into a ball, trying not to think about the half-century-old sex ghosts haunting the room, trying only to think about how we're never really touching anything, because there's at least an atom separating us from everyone and everything we want to get close to.

By that metric, I'm floating over the bed. A bed that has no idea who Sadie is, and doesn't care.

Somehow, despite the sex ghosts and the cold, I fall asleep.

Ancient Creature of the Deep

When my alarm goes off at seven the next morning, everything feels like a mistake. The first seven o'clock of the day is not a time you should have to witness during a school break.

Why did past Shani think this internship was a good idea? Past Shani was a naive fool.

No. No, we're not thinking like this. The internship is important.

And yet.

My mom's refrain from yesterday plays on repeat in my head, a chorus of overbearing Jewish mothers chanting, "You can still come home!"

But the thought of sitting in my childhood bedroom for a month, stewing in anger and sadness, is worse than the thought of getting out of bed. So I do the latter.

My whole body cracks when I stand up, like it knows I'm living in a ninety-six-year-old woman's house. I get dressed quickly and quietly, then head down to the kitchen.

It's empty, which is a huge relief. I would do anything to avoid having to make breakfast-adjacent small talk.

I try to turn on Beatrice's coffee maker, but the screen keeps flashing, "NOT READY," followed by "BREW LATER" over and over, so I don't even attempt to use the poor, unprepared appliance. Instead, I cut my losses, grab my bag, and walk through the quickly melting snow to The Big Blue Dog.

The same kid from yesterday is behind the counter, but the rest of the place is livelier. There are parents arguing with their toddlers over croissants, people wearing round glasses and reading giant tomes, and Christmas music blasting from the speakers.

I know that I complained to my mom about how Hanukkah isn't a real holiday and how I don't want to assimilate into mainstream Christian America, but the thing is . . . I fucking love Christmas music. I start listening to it in early November, before Thanksgiving. I know—I'm a monster.

It helps that all the best Christmas songs were written by Jews: "Rudolph the Red-Nosed Reindeer," "Let It Snow," "Santa Baby," the one that's like, "Chestnuts roasting on an open fire." The list goes on. It's incredible how cozy Christmas music can make me feel. I hate that I'm so into it, but that's the point. It's tailor-made to make you want to cuddle with someone (gross) and then buy overpriced gifts for them that they'll never use.

When I walk up to the counter, the kid asks me what I'd like.

"Just a black coffee, please."

"Where's your mom?"

I look up from searching for my wallet in my huge jacket pockets. "What?"

"The woman you were with yesterday?"

"Oh yeah," I say, still searching for my debit card. "She left last night."

"Why didn't you go with her?"

I can't tell if this is something they taught him to do at barista training ("People love it when you ask probing personal questions!") or if he's just nosy.

"I'm living here for the next month," I tell him, even though it's truly none of his business.

"Cool, so I guess I'll see you around," he says, and his face flushes.

Oh shit—is this kid . . . flirting with me?

He's certainly no older than fifteen, and more important, I'm gay. I've been forgetting this fact more and more in the days since Sadie broke up with me. It's like I've regressed to the early high school, closeted version of me, the one who would've immediately texted Taylor if this boy so much as glanced in my direction.

I find my debit card and hand it to him, but he puts a palm up and says, "On the house," looking too proud as he pushes the coffee toward me.

I grab it, then smile and thank him, hoping my smile says, "I'm an age-appropriate crush for you, and also I for sure like boys."

Hey, if he wants to give me free coffee, who am I to stop him?

The Metro is right by the café, and I'm grateful for the relative warmth of the station. I get on a huge escalator, holding my free flirting-hormonal-kid coffee and feeling pretty good about myself.

The Metro platform is beautiful—vaulted ceilings, soft yellow light—it looks more like a movie set than a functioning public transit station. I'm so used to the pee-riddled, claustrophobia-inducing New York City subway that this feels almost magical.

I traced out my commute on Google Maps yesterday, planning where to transfer and where I need to get off so that I'd look like I'd been commuting in DC all my life.

It's good that I don't have to concentrate on directions, because I'm entirely focused on how nervous I am about the first day of my internship. I applied back in July, before

I started college. Before I met Sadie.

When I got the acceptance email in November, I had forgotten I'd even sent in an application. It was like I'd had amnesia. Nothing before Sadie had mattered. And I had been convinced, right after she broke up with me, that nothing after her would matter either.

But it does. I keep having to remind myself that it absolutely does.

So, the moral of the story is that I'm going to do so fucking well at this internship that I'll prove to myself and Sadie and the entire world that I'm moving on.

I am moving on.

When I was a kid, my mom would take me to the natural history museum in New York. I loved those days because they felt like time travel. Like we were entering a different world just beyond the white pillars: where fifty-foot sharks bit the heads off extinct whales; where animals that had been buried under volcanic ash for millions of years were unearthed so they could stand before us, whole and spectacular.

I've missed that feeling of awe, of seeing how many creatures have lived and died and been reborn over the course of our planet's four-and-a-half-billion-year existence.

What I *haven't* missed is the fact that natural history museums were founded to glorify empires and display specimens collected during colonialist expeditions. I didn't know this when I was a little kid—I didn't know much beyond "BIG BONES, WANT TO TOUCH AND/OR PUT IN MOUTH"—but I sure as shit do now.

But, at the bare minimum, the place where I'll be interning—the Smithsonian National Museum of Natural History—has a repatriation office devoted to returning objects to the communities they come from, and it's made its collections and programs available online to anyone who wants to view them.

I spent hours on their website in high school looking at 3D images of fossilized fish and feeling like I was actively *doing* science. They've worked to make sure the museum isn't an intimidating institution but a place where anyone who wants to learn and participate can do so.

It's a work in progress, and maybe it's naive, but I'm glad I get to be a part of this positive change, of making science accessible to everyone.

I'm standing outside the museum now, practically buzzing as I reread the instructions on the email I received from the internship program last week. I have to pick up a badge from the security desk and wait for someone to escort me to the lab.

I walk past the early-morning tourists and a giant elephant until I find the right desk and tell the staff person the reason I'm standing here so awkwardly.

"All right, we'll get you set up," the guard sitting behind the desk tells me. "Now, smile."

I don't know why she's telling me to do that, but I don't want to disobey, so I turn my lips up a bit, and a minute later she hands me a badge.

"That's your ID. Please wear it at all times." She types something on her keyboard. "Someone's coming to pick you up in a few minutes."

"Oh, uh, thanks," I say, and turn the badge around to look at it.

On the thin plastic card is a picture of me looking—there's no other way to describe it—extremely constipated. I should've realized that the security guard wasn't asking me to smile in the "Give me a smile, honey!" way.

I flip the badge to the side without my picture and try to make my actual face look less constipated than the small square version of me.

It doesn't really matter how I look, though, because everyone in the atrium is in their own little world. It's loud and crowded despite the hour, and kids are running around the elephant, turning their arms into trunks and evading their parents' grasps.

I don't remember ever being that small. Actually, I don't remember much from birth to middle school, but what I *do* remember is that I've always loved fish.

It started with a documentary called *Ancient Creature of the Deep*. The movie was about the coelacanth, which is this giant fish that scientists thought went extinct with the dinosaurs, until they found one alive in the early 1900s. It's pronounced "see-LUH-canth," and I was a little too proud of being able to say the word when I was a kid. I would annoy my mom by repeating it over and over while she was doing the dishes or trying to nap.

I loved the shot from the documentary of the spotted fish being caught on camera, its eyes glowing red from the diver's flashlight. But the thing that fascinated me most, the thing I couldn't wrap my tiny head around, was the fact that this fish's ancestors lived at a time when there was no life on land at all. And not only that, but *all* of our ancestors came from the ocean. We're all fish.

"Shani?"

I shake the fish thoughts out of my head and turn around. A person with cropped, curly black hair (that's much better maintained than mine) is waving at me.

"Shani?" she asks again.

"Uh, yeah."

"Mandira!" She says her own name like she couldn't be more excited about it and then extends a hand for me to shake. When she does, the short sleeve of her black-and-white-striped button-down pulls back, and I see a tattoo of a black mammoth skull covering the brown skin of her upper arm.

"That's awesome," I say, pointing to the tattoo.

"I know," she says. "I got it a few months ago. I named her Margaret."

"Who?"

"The mammoth," she says. "Let's go to the lab! Do you need anything? Coffee? Tea? Seltzer? Juice?"

"I'm fine," I say when she's done listing beverages. "Excited to get started."

"Well, we're excited to have you," she says, and walks through a door marked, "Employees Only."

We enter a long, narrow, windowless hallway, and Mandira walks a few paces in front of me. I try to remember the order of the turns we take—left, right, left, and left again, but after a minute I decide it's pointless and that I live here now.

"On my first day I asked if I could leave a trail of bread crumbs so I'd be able to find my way back to the lab," Mandira says, reading my mind. "But Dr. Graham told me that wouldn't be sanitary." She laughs and so do I, glad to be in the same Hansel-and-Gretel–based boat that Mandira was. "He's a genius, you know. Not exactly a people person but a genius." She turns around to walk backward as she says, "So if you think he doesn't like you, don't worry. He doesn't like anything that was born in the last three hundred million years—Devonian joke." Mandira snorts; it's nice that this is the kind of place where people make jokes about geologic eras.

She stops laughing and says, "But seriously."

We arrive at a door marked "The Graham Paleoichthyology Lab," and Mandira pushes it open.

The room is the opposite of a museum exhibit built for the public with perfectly preserved specimens in glass display cases. There are three long stainless-steel lab benches, and on each are hundreds, maybe thousands, of loose fish fossils piled haphazardly on top of one another. Most are covered in dirt or plaster casts, some are parts of fish I can't identify, and some are just teeth.

I'm entirely amazed. I want to touch them all. It's a primal urge.

"Isn't it the best thing you've ever seen?" Mandira asks.

"Yeah," I say, still in awe.

"That's the correct response," she says, and I beam, happy to have already gotten something right. "So, you'll mostly be preparing the fossils for me and Dr. Graham." Mandira walks over to one of the benches, picks up what looks like part of a lungfish, and turns it over in her hands. "You ever work with fossils before?"

"Not really," I say, ashamed. What kind of aspiring paleoichthyologist hasn't worked with fossils?

"Don't even worry about it," Mandira says, and the shame is instantly gone and I'm convinced that she's the nicest person who's ever lived. "You can teach fossil prep, but you can't teach the rest of it. Your application was the one about coelacanths, right?"

"Yeah."

"Come look at this." She takes me to the third bench and points to a large plaster cast. "Open it up."

The cast is already sawed in half, so I lift the top and gape at the half still sitting on the bench.

"Holy shit," I say, then quickly add, "Sorry! Sorry."

"No, that's *also* the correct response." She stares lovingly at the fossil: a coelacanth so well-preserved it makes my heart flutter.

"What era is it from?" I immediately need to know everything about it: where it came from, how they found it, what species it is.

Mandira smiles and arches her eyebrows. "What do you think?"

I stare at the fossil for a minute. "Well, I guess it's probably pre-Jurassic, because it doesn't seem to have any of the internal breeding structures that evolved in the later species." I glance over at Mandira, whose face is startlingly impassive. I keep going. "Also, it's really small, isn't it?" It's way tinier than any other coelacanth fossil I've ever seen. They can be up to six feet long and weigh over one hundred pounds, but this one's only a foot long or so."

To be fair, I've only seen a few real specimen, and they've all been in museums. This one is right in front of me. I can reach out and touch it.

My heart's racing from the joy of loving dead things, the detective work of figuring out as much as you can about the circumstances of their demise.

But Mandira doesn't say anything, and after a horrifying moment when I'm convinced I got 100 percent of that wrong and she's going to kick me out of the internship program on my first day, her face breaks into a grin. "I knew we picked well." I almost vomit with relief. "You're right that it's pre-Jurassic. It's Devonian, like a lot of the fish in our lab."

I want to run my hands against the imprint its scales and fins left behind 350 million years ago.

"*And* you're right that it's small. We're pretty sure it was a juvenile." She says this part softly, as if we might wake the baby coelacanth.

"I'm, like, flustered by this fish—is that weird to say?"

Mandira's somehow already made me feel comfortable, which is usually a hopeless endeavor.

"Not at all." She laughs. "So, this is pretty much what you'll be doing: admiring fossils and then cleaning and preparing them for me and Dr. Graham." She goes on to tell me about PaleoBOND, which is a fossil glue, and then she shows me my spot at the bench. "All right," she says when she's done. "I'm gonna bring you into the other room to meet Dr. Graham."

Holy shit.

I'm about to meet a rock star, a man I've wanted to work with for years. The guy I completely forgot about when I was with Sadie.

I've watched his TED Talk about how we're all fish, like, ten thousand times. I'm obsessed with him. "Life doesn't evolve in a line," he says at the beginning of the video. I love the way he explains that humans aren't the pinnacle of evolution. That we're just one small part of the animal kingdom, and an even smaller part of all life on Earth.

"Sounds good," I say to Mandira as casually as I can.

She lowers her voice. "Just remember, he's not a people person. He's a nerdy, middle-aged white guy who loves fish."

Mandira knocks on an unmarked wooden door and presses her ear to it. She must hear some confirmation that we can enter because she turns the doorknob.

I peer inside, and there's a man with his back to us, hunched over a tray of fossils that are even more disorganized than the ones in the main area of the lab. His wiry hair has mostly gone gray, and he's much too tall for his desk.

"Dr. Graham," Mandira says loudly. "Do you want to say hi to our new intern, Shani?"

He spins around on his stool, and I almost laugh. He's holding a fossil in one hand and a toothbrush in the other. "Hi," he says, barely looking up. "I find that dirt on jaws responds best to a good toothbrushing, but don't discount it as a tool for any number of fossils."

"Um, I won't."

"All right, I've got to get back to this."

With that he turns around, and Mandira shuts the door.

"He's obsessed, you know," she says, sitting at a chair in front of one of the lab benches. "The fish are his whole life. Sorry that he didn't talk to you for longer, though. He's really bad at small talk. But I think he's a pretty good person, deep down."

"It's fine." I can understand the obsession part. In fact, I can see the lab being mine.

But maybe I just have an obsessive personality.

Mandira gives me a paddlefish skull to start cleaning, and I lose track of time trying to get the tiny specks of dirt out of the cracked and scaly surface of the fish. I'm carefully scrubbing its giant, protruding nose when Mandira says, "I think that's enough for today. Why don't you take off a bit early?"

Somehow, it's already four o'clock. We breezed right through lunch.

"Wait, what?" I double-check my phone. "That went so fast."

Mandira smiles. "Time flies when you're preparing specimen. I'll see you tomorrow."

When I get back to Beatrice's house an hour or so later, I open the door as quietly as I can. After my first day of work, I just want to go up to my room and not have to talk to anyone.

I'm almost up the stairs when I hear, "Doll, is that you?"

I hold my breath, hoping she means one of the other dolls.

"New doll? Come to the kitchen, angel."

I wince. My cover's blown. Beatrice, Lauren, and Tasha are sitting at the kitchen table, the three of them looking giddy.

There's a bottle of Baileys Irish Cream and a pint of vanilla ice cream placed between them, and they're all eating out of those fancy old-fashioned ice cream glasses. Beatrice is slurping what I can only assume is a Baileys-ice-cream combo. It's spilling all over her shirt, but she's making no effort to clean it up. I guess when you're ninety-six you don't really have to.

"Shani!" Lauren says. "We've been wondering where you've been. Beatrice told us you're working somewhere downtown? She said something about you being a mad scientist, but honestly I don't listen to a thing she says." This earns her a playful slap on the arm from Beatrice, one that splatters ice cream and Baileys everywhere. "Was it your first day?"

"Uh . . ."

"Well, don't just stand there," Beatrice says before I can respond to Lauren. "You expect us to get you a glass?" She stands up and wraps her arm around me, which barely reaches my upper butt/lower back area. "In this house we help ourselves."

I feel slightly overwhelmed by the barrage of words being thrown at me, but I grab a glass, sit between Lauren and Tasha, and scoop myself some ice cream.

"What, no Baileys?" Beatrice asks.

I've drunk before but not in front of adults. So I decide to be honest. "I'm not twenty-one."

"What does that have anything to do with it?"

"That's the drinking age," I tell her.

"Well, it wasn't back in my day."

"That's because alcohol wasn't invented yet," Lauren says, and Beatrice laughs boisterously.

"You have yourself a bit of Baileys," Beatrice tells me. "It's good for you. Helps you grow big and strong." She winks, and I pour a drop over my ice cream. "Well, you have to have more than that, doll," she says, shaking her head.

I pour a bit more.

"So, how's Sandy these days?" Beatrice asks after a minute of all of us slurping our Baileys-ice-cream combo.

I cough, and Irish cream sputters out of my nose. "She's, um," I start. "She died about ten years ago, when I was a little kid."

"Of course she did, doll," Beatrice says sympathetically. "I should've known. But then again, everyone my age is dead." She lets out a bark of laughter.

"How did you meet my great-grandma?" I ask, ignoring the death comment.

My mom mentioned that they knew each other from college, but I want to know the whole story. I'm always interested in learning new things about my great-grandma. I called her my "alte bubbe," and I don't remember much about her, except that she hated to cook and loved to sit me on her lap and just squeeze. I always tried to wiggle away, but after a while I would give in. I remember liking the way it felt to have someone protecting me with her whole body.

"Well, we both went to Barnard College, and we fancied ourselves radical, free women, but really we were just babies. Not a day over eighteen." Beatrice pauses to take another bite of ice cream. "She had come over from the Soviet Union just a few years earlier, and she was whip smart and loved New York to pieces. She was more of a New Yorker than I was, and I'd lived there my whole life. I was born on Staten Island, and going to school in Manhattan was a big adventure for me. I met all these new friends: immigrant Jews, Chinese people. Anyone who wasn't Italian, I would just gravitate toward them because I considered myself quite worldly. And oh! How I loved your Sandy. She would write in *The Bulletin* about birth control, and she acted in all the plays. She made me do *Twelfth Night* with her, and of course she was the lead—the man, whatever his name was. I had one line. But when she wooed that girl in the show, boy, I'll tell you . . ."

Beatrice stops there, just trails off. She takes another slurp of ice cream and smiles to herself. It's weird to think of my great-grandma as a "radical, free woman," just like it's weird to think that my mom had a life before me. But I love that Sandy played a man in *Twelfth Night*. And I love that she wooed a girl, even if it was just onstage.

I can't imagine my great-grandma ever being eighteen. I wonder if she had her heart broken, too. I wonder if she was horrible to her mom. Maybe these are just inherited traits, and I'm not a complete screwup.

"So, what are you doing for work, though? Like, actually?" Lauren asks after a minute of silence. "I know you're not transferring. Sorry about the crudités thing, by the way. I'm gonna bring a platter myself."

I laugh and tell them all about my internship—nothing too in the weeds, just the extinct-fish basics. "Are you at American too?" I ask Tasha.

She nods. "Yeah, but I'm in grad school. I did my undergraduate studies in Moscow, where I grew up."

"Cool," I say, glad to be able to place the accent.

"Also, I'd like to apologize on behalf of these two." She gestures to Lauren and Beatrice. "They are . . . not quiet."

Perhaps the understatement of the last 350 million years.

Beatrice chortles and reaches across the table to try to whack Tasha, but she can't reach. "Doll, you need to loosen up."

"I think you two need to tighten," Tasha says, and everyone laughs.

After that, I eat more of my ice cream soup and listen as Beatrice tells stories and Lauren makes fun of Beatrice. Tasha and I don't say much, but I start to feel warm and cozy. Maybe it's the Baileys, or maybe it's Beatrice's aura; she sucks everyone in.

"Well, I'm going to turn in," Beatrice says after a while. "You dolls don't have too much fun without me."

I look at the clock—it has an Italian flag on its face—and find that it's only seven. I thought it was later than that, somehow.

When I turn back to the table, Lauren is leaning forward, grinning. "Hey, Shani, do you wanna make a few bucks?"

It's possible she's just posing a philosophical question so I say, "Sure." As in, "Sure, who wouldn't wanna make a few bucks. In this economy?"

"Okay, amazing," she says. "I have this regular dog walking gig, but I'm leaving to go to my boyfriend's family's place in Houston for Christmas, and I need someone to take over for me."

"She already tried to get me to do it," Tasha says. "But I'm allergic to dogs."

"And I keep telling her that you don't even have to touch him, you just have to walk him."

"I'll do it," I say before Lauren and Tasha can bicker about it anymore.

"Really?" Lauren asks. "Holy shit, I did *not* think you were gonna say yes. You seem so quiet and brooding. I mean, not so much right now, but . . ."

It's a fair point, though I'm glad Baileys and ice cream is making a slight dent in the brooding vibes I've been giving off.

I want to keep this new, fun, non-brooding image alive, so I say, “No, yeah, I’m happy to walk the dog.”

“Thank goodness,” she says. “I had promised this guy weeks ago that I’d find a replacement, but I’ve been sitting on it till the last minute.”

“I’m super happy to do it,” I tell her. “When should I start going over there for walks? When are you leaving?”

“Uh . . .” She turns her gaze to the corner of the kitchen, and for the first time since coming home I see the giant suitcase sitting there like a large child in time-out. “Tonight? Can you start tonight?”

“I—”

“Because you’d literally be saving my *life* if you did.”

It’s always nice to be needed. “Yeah, I’m on it.”

“Okay, great. Lifesaver! I’ll text you the address so you have it, but it’s, like, a block away.” She pulls out her phone, and as she types, she says, “It’s a pretty cool job because the guy’s kind of a DC celebrity.”

“Really?”

“Oh yeah.” She puts her phone away as I receive a text with the address. “He’s our local weatherman. You know Greg Stern?” I shake my head. “You haven’t seen those bus ads? The ones that are like, ‘Greg Brings the Umbrella to You,’ and it’s this guy holding out an umbrella like he’s giving it to you?”

“Uh, no. I haven’t.”

"Well, it's a great ad, and everyone's obsessed with Greg."

"Yeah, he's kind of a DILF," Tasha adds, and I try not to choke on my own saliva. They don't yet know that there are approximately zero dads I'd like to fuck.

But even so, I'm now even more excited to walk the dog, because I'll be in the presence of a local celebrity, which is the exact right amount of celebrity. "I guess I'll just go over there now?"

"That would be *amazing*. Really, thanks so much."

"No problem at all." I put away my ice-cream glass (remembering the clean-your-own-messes rule), then head out.

The house that matches the address turns out to be another cute brick three-story with snow-covered bushes that give the place a nice wintry feel. There's even a menorah in the window, which makes sense for the house of a man named Greg Stern (even if the menorah's a bit past its expiration date for this year).

I knock on the door, but no one responds, so I ring the doorbell. After a minute, a light turns on in the main entrance, and the latch clicks.

And then: "You've got to be fucking kidding me."

Because who opens the door other than the girl my mom and I bumped with our car. She's not wearing the red beanie this time. Her brown hair is long and wavy and very bushy, like it's trying to overtake her head, and she's wearing a soft-looking black turtleneck and purple flannel pants with her phone tucked into the waistband.

"Okay, seriously, what the fuck?" she asks, taking a few steps back. "Aren't you the girl who almost killed me the other day?"

"No, I didn't—"

"You here to finish the job?"

"No." I scrunch my nose. "And . . . technically that was my mom."

She rolls her eyes. "But you were in the car."

"That doesn't mean I was responsible for it."

"Are you saying that it's okay to do something if you're just going along with it?"

"That's obviously not what I'm saying."

She stares at me for a moment. "Okay, so, I'm going to close the door now."

"No!" I shout at her, and she stops. "I'm, um—" I take a deep breath. "I'm here to walk your dog."

"I don't have a dog," she says just as something barks inside.

"Is that perhaps . . . a dog?"

Her eyes dart behind her. "No."

I'm about to head back and tell Lauren that I tried but it's not going to work out, when an extremely telegenic middle-aged man—Greg Stern, I'm sure—walks up to the door. He's wearing a suit and a sleek, expensive-looking backpack.

"Are you Lauren's replacement?" he asks, barely glancing at me.

"Yeah."

"Great, great." He types something on his phone. "I have to run for the nightly news, but thanks so much for walking my boy. I left the money in the mailbox. You can just pick it up after the walk." He heads down the path and adds, "Also, give my daughter your phone number. I need it in case of emergency. Okay thanks you're great." He says that last part in one breath while still looking at his phone.

"Thanks?" I say as he unlocks his tiny chrome car and gets in. I turn back to the door after he drives away. "So, should I come in and grab the little guy?"

"Absolutely not," Greg's daughter says. "I'll get it."

She slams the door and goes to find the dog, I guess, though she could just be locking me out.

A minute later, she comes back with a fat corgi trailing behind her and hands me a leash and a plastic bag. "I guess you know what to do?"

"Like how to walk the dog? Yeah, I'm pretty sure I can figure it out."

"You know how to get the poop and everything? Because I think they do that sometimes."

"You *think*? Have you never walked a dog before? Or encountered a living creature?"

"I don't like dogs. And I especially don't like *this* dog." She stares down at the corgi with so much malice, and the corgi gazes up at her with a dangling tongue and nothing but love.

"That doesn't answer my question," I say. "Also, that's outrageous. Everyone likes dogs."

The corgi wanders outside, and I bend to pet his perfect cylindrical body and strap on his leash.

She sighs. "Fine, no. I've never walked a dog. And I never *plan* on walking a dog." She shakes her head. "People have such a weird fascination with these things, but they're just inbred wolves."

We're both staring down at the corgi, who's running in circles trying to capture his fluffy white butt.

I give the girl a look. "So, just to be clear, you have a dog but you've never walked it?"

"*I* don't have a dog. My dad has a dog." She starts to close the door once again, as if she's answered my question perfectly and this was a satisfactory human interaction.

"Wait," I say, and I can practically hear her eyes rolling through the door. She opens it yet again. "Should I, like, give you my number?"

Even though she's only the conduit and the number's for her dad, I'm nervous.

I remember when I gave Sadie my number. I fabricated some wild excuse, because I didn't want her to know I wanted her to have it. I told her she'd never be able to find the fire safety orientation, and I sent her directions.

Nope.

This isn't like that. It's for the corgi.

"Sure, fine," she says, pulling out her phone. I tell her my number as I pet the dog, whose little tongue is sticking out as I give him a good scratch behind the ears.

"Does this sweet pup have a name?" I ask, more to the dog than the girl.

"Can't you read the collar?"

"Can't you tell me?"

When she doesn't say anything, I relent and read the dog's collar: Raphael. "Hey, Raphael," I coo, and he flops his long body onto the ground so I can rub his belly. After a few seconds he pops back up and pants and wiggles his little corgi butt. "So, the dog has a name," I say, feeling even more nervous. "Do, um—do you have one?"

"Sure."

"What is it?" I stand up and grab the leash as Raphael brushes against my calves. He looks up at me, ready for a walk.

"Why should I tell you?"

"Because I'm walking your dad's dog now, so I'll be seeing you around. And it's what decent human beings do."

"I'm pretty sure decent human beings don't hit people with their car," she says, and I roll my eyes. "And anyway, you haven't told me yours."

"It's Shani."

"Cool," she says, then shuts the door for real.

I can't even bring myself to feel angry. I don't know

what it is about being around this girl, but I still feel that exhilaration that coursed through me after my mom and I bumped into her.

I glance down at the corgi. "Your roommate's kind of mean," I tell him as I coax his tiny legs down the stairs and onto the street.

Raphael gets easily distracted and buries his sweet little nose in the dusting of snow until his muzzle is all white. I ask him who's a good boy a number of times (he is, he is), and then glance at my phone to see if it's time to start heading back.

There are three texts from a number I don't recognize.

Don't kill the dog

202-555-8179

^Vet

Then a minute later:

May

And a few seconds after that, one more:

My name is May

Why Would I Bring a Poop Bag?

When I wake up to my alarm the next morning, things are hazy. For a moment, I'm convinced that seeing the girl yesterday—May—was a dream. But I'm pretty sure it wasn't. I'm pretty sure she texted me, told me her name.

I'm pretty sure she wanted to throw me facedown into the snow and leave me there to die.

I grab my phone from Beatrice's bedside table and find two texts, one from my mom and one from Taylor. The text from my mom says, "u 4got slipperz, wud u like me 2 send them? I no ur feet get burr."

It takes me, like, five minutes to decipher the message in my half-asleep state, but I finally realize she's asking me if I want slippers. I write back "no."

Until I remember that she's all alone, so I add, "ty."

Yes, I'm the worst.

The text from Taylor is a screenshot of this kid Gavin from our high school posing with his newborn baby and the baby's mom.

TAY: this could be you lmao

I *ha ha* react it but don't add anything else, because she's definitely asleep, like most people should be at this hour during their winter break.

She wrote, "this could be you," because Gavin tried to ask me to homecoming junior year, and instead of rejecting him like a decent human being, I ran into the bathroom and locked myself in a stall.

I had just started thinking that there was a strong possibility I wasn't interested in men, and there was Gavin, trying to renew that interest.

Taylor followed and locked herself into the stall next to mine, and that's where I came out to her. In the bathroom, staring at the writing over the toilet that told me, "CALEB MCMAHON HAS A THIRD LEG." I didn't use the word *lesbian* to describe myself until this year, though, which is when I chopped off all my hair and flirted with veganism (I know).

Taylor proceeded to tell me all the right things: that she

loved me, that she was proud of me, and that we were going to homecoming together (platonically, of course). She even rejected Gavin for me.

That's what I left behind when I started dating Sadie: my token straight best friend who wore a tux to homecoming after I came out to her in the school bathroom plastered in discarded tampon applicators and stale gossip.

And then she took me back post-Sadie, no questions asked.

Which somehow makes me feel even worse.

To avoid wallowing, I get dressed and head straight to The Big Blue Dog.

I smile at the boy, hoping it's enough to get me free coffee. It is, but after he hands me the drink he says, "Well, have a good one— Wait, I don't think I caught your name," in a way that makes it sound like he'd been practicing that line in the mirror all night.

"It's Shani," I tell him. "And you're"—I glance at his name tag only to find the most goyishe name in history—"Luke. Nice to officially meet you." I add the last part to really personalize the whole thing. I want to *earn* my free coffee.

"You too, Shani."

I don't love the way he says my name, how he tries to imbue it with meaning. I take my coffee and walk quickly out of the café into the freezing winter air.

When I get to the museum, I go straight to the staff

entrance and scan my badge facedown. Then I stumble through the labyrinthine hallway in an attempt to find Dr. Graham's lab.

After at least fifteen wrong and disheartening turns, I'm ready to give up and go home when I see Mandira walking in the opposite direction.

"Mandira!" I shout, and she turns around and waves. I run to catch up to her until a man passing by in a lab coat says, "No running!"

"Were you in here long?" she asks.

"No, no," I lie. "I just got here."

"Perfect, let's head over!"

I follow Mandira, grateful for the guide.

"So, you're a first-year?" she asks.

"Yeah, it's my winter break."

"This is sort of a wild way to spend a break."

"I guess."

"Do you live around here?"

"No, I'm from New York."

"Go to school around here, then?"

"Nope, school's also in New York."

"So you're just here for the month? You didn't have anywhere else to be?" Then she looks at me and says, "Sorry, that came out super harsh— I didn't mean . . . It's just that the people who do this internship are usually from around here so that they can see their family over the holidays."

"I don't celebrate Christmas, so it's fine."

"Yeah, I don't either," she says, "but it's still nice to be around family."

Why does the whole world think I'm not fine? That I need to be surrounded by people to be happy? I want to tell everyone that things are great when I'm alone. That they're *better.*

"Sorry, that was kind of shitty of me," Mandira says after a minute. I want to tell her it wasn't, but she adds, "Don't worry, I'll keep things festive in the lab. Maybe put a Santa hat on one of the fish. That might be fun, don't you think?"

"Yeah," I say because, honestly, it would be.

When we get to the lab Mandira says, "Dr. Graham's already here, so I'm just gonna check in with him and see if there's anything in particular he needs us to do today."

"Sounds good."

While she does that, I look around the lab. There are a couple research posters from the past few years, one with Mandira's name on it and another with the names of grad students past.

One of the posters is from a paper that looks at how live birth evolved in living coelacanths by studying fossils. The other one is about coelacanth locomotion—apparently the huge scaly fools will do *headstands* instead of swimming—and what it can tell us about the evolution of walking in land animals. Absolutely wild.

I still can't believe I'm here, and that it's this chill. I

thought paleoichthyology would be way more intense, but I like that it's mostly cleaning fish and hanging with Mandira.

"He just wants us to do some more prep work today," Mandira says when she comes out of Dr. Graham's little closet workspace. "We can put on music or something."

"Cool."

"Any requests?"

"Not really," I tell her, hands shoved deep in the pockets of my men's department jeans.

"Would you be mad if I put on Christmas music?"

I smile. "Not at all."

Mandira plays "Jingle Bell Rock," and we talk for a while as we scrub down the fossils. She tells me about what she studied as an undergrad and that she chose this fellowship because she wanted to be closer to her girlfriend, who lives in Virginia.

I'm not at all surprised that Mandira's queer, because she's incredibly cool and has short hair and wears button-downs and has a mammoth tattoo. Not that any of these things mean someone *has* to be queer, but taken together they're a pretty good indicator.

Meanwhile, I'm over here looking like a mess in my black sweatshirt and jeans, my hair doing whatever it pleases. A few months ago, I seriously considered getting an undercut because Sadie said it would look good, but it never happened while we were together, and I'm obviously not getting one now that we're broken up. But at the very least it would probably make it more obvious to people that I'm queer, rather than just disheveled, which is what my current look is projecting to the world.

"Wanna get lunch?" Mandira asks after a while of scrubbing and chatting and Christmas song humming.

"Definitely," I tell her.

"There are some good carts outside. There's halal or burgers or tacos. And sometimes there's a grilled cheese truck, which people here go kind of wild over—including me, obviously. I can't even tell you how lactose intolerant I am, but I would never let that stop me."

"Of course not," I agree, because I, like almost every other Ashkenazi Jew on the planet, am deeply lactose intolerant but will never admit it to myself.

She takes me outside (I pay extra attention to the hallway directions this time), and when we exit the museum there's a whole block's worth of carts and trucks to choose from.

"Oh, hell yeah," she says, leading me toward a red and yellow truck. "Grilled cheese time."

We wait in line, and when we get to the front she offers to pay. "Don't say no. It's the least I can do for an intern."

I *don't* say no (who would turn down free grilled cheese?) but I do thank her, and we eat our sandwiches sitting on the cold, wet steps leading up to the museum. It's nice to breathe in fresh non-lab air, even if it's freezing. And the grilled cheeses live up to the hype.

"How long have you been working in the lab?" I ask Mandira after I wipe an embarrassing amount of cheese off my face.

"About a year," she says. "Honestly, I applied to a different lab, but Graham was the one who took me." I don't know what to say to that, because I'd donate a kidney to Dr. Graham without him so much as asking, and she must see that on my face because she adds, "I'm super happy he took me on, though, because his research is incredible. And he actually cares about paleoichthyology not being entirely dominated by white men."

"Yeah, he's so cool," I say. "Have you seen his TED Talk?"

"Oh, of course. It's the first thing I watched when he brought me on— 'The Earth wasn't made for you, and we're all fish—'"

"'—deal with it!'" I finish the quote for her, the one his talk ends on. "He's, like, my idol."

"He's completely different when you get to know him, though. Different from the TED Talk guy, at least," she says. "Like, he's great and so, so smart, of course, but I think he's probably a little lonely. I might be projecting, but he's at work *all the time*. He doesn't have a wife or kids or even a dog." She takes a practiced bite of grilled cheese. "It's good to have people to look up to, but maybe don't *idolize* him."

I don't tell her that it's too late. That everything in my life seems to be all or nothing, and I need the lab and Dr. Graham to be *all* because right now too much is *nothing.*

We switch gears and talk about which made-for-TV movie, *Dinoshark* or *Piranhaconda,* is more realistic. (We decide on *Piranhaconda,* because at least both of those animals are still alive today.)

After that, the rest of the afternoon goes by as quickly as the last, and I'm sad to leave Mandira and the fish at the end of it.

But I have to get to Greg/May/Raphael Stern's house. So I thank Mandira again and head out on the Metro.

I make it back to my neighborhood in record time, and I'm ready to see Raphael's wagging tail nub and perfect triangular corgi ears—even if it means going through May—when I hear something inside the house that stops me from knocking.

It sounds like a screaming match.

The part of me that's scared of confrontation wants to leave and come back when the yelling's done. But the part of me that needs to know what's happening at all times tells me to stay and eavesdrop.

After a moment of debate between these two parts of myself, the latter wins by a landslide, and I hold my breath and flatten myself against the door to listen.

A man's voice—Greg: "That's really too bad, because it's not up for discussion."

May's voice: "You didn't care last year!"

Greg: "That's because your mom had custody of you for the holidays last year."

May: "You barely have custody of me now! You're at work all the *fucking* time—"

Greg: "Do not curse at me."

May: "All the fucking time, so it doesn't matter if you have custody if I never even see you!"

Greg: "That's not how custody works. It just means that you need to be here."

May: "So suddenly you're the expert?"

Greg: "On this? Yes. I'm your father, and what I say goes."

May: "Do you realize how stupid you sound right now? 'What I say goes.' Do you think you're arguing with a five-year-old? Like, I don't get it."

Greg: *(frustrated grunt)* "This is the arrangement your mom and I have. If you don't like it, take it up with her."

May: "I literally have. I've told her a million times I wanna stay at her place."

Greg: "Well, you 'literally' can't. You're here for break."

May: "I'm in college. I'll be eighteen next week. How is this fair?"

Heavy footsteps approach the front door, and I don't know what to do because if I move they'll see me, and if I stay here they'll know I was listening.

I don't move.

And the door doesn't open. Yet.

May: "The second I turn eighteen I'm going back to Mom's. Just gonna hop on a bus and leave."

Greg: "And you're the one calling me childish? You're going to run away from home like when you were a little kid?"

May: "I can't do this right now." *(Stomping.)*

Greg: "Fine. Do what you want. I'm not stopping you."

May: "Except you fucking are."

Greg: "Language."

Then a third voice enters the mix.

Raphael: "Bark. Barkbarkbark—"

Greg: "Raph, shh, please. Puppy, please."

May: "Right, great." *(scoff)* "You care more about the fucking dog than you do about me."

Here there's a pause, and I still don't know what to do. I'm frozen to the porch, trapped against the door. I know it's wrong, listening to this father and daughter who I barely know fight with each other over something so big. But I can't move.

> After a minute, Greg says, "You know that's not true."
>
> Then May says, "Whatever."

And then it's over.

If I was May, I'd be mortified if I knew someone overheard that fight. Sure, I'm a bitch to my mom, but I would never be a bitch to her in front of other people.

I don't know what it's like to fight about custody with a dad—I don't have one, my mom had me from a sperm donor—but I know what it's like to feel powerless. To feel like you don't have any say in your own life.

So instead of knocking on the door right away and pretending everything's fine, I sneak down the path as quietly as I can, hoping to reach the bottom unnoticed. Then I'll walk back to the door, and no one will have to know I heard anything.

"Where are you going?"

I turn around, and there's May. She's silhouetted in the entryway, and I have no idea what to do. She closes the door and steps outside. A leash-less Raphael is jauntily bouncing at her heels, unaware that anything bad has ever happened in the world.

I sprint to grab him before he does his little corgi butt-shuffle directly into traffic. "Do you have his leash?"

"No."

"That's kind of an important part of dog walking." I adjust Raphael in my arms, and he squirms a bit, then settles. Holding him is like carrying a really dense loaf of bread with legs.

"Well, we're just gonna have to do without it, then," May says as she walks ahead of me toward the sidewalk.

Our path's only illuminated by a few dim streetlights, so I step carefully as I jog to keep up. I'm also trying not to jostle Raphael too much—though he looks like he's enjoying himself, or at least has no idea what's going on. Which, same.

Without looking at me, May asks, "Did you hear any of that?"

"Uh—"

That must be answer enough, because she says, "Fuck me."

"No, no. It's fine. Or— I'm sorry?" We reach a tiny park—it's mostly just a bench—and I put Raphael down so he can at least stretch his stumpy legs.

"You really keep showing up at the worst times."

"I'm sorry," I say again, and it's not a question.

Neither of us says anything for a minute. Raphael

bounces around the bench, and I have no idea how to fill the silence—it's much easier to talk when we're arguing. But I guess she got all her arguing out during the fight with her dad.

Finally, I settle on, "So, you're Jewish?" I know it's silly the moment I say it, but it's not like she was offering anything.

"*That's* what you're asking me right now?"

"I am too—well, maybe you're not, but I am—I just saw the menorah in your window and I was curious. I thought maybe—"

"Yeah, I am. But I'm not really that religious. My dad just pulled out any decorations and holiday shit he could find to try to cozy up the place while I'm staying with him."

I figure since she knows I overheard the fight with her dad, I should say something supportive. "Oh, that sucks. Screw Hanukkah, right?"

She stares at me. "What?"

"Because it's, like, a corporate holiday? And your dad is buying into the corporate overlords?"

"What? No," she says. "Are you kidding me? Hanukkah's amazing. I love it."

"You love the fact that we turned a religiously nothing holiday into this huge deal just so we can fit in with"—I almost say the Christian hegemony, but think better of it—"the whole winter holiday season?"

"I love the fact that we basically have a new holiday

because Jewish kids in America felt sad about Christmas. I love that it's a big deal." She's getting more excited now, and she gestures with her whole body as she says, "And it's all about the marketing. Hanukkah PR is amazing. Like, everyone knows about Hanukkah, which you definitely can't say about any other Jewish holiday." She folds her arms over her stomach and looks down at the last dregs of snow. "Plus, I *really* fucking love latkes."

"Well, same, obviously."

And, as if he wants to be part of the conversation as well, Raphael trots over to me, looks directly into my eyes, and takes a shit.

"Really?" I ask Raphael, who's now wagging his nub. I turn to May. "Do you have a poop bag?"

"Why would I have a poop bag?"

"Didn't we go over this yesterday?"

"I didn't even bring a leash; why would I bring a poop bag?"

"I don't know." I bend to inspect Raphael's gift. "But I need one. I think it's illegal to leave dog shit on the ground."

"How could you possibly know the DC dog shit laws?"

"I don't know!" I say again, a bit too loudly. Raphael barks.

Then May says quietly, "I can't go home to get one right now," and I feel weird for asking about the poop bag in the first place.

So the poop stays on the ground.

After a minute: "Can I ask what happened?"

"No offense, but I'm not talking to you about it." She stares at Raphael like she's contemplating petting him, then thinks better of it. "Just because you heard something you weren't supposed to doesn't mean I have to tell you anything."

"I know," I say, feeling a little hurt. Which is silly. It's not like I thought we were friends just because she almost willingly came on this walk.

But I thought there would at least be some sort of truce.

"I don't want to be here, you know," May says after another minute of Raphael zooming around.

"You've made that abundantly clear."

"In DC, I mean." She meets my eyes, and I realize that she might actually be answering my question about what happened (in her weird, roundabout way), so I shut up. "I don't live here. I visit, sometimes. That's why I barely know this dog, or this neighborhood. I usually live with my mom."

"Oh," I say, feeling somehow worse, because she *wants* to be with her mom for the holidays but is being forced to stay here, and I'm *choosing* to stay here when I could be with my mom.

"Yup."

A car drives by, and Raphael almost runs into the street to chase it, so I scoop him up again. "So just to circle back—no poop bags?"

"It's natural. Leave it."

"It's rude to leave it."

"You wanna pick it up with your hands?"

I glance down at the surprisingly large pile of poop. Maybe I'll come back for it tomorrow.

I carry Raphael all the way back to May's house. It's only a couple of blocks, but he gets heavy, fast. May and I don't say anything to each other, but when I gently drop the pup in front of May's door she says, "Thanks."

I don't know what she's thanking me for, let alone that she was capable of gratitude, so I just say, "Sure."

"But don't expect me to come with you tomorrow."

And with that return to normalcy, she ushers Raphael inside and slams the door.

Hall of Human Suffering

On the first Friday of my internship, I decide to treat myself and spend my lunch break wandering aimlessly around the museum.

When I get back to the lab, Mandira has her jacket on. "Why don't we get coffee?"

"I just got back from lunch."

"Well, I need coffee. So come with."

I don't argue, and Mandira leads us to a nearby Starbucks.

"How's your first week in DC been?" she asks once we're outside.

"Pretty weird," I say, then immediately try to qualify

that statement. "Not because of lab, though. That's been great. The best part, actually."

"What's been going on, then?"

Out of everyone I know in DC, which, at this point, are Mandira, my roommates, a ninety-six-year-old with a potential drinking problem, a teen barista, a weatherman, his corgi, and a girl who hates me—Mandira feels like the person I can trust the most.

And, sure, maybe that's a little pathetic.

Scratch that: it's *definitely* pathetic that my closest friend in our nation's capital is also sort of my boss. But I'm tired of keeping stuff in.

"Did I tell you that my mom and I almost ran over this girl with our car when she was dropping me off?"

"Wait, really?"

We arrive at Starbucks, and it's a peppermint-scented nightmare.

"Yeah," I say, continuing the story once Mandira and I are in line, "it was really snowy and the girl came out of nowhere. She was just taking a walk or something. It was pretty scary. Like, we could've killed her."

"Is she okay?"

"Oh yeah," I say, then amend my statement: "Well, she was angry, but she's fine."

"That's good."

"Yeah, but wanna know something wild?"

"Of course."

The line is barely moving, and all the suit-clad DC businesspeople tap their feet while the tourists hold up the line debating whether they should buy the limited edition "DC at Christmas" mugs or a decades-old Alanis Morissette CD.

"The other day my roommate asked me if I could take over her dog walking job, and guess whose dog I'm walking?"

"The girl you almost ran over?" Mandira asks, sounding appropriately shocked.

"Yup. May. Is her name."

Mandira smiles a little, starts to say something, then stops. After a few seconds, she tries again: "That honestly sounds like the start of a Hallmark movie."

"What? No." *Absolutely not.* "It's just weird, right?"

"Yeah, definitely weird."

The conversation stops after that as we move closer to the front of the line.

I shouldn't have brought it up in the first place.

But I can't talk about this with anyone else. I don't want to tell Taylor, because she'll make it into a *thing*. She'll try to look May up on IG or she'll find some weird but ultimately charming old YouTube video of an assignment that May had to make for Spanish or French class in high school or something heinous like that. And I can't deal with that right now.

"All right, you need to help me brainstorm," Mandira says.

"Okay. What?" I ask, grateful for a new conversation topic.

"I have this joke with Dr. Graham—well, it's funny to me, anyway—but it's this joke where I like to buy him the sweetest, most outrageous drink on the menu. And he *always* drinks it, no matter what I buy."

I try to imagine serious paleoichthyologist Dr. Charles Graham slurping down a peppermint mocha. It is, in fact, hilarious. "What should we get him?"

"Maybe a holiday drink."

"Obviously," I say, playing along.

"And it has to be giant."

"A trenta, for sure."

"Genius," Mandira says.

"What about"—I point to a sign displaying this year's holiday flavors—"a caramel brûlée latte?"

"Oh, he won't know what to do with that," she says. "It's perfect."

A perky barista calls us up, and Mandira gives them the order. When the barista asks if we want whipped cream, Mandira looks at me, nods solemnly, and tells them, "Absolutely."

We head out of Starbucks holding two normal coffees and an outrageous coffee-adjacent drink that's larger than a small child.

I can't help but laugh. Not just because of the drink, but also because a week ago I thought my life was over, and now I'm getting overly sweet lattes for an award-winning scientist and preparing specimens that have survived millions of years longer than I've lived with a broken heart.

Even though the museum is only a few blocks away, we take our time walking back. After a minute, Mandira says, "So, can I tell *you* something kind of funny?"

"Yeah," I say. Because of course I want Mandira to tell me something kind of funny. Every time I've met a cool, older queer person, I've been desperate for them to be my friend, and she's no exception.

"Back to what you were saying about that girl." When she says this, I have a thought that's like, *Thank goodness we're back to talking about me.* I hate that I do but yeah. "When I met my girlfriend, we were at a bar, and she yelled at me for cutting in front of her to order. But then we started talking and I bought her a drink and we hit it off." She does this exhale-snort-laugh thing. "We still joke about it because she said so many wild things while she was yelling. Whenever we go out, we still quote her. We'll be like, 'You cut in front of me for a *spiked Shirley Temple*?'" And then Mandira laughs for real, and I laugh weakly along with her.

Of course Mandira is cool enough to get a girl to go from yelling at her to flirting just like that.

When she doesn't say anything else, it feels like an invitation to talk about May, which, fine, maybe that's a selfish impulse, but I *want* to talk to Mandira about her. I need Mandira to know that I'm queer and cool, which go hand-in-hand, obviously.

"It's really not like a Hallmark movie—the thing with that girl. With May."

"Oh?" Mandira asks.

"Yeah, I sort of just went through a breakup." And then I tell Mandira about Sadie, about falling in love with her and how I had planned our wedding and all the gay babies we were going to have.

After I tell the story and we're back in the lab, Mandira says, "So, why'd you break up, then, if you don't mind me asking? Sounds like things were pretty good?"

This sets my face on fire.

Whenever I talk about Sadie, I can't help but gloss over the bad parts.

I haven't said the real reason for our breakup out loud to anyone. And it's not an appropriate thing to say to the person who is technically my direct boss.

I try to skirt around the real reason, but ultimately, I need to tell Mandira at least part of the truth or I'll explode. "It was maybe like a"—I pause and lower my voice before I say the last part, in case Dr. Graham is listening—"a sex thing."

Mandira smiles, and I want to die. She must see the look on my face because she says, "Sorry! Sorry. But she broke up with you over a sex thing?" She's clearly trying not to laugh.

I glance around the room, praying that no one's walking

directly outside the door, or if they are that it's the grim reaper here to remove me from this mortal coil. "Not *a* sex thing. Just, like, sex— I probably shouldn't talk about this. I don't even know why I brought it up." Then I add, "I'm the worst intern of all time," for good measure.

"No, the worst intern of all time sat on his phone and blasted 100 gecs all day." Mandira stops cleaning and looks up at me. "We don't have to talk about this—we probably *shouldn't* talk about this—but just let me say one thing: sex can be amazing. Especially queer sex. And especially if you communicate what you want with your partner."

My face is so hot that my skin and muscle are both burning off and soon I'll be a skeleton for the museum to display in the Hall of Human Suffering.

"Please don't report me for talking to you about this," Mandira says, and it only seems like she's half joking.

"Same," I say. Then: "Can we not talk about this anymore?"

We work in an awkward silence for a few minutes, until Mandira says, "Christmas music?"

And I say, "Yes, please."

I wake up to a warm patch of sun bathing my face from a large dusty window.

Oh, shit.

I bolt out of bed. I'm late for work. Crap, crap, crap. I've woken up before the sun every day this week, and now I'm going to be late and Mandira will be disappointed and Dr. Graham will sigh and keep washing fossils with his toothbrush and they'll both think about how they should've hired a punctual intern and on top of that my Sadie-addled brain made things too awkward with Mandira for me to ever return.

Then I check my phone.

. . . It's Saturday.

I had been planning on getting up early and spending the day alone wandering around DC, but the getting-up-early part clearly didn't work out too well. I get dressed so that I can start on the second part.

Until I hear chatter and music and laughter downstairs. It's not weird that people are visiting—they pop by all the time to see Beatrice. But I don't want to see them. It's one thing to fill up my water bottle in the kitchen in the morning before work, when the house is quiet, but it's another to join in on a Saturday morning get-together.

I grab my jacket and backpack and try to sneak out. An Ella Fitzgerald song is playing, which I figure should drown out the door opening. I reach my hand out to grasp the doorknob, inches from escape—

"Doll!"

I turn around and there's Beatrice, standing approximately forty feet below me.

"Hi," I say. Then, quickly, with my hand still on the

door: “I didn’t want to be a bother, so I’m just gonna head out.”

“Nonsense!” Beatrice says. “Stay, stay.” She grabs my waist and pulls me into the throng. There are people of all different ages scattered everywhere throughout the living room and kitchen, all of them holding a drink or a snack plate or, if they’re profoundly wild, both.

We end up standing between a cool, vintage-looking record player and a stocky man who’s probably in his early seventies.

“George,” the man says in a gruff smoker’s voice. He reaches his hand out for me to shake.

I reach mine out, too. “Shani.”

“He’s my baby.” Beatrice squeezes my waist and his non-shaking arm at the same time. “The runt of the litter.”

I stare at the man for a beat too long. This *elderly* person is Beatrice’s youngest son? My mind is boggled.

“Doll, make nice with George for a while, won’t you? I’m going to speak with my great-grandson.” She lets go of my waist. “Tony owes me thirty bucks.”

“So,” George says once Beatrice leaves. “You’re sleeping in ma and pa’s room, right?”

My eyes go wide. “Oh, um, yeah,” and then, of course, I’m struck by a nasty case of verbal diarrhea. “It’s fantastic. Super comfortable. Very . . . homey. You know?”

George ignores me, thankfully. “Our dad haunts that room—did my mom tell you?”

It's possible I misheard, so I ask, "He does what with the room?"

"Haunts it, kid. He haunts it." George laughs like it's a wonderful joke that his dead father's ghost is watching me sleep on the bed where George was conceived.

"Well, excuse me while I head to the little boys' room," George says, starting to open his belt buckle unceremoniously.

And then I head out too, happy for the excuse.

When I step outside, everything is quiet, muted. I feel untethered.

No one besides me knows where I'm going. And now that I've escaped, I have a whole day to do what I want. I could walk across all of DC, or I could sit in a bookstore and read for eight hours. No one would care either way.

I've been to the natural history museum every day this week, so I figure I should branch out and go to a different one. All the Smithsonian museums are free, and I want to see as many as I can before I go back to school.

Before I hop on the Metro, I look inside The Big Blue Dog to see if my boy Luke is there—I got a free latte out of him yesterday morning, which was a big accomplishment—but he's not.

So I skip the café and get on the train. I don't transfer lines like I've been doing during the week and instead go straight downtown to the Gallery Place-Chinatown stop, because "Gallery Place" sounds pretty museum-y.

The escalators at Gallery Place are just as freakishly tall as the ones at the other stops, and it's like a wind tunnel as I try to get out. I don't know why, but every station on the DC Metro has hurricane-level gales trying to keep you from getting onto the street.

In the end, I make it to the surface, but the sight my eyes behold makes me wish the wind would drag me back down into the underworld.

I escaped one Christmas party, yet somehow, I've landed smack-dab in the middle of another one.

Well, it's not a party so much as a Christmas market. There are string lights and oversize plastic candy canes hanging above little shops in red-and-white striped tents. The vendors are all wearing Santa hats and creepily large smiles.

I don't know what it is about the weeks leading up to Christmas and people wearing Santa hats. Isn't that confusing for kids? Maybe it's like how bridesmaids used to have to wear white dresses and stand around the bride to ward off evil spirits who wanted to kidnap her. Does wearing Santa hats ward off Santa? Like, the guy's pretty creepy. He straight up breaks and enters, and also he can somehow look inside a home and know if there's a Christian kid or if there's just some other kid who doesn't deserve his love and presents (and crimes).

Anyway, I locate the museum, a large square beige

building, but it seems that the only way to get to the front entrance is through the market.

So I take the plunge.

There's a band assembled under one of the vendor tents; it's made up of four middle-aged white guys doing bad rock covers of Christmas songs. I stop and watch for a minute as the drummer pounds his sticks together and they start on "Good King Wenceslas." It's the worst thing I've ever heard.

Once they've finished butchering the song, the front man shouts into a feedback-y microphone, "We've been The Naughty Elves! Thanks for your time and MERRY CHRISTMAS."

They're met with no response, except from a visibly intoxicated man walking by with what is clearly a beer wrapped in a brown paper bag. He whistles and shouts, "WOOOOO," at the top of his lungs.

I keep walking but stop when I smell something fried and wonderful. There's a tent with a guy selling powdered donuts and hot beverages, which immediately makes up for The Naughty Elves.

When I get to the front of the line, the person running the stand barely looks up as he says, "And what can I get for you, young man?"

I smile and order powdered donuts and chai. He responds, "Yes, sir," still not looking at me.

This happens sometimes and even more so when my hair was a bit shorter. If someone glances at me for a moment, they might think I'm a prepubescent boy. Or they might look and see that I'm an eighteen-year-old lesbian. It's like the rabbit/duck optical illusion. There's a case to be made for both.

"Here you go," the man says as he hands me a bag filled with donuts and a steaming paper cup of chai. He pauses and stares at me, and I see the gears turning in his head as he begins to realize that I might not be the young man he greeted.

That's my cue to thank him and run up the steps to the museum. On one side there's a sign that says, "Smithsonian American Art Museum," and on the other there's one that reads, "National Portrait Gallery." It's like a two-for-one museum experience, even though it's free, which is music to my cheap, cheap ears.

"No food in the museum," a guard yells before I'm fully through the door. "Are you going to the courtyard?"

"Uh, yes," I say, and he nods, pointing to an entryway past the information desk.

I open a set of elegant glass doors, and when I step inside the courtyard, I'm in another world. It's huge and warm, with a giant glass ceiling that must be sixty feet in the air, held up by old, beautiful museum walls on all four sides. It's like being outside but without the cold. There are trees and poinsettias and fountains and tables and families, but it doesn't feel crowded like the Christmas market. The space is so huge that even with all the people, there's room to spare.

I take off my jacket and lift my face to the rippling glass ceiling and the winter sky above. I'm happy to have nowhere to be as I walk around and get powdered sugar all over my clothes, then wash the donuts down with the hot chai.

There's a slightly removed area with a marble bench in front of some trees, and even though I've never been here before, it's like it was made for me. There's no one around, so I pull a book out of my backpack, then stretch out on the bench, resting my head on the padded part of the bag.

I extend my arms in the air so the book is looking down on me. All I see are the words on the page, leaves stretching over me, and the glass ceiling keeping the cold out. It's so peaceful, so perfect, so—

"I was hoping I wouldn't find you here."

At the sound of a voice coming from directly above me, I sit up so quickly that I have spots in my eyes. When the floaters clear, I see her.

Of course.

"You know there are seven hundred thousand people living in DC?" I ask once the initial shock has worn off and my heart rate is somewhat normal.

"Plus tourists," May says. "And neither of us count, really." She's looking down at me with one hip popped, red beanie in hand.

"Can't you see I was reading?" I stretch and start to put the book away.

"I've read that one," she says, pointing to the cover. "The demon is her brother and she fucks the merman."

"Seriously?" I shove the book into my bag. "I barely started it."

She shrugs.

"Did you follow me here?" I ask, because that seems like the only logical explanation for her standing in front of me right now.

"Why would I do that?"

"I don't know."

I think about what Mandira said, about all my run-ins with May being like a Hallmark movie.

But Mandira was wrong.

It's not like a rom-com. It's a series of coincidences in which a girl—a cute girl, fine, yes, sure—ruins my chances of having a monk-like, quiet, lab-focused month where I get to wander around DC alone to my heart's content.

When I got together with Sadie, *that* felt like a movie. Like a Nora Ephron film, if she ever wrote about queer girls. It would take place in the nineties, somehow. It would be something people quoted.

But maybe that's how everyone feels when they get into their first real relationship.

"Are you here with your dad, then?" I ask May. I can't figure out why else she'd be at the museum.

She laughs but not like you would at a joke. "I'm here to get *away* from him."

"And to follow me, apparently." I put my elbows on my knees and spread my legs apart. "Did you, like, trail me?"

"No, we just got on the Metro at the same time. It's allowed."

"And then you saw me get off and followed me here so that you could spoil my book?"

"Again, no. You just have a useless superpower where you can anticipate where I'll be and how to annoy me and then you're there and doing that."

I wait until I'm sure she's done reprimanding me for existing. "So, I annoy you?"

"Terribly."

"Good."

She plops down on the bench next to me. We both sit there, not talking, watching people stroll by.

"All right, listen," May says, staring ahead. "I know that, because it's us, you're gonna bump into me and knock down some priceless masterpiece if I let you wander around the museum by yourself—"

"How kind," I say in what I hope is my most biting voice. But my heart is pounding because she said "us," which like . . . Body, why? It's an automatic reflex. Like gagging. "I'll call my mom and tell her she doesn't need to find a babysitter for tonight."

"—so I might as well have you under my supervision,"

she continues, not responding to my comment. Then she stands up, faces me on the bench, and nods her head toward the museum door. "Come with me."

I stay where I am, arms crossed.

"Really?" she asks. "Come on. Just get up. You're fine." And she reaches out her hand.

I pretend like I have to think about it. But I don't, really.

I grab it.

The second I do, she yanks my arm so hard that she must've dislocated my shoulder.

"Stay with me. I can't have you loose in the portrait gallery."

"I'm not *that* much of a hazard."

"Personal experience would beg to differ."

I hate that I *don't* hate the way she talks to me.

I hate that I sort of like it.

And, I don't know, maybe it's possible that she's into me? Is that such a wild thought? Though it's even likelier that she's straight and I'm overthinking everything.

Not that it matters, though. If she was queer, nothing would happen.

I don't *want* anything to happen.

Seriously.

"All right," she says, once I'm up and rubbing my shoulder. "Let's go."

May runs ahead of me, out of the courtyard and up a

spiral staircase, weaving through the other museum-goers as they observe the art at a leisurely pace.

"I don't believe in *wandering* through museums," she says as we emerge two floors up. She's a few steps ahead of me. "I know where all the good stuff is, so that's where I go. Like, I don't care at all about the presidential portraits, but I always visit Michelle Obama." She power walks away, like an elderly woman who goes to the mall for exercise. "Keep up."

I jog a little as I try not to lose her, but she walks with such purpose that I find myself apologizing to families as I nearly mow them down.

Her big puff of brown hair turns into one of the side galleries, and I run in after her.

May's standing in a large crowd, in front of which is the portrait of Michelle Obama.

I stare at May staring at the painting, her jaw slack and eyes glazed over. She stays like that for a full minute.

"I can't believe Michelle took away our vending machines," I say, trying to elicit literally any response from a frozen May. "I miss the Doritos." After another moment of silent gazing, May still doesn't respond. "And I can't believe she likes to crush puppies with her powerful arms in her spare time."

"Yeah," May says, dazed.

"Did you hear what I said?"

"What?" May shakes her head a little and blinks. "Not really. On we go."

"That's it?" I ask. "You went into a trance in front of Michelle Obama and now we're moving on?"

"Yup," she says. "We stay at a painting for as long as we need to see it. That's all we need for Michelle."

"I kind of want to look a bit at the other—"

But she's off again, and, against my better judgment, I follow. This time she turns around once to make sure I'm there. I give her a thumbs-up, and she rolls her eyes, but she's smiling as she turns to guide us through the museum.

We cross over from the portrait gallery to the American art side, and she stops at the entrance to a large room. There's a giant translucent column that stretches from the floor all the way to the tall ceiling. It's not solid, just a projection of light scrolling to display different words. It's spinning and spinning and spinning, repeating a phrase over and over again: "Being alone with yourself is increasingly unpopular."

Or just impossible, I think. But I say, "I like this," as I point to the cylinder of light and truisms.

"It'll rotate through different phrases," May says. "Last time I was here it said, 'Bad intentions can yield good results.'"

Of course that's what it said for May.

"Come in here," she says while I'm still transfixed by the glowing cylinder.

May walks into an empty, dark area of the gallery. But when she sits on a bench, a red light turns on and illuminates the piece. With the light, I see we're in a three-sided room, staring at something like a stage that's filled with abstract shapes and sculptures. Some of the shapes are illuminated, and others are making dark red shadows along the walls.

I sit on the soft, black-cushioned bench with her, but as far away as possible, and watch the display.

The red fades away, and the stage is plunged into darkness once again. But then another light comes on and illuminates a small leaf-shaped painting on the floor, one I didn't see when it was bathed in red. This time the light is purple, and the stage looks completely different.

Watching it feels like sitting in a kitchen on a bright Sunday morning, drinking steaming-hot coffee as sunlight progresses across the room. It's color, light, and emotion.

"Last time I was in DC, I brought a friend from home," May says after a while, leaning back on her hands and watching the colors change. There's a green light being thrown into the mix now, and even more of the sculpture comes to life. "We watched this for a long, long time."

"It's mesmerizing," I say. Something about the changing lights and the dark room has mellowed both of us out. After another minute I ask, "So, where's home?" because I think she might actually tell me. And I want to know.

"Ithaca." Her face is covered half in purple light and half in green. "I go to school there, too. Cornell."

I sit up and shake my head, shocked. "Wait, dude, I go to Binghamton." I immediately feel weird for calling her dude even though there's nothing going on between us.

"And? That's not very close," she says. "An hour away, at least."

"It's not far by upstate standards," I say, and lean back again. "I'm from Queens, and before I left for school, I thought Westchester was upstate. So Ithaca and Bing are pretty much the same area."

"Fine," she says. "The same *general* area."

It's funny that we're arguing about this—the specifics of Upstate New York geography. Of all the places she could be from, and of all the places I could go to school, of course they're only an hour apart.

Mandira pops into my head again, saying, "*Hallmark movie.*" I shake the thought away.

The light cycles back to red, and May still doesn't move.

"Read the plaque," she says.

"The what?"

"The plaque thing, by the entrance. It's interesting. You know, stuff about the piece."

I heave myself up from the bench and read the text.

"David Hockney made this?" I ask, stunned.

I'm obsessed with him. I don't know much about art, but I know about Hockney. He was a gay icon. He painted men showering together, abstract dicks, men in love, living with each other. Quiet intimacy.

It doesn't surprise me that he designed this. It's an invitation to sit, maybe with someone, maybe alone, and look. Just observe and experience.

"Do you like him?" May asks, and when I turn, she's watching me.

She looks back at the painting.

"I love him."

"I love him, too," she says, still staring at Hockney's work. "I love what it says on the plaque. He wrote something about how it's art's job to overcome the sterility of despair."

Sure enough, that's what it says on the sign. Almost word for word: "*Snails Space* is both a summary of Hockney's career and a poignant example of his belief that art should 'overcome the sterility of despair.' It grew out of his practice of arranging separate canvases around the studio, painting the floor, and inviting his visitors to step into the world of his paintings."

I think over the words *sterility of despair.* I think of sitting alone in my room: at home in Queens, at Beatrice's place. I think of not talking to my mom on the car ride here, of staring out the window, of the white snow obscuring the highway.

Then I look over at the painting: the stage, bright lights, warmth. The bench, made for two.

It's embarrassing, but a few tears form at the corners of my eyes, and when I turn back to *Snails Space* it's just a block of fuzzy reds and purples.

I covertly wipe the tears away and sit back down on the

bench. "Why didn't you bring your friend to DC this time?"

It's something I've been wondering since she mentioned the friend. If she's trying to avoid her dad and hates DC so much, it seems like she should have a buffer. That she shouldn't be watching *Snails Space* with me if she could be watching it with someone she likes.

She frowns a little, and her face is thrown into shadow as the piece goes into one of its dark periods. "We're not really friends anymore," she says. "Me and the girl."

She doesn't say anything else, no short, quippy comeback. She just stares and stares.

I know I'm pushing it, but I ask, "How come?"

"Oh, you know." She gathers her hair at the nape of her neck and releases it. "Just because."

Something about the way she says it makes me wonder: is this "friend" a friend (with scare quotes to infinity) like Sadie was for me?

"I'm sorry," I say, and I mean it. Because if she was a "friend," I know how it feels.

"It's fine. I'm fine now."

Red turns to purple turns to blue turns to green. I don't respond.

After sitting in front of the Hockney piece for a while, we leave to explore the rest of the museum. May's still running ahead, but now she watches for me and sometimes waits.

When we stop in front of a painting or a sculpture, she'll tell me about it.

"I really like this one," she says as we look at a painting made of brightly colored vertical stripes. "The artist wanted to make it so that it didn't look like anything, so that you couldn't *make* it look like something. You can read on the plaque." She glances over at me. "I don't know, I kind of like that."

I examine the text under the painting, and it says almost exactly what May told me.

"How do you know so much about this museum?" I ask after she tells me about a horse sculpture that looks like it's made of tree branches but is really bronze.

"It's my favorite place in DC," she says. "It's the only good place."

"Um, that's obviously false," I tell her. "Have you ever been to the museum of natural history?"

"Never."

"That's why I'm here. I'm working there over break."

"I was wondering about that," she says. "I thought you came just to annoy me. As a holiday treat."

"I mean, yeah, that was the other reason." We stop in front of a portrait of Muhammad Ali. "But we'll have to go to the natural history museum sometime."

And then I realize what I said and blush. One good morning in the portrait gallery, and suddenly I'm planning a future activity.

She looks over at me, tilts her head a bit. "Sure," she says. "We should."

I smile at Muhammed Ali.

Then she adds, "It's not like there's anybody else to go with."

A couple hours later, I'm exhausted in the way that only a museum can make me, and May and I take the Metro home together. We're quiet for a little while as the train makes its northbound journey, silent and smooth.

I don't know how or why (I never do), but Sadie pops into my head. And when she does, I realize: I haven't thought about her in hours.

A week ago, I was thinking about her every second of every day. She lived in my brain.

Then it decreased to every ten minutes, and now, magically, it's only every couple of hours. Maybe one day it'll be never. Or, at least, it won't hurt so much when I do think of her.

Maybe this means I'm moving on.

The thought makes me smile, and as I'm smiling, I turn toward May.

She turns to me and smiles back. A real one, from the girl I almost ran over less than a week ago.

As the train bends slightly on its path, she's pushed closer to me. She doesn't move back to her spot near the window.

Having her this close makes my heart beat faster. It makes my palms sweaty.

Oh, fuck.

No. We're not doing this.

Because I'm pretty sure my body thinks something that my brain certainly does not.

That maybe, possibly, unbelievably, my traitorous nervous system has developed a crush on someone when I explicitly told it not to.

The train announcement comes on: "The next stop is Tenleytown-AU."

"That's us," May says, putting her jacket back on.

I stand up to get away from her. "I guess it is."

Gory Details About This Guy's Ass

Pretty much the last thing I want to do today is go over to May's house and walk her dad's dog. Because if I do, I'll see May. And if I see May, there's a strong possibility that my body will once again betray me.

So instead, I'm sitting in my room. The current plan is to not move from this spot—on the bed, over the covers—at all today. I'll spend my entire Sunday cloistered up here.

And, later tonight, when Beatrice's family leaves and May is most likely asleep, I'll take Raphael out for a midnight walk. Is that a bit unconventional for a dog walker? Sure. Will May's dad think someone is dognapping his corgi? Possibly.

I open my book—I'm going to finish it out of spite even though May spoiled it—and end up reading the same paragraph four times. So, of course, I reach for my phone.

MAY: what time are you coming to walk the dog?

Well.

Great.

ME: are u asking bc u wanna make sure you're not there?

MAY: ha ha.

ME: idk i was gonna come later
like much later
i'm pretty busy today

I send that last text from a fully horizontal position with my book on my chest and not a single item on my agenda. But May doesn't need to know that.

MAY: gotcha

I switch over to IG, thinking that's all she has to say, when another text comes:

MAY: i actually had a pretty good time yesterday

I stare at my phone for an entire minute. Then my fingers type before my brain can think.

ME: i did too

even if you did follow me there

MAY: uh DID NOT follow you

!!!!!

ME: i don't know . . .

signs point to yes

MAY: are you a magic 8 ball

ME: yeah srry wrong number

this is a sentient ball

MAY: oh shit

i knew something was up

I smile down at my phone.

No!

I wipe the smile off my face.

But here's the problem: if someone's good at texting, that's ten thousand points in their favor.

Sadie was a horrible texter, but it didn't really matter because we were always together. Always. Like, people would ask me where she was if I showed up anywhere without her. After a while I started to resent how everyone assumed that I should be following her at all times, like a lost puppy.

Mostly I resented it because it was true. I needed her near me—next to me, even—to feel safe.

But May is not Sadie. And nothing is happening here. You can send a few flirty texts to someone without it being a *thing*.

And May is pretty good at it.

Texting, that is.

ME: yeah
so rough for you that you spent the entire day yesterday with an inanimate object
a stocking stuffer, one might say

MAY: and here i was thinking you were anti christmas
or is that just hanukkah?
i forget
do you like ruining the holidays for all kids or just some?

ME: i like ruining the holidays for every child
even the christian ones
i don't discriminate

MAY: so brave of u
calling the nobel peace prize committee rn

The sound of Beatrice's laugh carries upstairs, and I burrow further into bed. The last thing I want to do is go down there. And texting May has become significantly higher on the list of things I *do* want to do.

ME: there's a large catholic family downstairs

so i'm hiding rn

MAY: ok remind me where you're living???

like i only get more confused the more details i hear about it

you're living in the place my dad's dog walker usually does?

but a catholic family broke in?

is this a home invasion?

should i be worried?

The ratio is so skewed toward May's words right now. It's nice to be on the receiving end of a huge block of text; it makes me feel like I'm in control. Or at the very least that May wants to talk to me.

Which wasn't the case just a few days ago.

Plus, she's wondering if she should be *worried* about me. It's like I'm speaking to someone doing a shitty impersonation of May.

ME: no need to be worried

i can take them

im GIFTED in the art of hand-to-hand combat

MAY: i find that

deeply hard to believe

but can u tell me where ur living

im on the edge of my seat

ME: lol ok so

im living w my great-grandma's friend?

she's 96

and her giant catholic family is here

MAY: she's 96??

like years old?????

ME: lmao literally what else would that mean

MAY: IDK THAT'S VERY OLD

I'M JUST SURPRISED

I look up from my phone and shake my head, laughing.

Then, from outside the room: "Angel, are you in there?"

I don't move or breathe.

"We're having cake, doll. If you're in there, why don't you come down and join us?"

I almost run into the en suite bathroom, but it would be pathetic for me to continue hiding from a ninety-six-year-old woman who wants to feed me cake, so I rip off my pajama bottoms and throw on a pair of jeans before sending May a few final messages.

ME: the 96 y/o is knocking on my door

asking me to come for cake

so gotta do that

MAY: she goes up stairs?????????

I once again grin at my phone, but quickly wipe the smile away.

"Cake sounds great," I say as I open the door, and immediately shut it behind me so Beatrice can't see the mess I've made of her marital bed.

"Oh, doll, you scared me." She puts a hand over her heart. "I didn't even know if you were in there."

"I was," I say. "But, you know, just resting."

"Are you not feeling well? I can give you an ibuprofen." She stretches a hand up to my forehead. "Would that help? I think I have a handful in one of my pockets."

"I'm fine, really," I say. "Just relaxing."

She grabs my arm. "You can relax when you're dead."

And just like that, I'm downstairs. The family crowd has thinned a bit, but George is sitting there, alone at the kitchen table. I grab a seat next to him.

"Shani! We missed you after you left yesterday." He

takes a bite of the chocolate cake. "Where'd you go?"

"Just out," I say. Then, because that's something I would say to my mom and not what I should say to the son of the woman who's letting me stay in her bedroom, I add: "The Portrait Gallery."

"Oh, isn't it the best?" he asks.

Beatrice sits down and takes a bite of cake. "What's the best?"

"The Portrait Gallery, Ma," George says loudly.

"It is!" She smiles wistfully at me. "One of the most romantic spots in the city. Perfect for a first date."

Sweat pools under my arms. I slice a piece of cake to give myself something to do.

"Do you have a beau, doll?"

"Uh, no." I focus all my attention on the cake. "This is delicious," I say quickly, mouth full.

"Thanks," George says, laughing a bit. "I got the recipe from a video on The YouTube. My niece emailed it to me. I'm testing out some desserts for Christmas."

"What are you doing for Christmas, doll?" Beatrice asks.

Staying as far away from anyone celebrating the holiday as I possibly can. "Oh, nothing, really."

"Nothing?" She grips my arm with her frighteningly strong fingers. "Come to George's, angel! He'd be happy to have you."

George seems hesitant. "Oh, Ma, I was thinking it would just be a family thing, you know. . . ."

"It's really okay," I tell him, because it is. The last thing I want to do is celebrate Christmas with a bunch of strangers. Or celebrate Christmas at all.

"This doll *is* family," Beatrice says, giving George a chastising look as her fingers tighten around my wrist.

I don't know how Beatrice has made it through life like this, where she considers moody girls who've spent less than two weeks in her home family. But maybe that's the secret to her longevity: inviting everyone into her life, indiscriminately.

If that *is* the secret, I don't think I'll live to be ninety-six.

"I'm okay, really," I say. "But thanks for the offer." I give George a closed-mouth smile to let him know we're on the same team, and he tries to distract Beatrice by asking about her aquacise class.

But she's back to an earlier question: "So, no beau? That's good," she adds. "Boys just distract from studies. You can get serious about dating when you're done with school."

If only she knew how much girls can distract from studies, too.

"You go to school in New York, doll?"

"Yeah, but not the city—"

Beatrice plows ahead: "The best date spot in the city? Wanna know?" she asks. "The best spot to bring a boy—or better yet, a *man*—is the Staten Island ferry. It's free *and* romantic! The river air, the wind. You even get a peek at the Statue of Liberty! That's one gorgeous broad, I'll tell you."

"Ma, Shani doesn't want to hear about this. Look at her." George gestures toward me as I shovel a large bite of cake into my mouth.

Beatrice only laughs. "Sure she does. Right, angel?" She doesn't wait for me to answer before she says, "Who wouldn't want advice on how to get a beau from someone who's never been divorced?"

"You were never divorced because Dad died, Ma," George says as he clears his throat.

"But it's still true, isn't it?" She chuckles and slaps George's arm. "My two cents? Don't let him take over your life—your beau. He should just be a part of it, doll. Never the whole thing."

Well, shit. That's actually good advice. I could've used it a few months ago.

I nod and smile as Beatrice pats my arm, then she and George start arguing about the Staten Island ferry schedule.

When I was with Sadie, I felt like I had become a second-class person in the relationship, even though I was dating another girl. I relied on her in a way I know she didn't rely on me.

And I don't like where this train of thought is going. The kitchen feels too small, and I feel too big, like I'm going to rip through my own skin, so I mumble, "I, uh, have to call my mom." It's stretching the truth a bit, but I can't be down here anymore.

"Say hi to her for me," Beatrice says. "Tell her I'm taking perfect care of you."

"Will do," I say, and wave to George as I run back to the comfort of Beatrice's bedroom.

When I get there, I close the door, put my pajama pants back on and hop into bed. I decide that I probably *should* check in on my mom, so I send her a text.

ME: beatrice says hi

It's not much, but it's something. A few minutes later, she responds.

MOM: Awwwwww . . . Tell her I say hi back . . . . . . R u eating?

The last part is such a classic Jewish mom question that I hardly think it's necessary to answer. I take a deep breath to stifle the unwanted anger rising in my chest.

ME: plenty

And now that I've communicated the bare minimum with my mom, there's something else I need to do.

Earlier this week, I didn't want to tell Taylor about May because I was worried she'd make a big deal out of nothing.

But now, it seems, there might be something to tell.

Taylor loves knowing everything about my life. It was a breach of our friendship contract to not talk to her about Sadie, to not tell her everything.

I definitely don't know everything about Taylor's life, though, but only because I have to repeatedly remind her that she should keep some things private. Take, for example, when she first saw a boy naked back in ninth grade. She started giving me the gory details about this guy's ass, and I covered my ears. She knows now not to describe her hookups in detail; I don't need to hear what my best friend is doing behind closed doors.

I need to call Taylor.

"Shani!" she says when she picks up the FaceTime.

"Tay!"

We smile at each other for a second and then burst out laughing for no reason in particular.

"How's my mom?" I ask.

"We just got coffee yesterday," the little Taylor in the screen tells me. "I made sure she used a dairy alternative."

"You're a hero."

She tips a fake cowboy hat. "Just doing my job, ma'am." Then she says, "How the fuck are you?"

I take a deep breath. "So—"

"I KNEW IT!"

"What?" I ask, alarmed.

"I *knew* you met someone. I KNEW IT. Ha! That's why you FaceTimed. I called it. I'm a literal genius."

"I didn't 'meet someone.'" But then I add, "There's just this girl," and Taylor laughs triumphantly.

I launch into the story of May, from the near–vehicular manslaughter to our day at the museum to texting her before I got on the phone with Taylor.

"All right, so you have a big ol' lesbian crush on her," Taylor says when I'm done with the story.

"What? Absolutely not." I smooth down the scratchy comforter. "I don't even know if she's queer."

"The texts are literally so flirty, though," Taylor says. "I would never text another girl like that."

"Okay, so like if I *did* have a crush on her—"

"I knew it!" Taylor says again.

"—and I'm not saying I do, but if I *did* . . . Is it too soon? Is it weird? Am I horrible? Do you hate me?"

"Well, let's address those questions one at a time." Taylor's always very good at making lists and doing pros and cons and being generally logical. "It may be slightly too soon, sure, but the statute of limitations is way shorter if you're the dump-ee. Is it weird? No. It sounds kind of exciting, honestly. As for the final two: you're not horrible at all. And wait, what was the last one again?"

"Do you hate me?" I ask quietly.

"Yes."

I smile at that.

"But I'm still mad at you for being in DC. I can't believe we're not spending New Year's together," Taylor adds when I don't say anything for a moment.

"I know." I fall back into bed. "Who's gonna wake me up when I inevitably fall asleep at ten thirty?"

Taylor and I have spent every New Year's together since we became friends. When we were little, we would join her parents and my mom, but once we got to middle school, we would celebrate with just the two of us. Then, for a couple years at the end of high school, Taylor got us invited to a New Year's party, which was a big deal.

After disappearing on her for a full semester, New Year's would've been the perfect time to make it up. To prove our friendship hasn't changed entirely.

"Oh, shit," Taylor says, and her screen goes black as she goes off FaceTime to check something else—she refuses to update her phone. "I promised my dad I would go see some documentary with him. Something about World War Two at the JCC."

"Sounds terrible."

"It will be. Keep me updated on the girl."

"There won't be anything to update you on."

Taylor comes back into the FaceTime just to wink dramatically at me.

"Have fun napping at the JCC," I say.

"Have fun texting your new gf."

"I'm hanging up now," I say, and smiling, I do.

Well, now that Taylor knows, I guess it's official: I have a crush on May.

People Love Al Roker

It's impossible to get any work done in the days leading up to Christmas. I blame (say it with me) the Christian hegemony. If Christmas weren't such an all-consuming holiday, we'd be perfectly productive capitalist cogs. But instead, we're perfectly unproductive capitalist cogs, awaiting the arrival of the most capitalist holiday of the year.

I tried to go above and beyond in the lab this week, to clean every millimeter of the fossils Mandira gave me, to impress Dr. Graham, to be a model employee.

But, along with everyone else, I lost steam about halfway through the week.

By Thursday, the twenty-third, things had devolved to

the point where Mandira tried to get me to wear a Santa hat, but for obvious reasons, I refused, so she laid it gently atop a fossilized fish skull. She also tried to get Dr. Graham to wear one, but I don't even think he heard her ask.

And, fine, there might be another reason I've been losing steam. And that reason might be puffy-haired, angry, and obscenely good at texting.

May's joined me on all of Raphael's walks this week. She'd grumbled a bit, sure, but she'd come along anyway.

"Why don't you hold the leash?" I had asked her on Wednesday evening. "Maybe if you held the leash literally one time, you'd like the poor dog a bit more."

We both turned our gaze toward Raphael. He stared up at us like he'd never been happier to do anything in his entire life than stand outside in the cold and stare at his part-time owner and substitute dog walker.

"If I held the leash then there'd be no reason for my dad to pay you," she had said.

"I think he'd pay me to supervise," I told her, and she bumped into me with her shoulder. "He wouldn't leave his precious son alone with you."

Her expression darkened. "You think you're joking, but that's not far from the truth."

"Well, then it's a good thing I'm here for supervision, isn't it?"

She smiled a little, then walked ahead of me and Raphael. "You tell yourself that," she called back.

I jogged to catch up, and Raphael sprinted a few steps behind on his stubby little legs. "I will."

"Good," May said, not breaking eye contact.

"Good," I said, doing the same.

"Bork," Raphael said, and May and I quickly looked away from each other.

Not only has May been joining me on walks, but we've been taking longer than Greg's mandated twenty minutes—sometimes as long as an hour. When we walk for that long, I have to carry Raphael home. He can't handle the intense exercise.

During that extra time, May tells me about her friends in Ithaca, or her mom's Hanukkah traditions (alternating latkes and jelly donuts each night), and I'll pick up the loaf boy and cradle his dense body in my arms, where he pants happily until we get home.

Sometimes I'll add something to the conversation, like how my mom loves latkes but hates the way they smell so she opens all the windows and doors when she's cooking them, making the house freezing. And sometimes Raphael will contribute a bark or a howl, but mostly we just listen to May.

Uh, yeah. So. Back to the lab.

The museum is open Christmas Eve, so all the labs are, too. *And* it's a Friday, which means that nothing is going to get done. Even Dr. Graham is out of his little closet workspace and sitting at the benches, humming along to

Mandira's Christmas music in a surprisingly dulcet baritone.

He's come out to join us a few times, and I'm always a little starstruck. That feeling lessened the other day when he was sitting with us and sorting fossils, so distracted that he barely seemed to notice when he let a tremendous fart rip. Mandira had to excuse herself to keep from laughing too hard.

To make matters even less productive, it started snowing this morning, and now Dr. Graham is telling us that Greg Stern said it was only going to get worse.

"He said to make sure to leave plenty of time for travel this evening," Dr. Graham says as he cleans a fossil with his trusty toothbrush.

"So does that mean you're taking off early?" Mandira asks him.

"Of course not."

"You know the fossils will still be here, right?" she asks. "They've survived a few million years; what's another night?"

It's cozy in the lab, with Mandira teasing Dr. Graham and Christmas music blasting from the speakers.

I haven't been adding much to the conversation, mostly because, even after the fart incident, I'm still a little intimidated by Dr. Graham. But after a minute I say, "You know I walk Greg Stern's dog?"

Dr. Graham puts down his toothbrush and looks at me,

really *looks* at me, for the first time since my internship started. "You know *Greg Stern*?"

I've never seen the man this excited. His eyes light up, as if Christmas has come a day early. "What's he like?"

In the one or two brief interactions I've had with Greg, he was running past me to get to his car or yelling at May.

"He seems pretty nice," I say. "And his dog is great. A little corgi. Very sweet."

"Of course he has a corgi," Dr. Graham says, laughing and shaking his head. "My intern knows Greg Stern!"

"I actually have to walk his dog tonight," I tell Dr. Graham, thinking this will be a fun little anecdote for him. "I told him I would the other day."

"Well, then you'd better leave soon," he says, looking at his watch. "Greg Stern himself is saying the snow's gonna pick up. Might even be a blizzard." He glances at his wrist again, this time with a panicked look. "Maybe you should leave now. The Metro might not be running so well in an hour."

"Let me get this straight," Mandira says. "You want Shani to leave at four in the afternoon to walk a dog"—she looks over at me—"which you absolutely should, seeing as it's *Christmas Eve*"—she turns back to Dr. Graham—"but *you* won't leave before six? In a blizzard?"

"It's *Greg Stern*'s dog," Dr. Graham says to Mandira, as if this explains everything. He turns to me. "You should go."

"Are you sure?"

"You really should," Mandira says. "But not just for the dog. You've been doing great work these past two weeks. It's Christmas, let's go home." She looks over at Dr. Graham, making it clear this advice is aimed at all of us. "As much as I love it here, I'm gonna dip soon, too. I told my girlfriend I'd make mulled wine for the party we're going to."

"I thought you didn't celebrate Christmas?" I ask, feeling slightly betrayed. We had our whole non-Christian solidarity thing going.

"Not, like, in a religious way," she says, "but my girlfriend does, and we're going to a Christmas Eve party. Plus, mulled wine transcends religion. Seriously, Shani, go home."

"All right," I say, even though it feels like a trap. "Um, thanks. Merry—you know."

"Merry Christmas, Shani," Mandira says.

I grab my coat, but right before I walk out, Dr. Graham shouts, "And if you see Greg Stern, tell him Dr. Charles Graham is his number one fan!"

Dr. Graham—and, I guess, Greg Stern—were right: by the time I get off the Metro, it's a true blizzard. The moon is bright, but it's struggling to glow through the thick snow clouds. I can barely see anything with gale-force winds and rogue snowflakes whipping past me.

"*Fuck.*"

I hold my arms above my face to stop the burning cold sensation and fight my way to May's house.

By the time I get to her street, my whole body's frozen and there's snow up to my calves. My pants are soaked through, and my jacket isn't doing much better.

When I spot the inappropriately timed menorah in the window, it's like reaching an oasis in the desert.

I walk up the steps to the house, but it's snowing so hard and the wind is so strong that even the porch is coated in inches of thick, wet snow, and I have to use my hands to shovel a path to open the glass door.

I knock, then ring, then knock again. My fingers are going to fall off and so are my toes and maybe my arms and legs too. I don't think I've ever been this cold in my entire life.

After an endless minute of ringing and knocking with my snow-numbed fingers, the door opens.

"Jesus Christ," May says when she sees me.

I stumble inside.

"It's almost His birthday, huh?" I say in response, slightly delirious.

"Are you okay?" she asks as I drip snow onto her dad's floor.

She closes the door and looks at me. "You're not walking Raphael like this."

"Sure I am," I say, teeth chattering.

"No, you're not. And my dad wouldn't want you taking

him outside right now, anyway. That dog is not very hardy." She points upstairs. "He's sleeping on the heated bathroom floor. Barely even woke up for dinner."

"Then why didn't you text me not to come?"

"I forgot you were supposed to walk him today!" She seems freaked out, and I'm sure I do too because I'm still freezing and my fingers are thawing but now they're burning and I might pass out.

May wraps her arms around her waist and rocks back and forth. "You need to get out of those clothes."

If there were enough heat in my body to allow my face to blush, it would.

But if May realizes what she said, she doesn't show it. "I'm getting you a sweatshirt." She runs upstairs. "Stay here so you don't drip on anything."

"I'm not staying," I call up after her. "If you don't need me here for Raphael I'm going home."

She stops at the top of the stairs, then bounces down a few steps so I can see her. "You most certainly are not."

"It's only a few blocks."

"Yeah, well, you almost died getting here from the Metro."

"So I'll be fine walking home."

"You literally won't be," she says. "My dad's been telling me to stay inside all day. The wind speed got up to forty-seven miles per hour. That's Strong Gale on the Beaufort scale. It's an actual hazard."

I glance around at the apparently empty house. "Where *is* your dad?"

"He's at the station."

"The Metro station?"

"Uh, no. Like, at work. At the TV station."

"He's working on Christmas Eve? At night?"

"If there's a weather emergency, they need him there. Plus, it's not like we really celebrate anyway." She stares me down. "And this *is* a weather emergency. So don't fucking go outside. I'm bringing you warm clothes so you don't get hypothermia and die."

And with that, she runs upstairs.

The thing is, I had been planning on having the night to myself.

I don't know if that's what I wanted, but that was the plan.

Tasha's at a school friend's Christmas Eve party, Lauren's with her boyfriend, and George whisked Beatrice off to the family-only Christmas festivities.

So, while May is upstairs, I try my hardest to open the door with my numb hands.

I need to go. I don't want to bother her. I don't want things to be weird.

But once I step outside, the force of the (apparently Strong Gale) wind and snow hits my already freezing face, and it's possible May is right, that I might really get hypothermia if I stay outside a minute longer. So I go back in.

When I do, May's right there, holding a pile of neatly folded clothes, hip cocked to one side. Raphael is bouncing around her feet, pawing at the ground and making little yaps.

"Trying to escape?"

"Tried," I correct her. "It's horrible out there."

"I already told you that." She hands me the clothes. "Bathroom's down the hall on the right."

I nod and walk there as fast as my frozen feet will carry me. I don't think about what this means, that I'm in May's house alone with her and Raphael on Christmas Eve. I just shut myself in the bathroom and take off my clothes, which are crunchy from the snow.

The sweatshirt and sweatpants May gave me both say "Cornell" on them. Of course she chose these—Binghamton and Cornell are sort of rivals.

"Any better?" May calls from down the hall as I carry my sopping wet clothes back into the entrance area.

"Much."

But now that I'm in warm clothes and thawing, I'm a little nervous and a lot awkward. What am I doing alone in some girl's house, wearing her college's sweats?

May gets up from where she was sitting at the bottom of the staircase and looks at my new outfit. "Let's go, Big Red," she says, stifling a laugh.

"Absolutely not."

"Should we do a quick chorus of 'Give My Regards to Davy'?"

"I'm leaving. I'm walking out the door—"

"'*Give my regards to Davy, remember me to Tee Fee Crane—*'" May sings at the top of her lungs. Raphael howls and sprints up and down the stairs, paws clattering on the hardwood.

"I'm gonna go outside and let the snow take me, I think."

"'*Tell all the pikers on the hill that I'll be back again.*'"

"How do you even know the words to this? Are you a big football fan? You really go all out for the games?"

"Not done," she says before getting even louder and singing, "'*Tell them just how I busted lapping up the high highball—*'"

"I'm sorry, is your fight song about getting wasted?"

"'*We'll all have drinks at Theodore Zinck's.*'" She takes a deep breath. "Big finish . . . '*When I get back next fall!*'"

She takes a dramatic bow, walks into the living room, and collapses onto a fancy-looking sectional couch. Raphael jumps up near her and she scoots away.

"I can't believe you know even a single word of that song." I walk toward where she's sitting, but before I get there, she puts up a hand to stop me.

"Don't bring your wet clothes in here, my dad'll freak. Just leave your shit by the door and I'll throw it in the dryer later."

"Fine." I toss the clothes on the doormat and pad into the living room.

Even though there's space, I don't want to sit on the couch with her, so I lower myself onto the floor. Raphael's much braver than I am, lying next to this frightening girl who outright hates him. Though maybe this is more his domain than May's.

I wrap my arms around my knees and rub my legs, trying to warm myself through friction.

"You want a hot beverage?"

I resist the urge to laugh at the phrase "hot beverage," mostly because I'm so cold that my bones have turned to ice. I nod.

"Come," she says, and stands up from the couch.

I give Raphael a pat, and he huffs and closes his eyes. I follow May into the kitchen. It's large but lived-in—being a local celebrity must pay the bills pretty well. There's a small TV over the kitchen table, and May switches it on to her dad's channel.

"The news of the hour?" a perfectly coiffed middle-aged newscaster asks from behind her desk. "Santa and his reindeer are going to be braving quite the storm when they land here in DC—but don't worry, kids, he'll still get to your milk and cookies. Giving us an update from Capitol Hill is our very own Greg Stern. How's it going out there, Greg?"

The screen switches to a shot of Greg being pummeled

by wind and snow. He's bundled in a huge parka and wearing giant gloves and earmuffs, but he still looks freezing.

"Well, Jen," Greg screams over the wind, "I'll just say that Santa's the *only* one who should be going out tonight." A large gust forces him to stumble and grab on to his earmuffs. "We have an advisory out, and if you're just tuning in: please, stay off the roads, and stay inside if you can."

"That's great, Greg," Jen says, shuffling papers from the comfort of her warm and dry studio. "Thanks for the update." The screen switches so that we see only Jen. "Next up, we have a cookie expert joining us remotely to give you some last-minute tips on treats that'll make Santa's mouth water. You won't want to miss this, folks."

A commercial for Harris Teeter, a local supermarket, comes on, and May mutes the TV.

"I can't believe your dad has to be out in that."

"Yeah, well, he does," she says, sounding upset.

"I'm sure he'll be fine," I say as gently as I can, because I think that's what she needs to hear.

"I *know* he'll be fine," she snaps. "But he won't be *here*." She pulls a saucepan out from a cabinet by the stove. "Whatever, he's there. It's fine. I'll spare you the details."

"You don't have to," I say. "You should talk about it if you want to. It's shitty that you don't get to see him today."

"It's fine."

I give her a minute. "It's not," I say finally. "It really, really sucks."

She lights the burner and opens the fridge to grab oat milk. "Thanks," she says quietly. "I guess I'm just mad because he told me he'd find someone to cover him tonight. But he couldn't, or didn't want to. It was silly of me to believe him, anyway."

"I don't know," I say. "I think you had every right to believe him."

I won't be telling her that the reason I'm being so forceful about this is that I've been feeling guilty about not being home with my mom, who *wanted* to be with me. I hate thinking that I'm the Greg of my own life.

But, at the same time, I like that May told me why she's mad. And I didn't even have to pry it out of her.

With Sadie, it was the opposite. If I didn't know exactly how she felt at all times, she would snap at me. So I would say nice things to placate her. She didn't want to open up to me, and I didn't want to hurt her. I just wanted everything to be okay. To be normal.

Obviously May and I aren't dating, but I'm glad I know how she's feeling. Maybe not exactly, but something close to it. And I want to help. Especially since it's too late to be home with my mom.

I lean against the kitchen island next to where May's tending the stove. She rests against the counter as she whisks the oat milk.

"I'm making hot chocolate."

"Perfect."

"But I'm making it the good way. Not with some cheap store-bought powder."

"Even better."

I stare, transfixed, as she stirs cocoa powder and sugar and chocolate syrup into the saucepan.

When it's ready, she taps the whisk against the stainless-steel pan and grabs two mugs out of a cabinet. She carefully pours the hot chocolate into each mug, then hands one to me. It's got her dad's face on it and says, "Greg Brings the Umbrella to You."

She shuts the TV off, and I take a sip of the hot chocolate as we sit at the table. The scalding hot liquid coats my internal organs.

"Does your dad really drink out of a mug with his own face on it?"

"It's the *only* mug he drinks out of."

"Oh . . . no."

"Yeah. . . ."

We sip our hot chocolates in silence for a moment, then May adds, "I don't, like, hate him, if that's what you're thinking. I love him, obviously."

"I wasn't thinking that." If she saw how I was with my mom, I might have to give the same qualifications. And I don't hate my mom. I love her maybe more than anyone on the entire planet, even when I'm being angry and horrible to her.

"Back when I was little, I wanted to be just like him," May says. "He's the reason I love weather."

"Like, the concept of weather?" I ask, incredulous.

"Well, kind of," she says. "But more the uncertainty of it. That even if you've studied the science, you still might not get it right. There's never a guarantee."

"Isn't that a bad thing? Don't most people not really trust meteorologists?"

"They might not trust them, but they love them," she says. "They recognize that they're human, too. Like Al Roker. People love Al Roker. And people love my dad. It's something about the imperfection." She stares into her hot chocolate. "I don't know, I think it's nice. The not knowing."

"I never thought about weather like that, but that's also why I love paleontology," I tell her, leaning forward. "Because you're never gonna know the full story, but you get to piece it together. Like, with coelacanths—this fish that everyone thought was extinct but it turned out they weren't. Scientists in the eighteen hundreds had all these wild guesses about what they looked like, and then when people realized they still exist, almost all the illustrations were wrong. But they did their best with the clues they had."

"I love that," she says, and I raise my eyebrows. "Really, I do! It's like how people get angry when they walk outside and it's raining even though the news called for clear skies.

Like, sure it's raining. The whole thing's based on chance. There's never 100 percent certainty that it'll be sunny . . . ever. So it's always safer to just pack an umbrella."

I smirk because that seems to sum up May's entire worldview. "I'll remember that."

"And it's *also* safer not to almost kill yourself trying to walk a dog in a blizzard," she adds, and her hand grazes my knee. I don't know if she did it on purpose, but now my whole body's awake.

I'm a coward, though, so I move my knee a bit and say, "That part I won't remember."

She snorts. "Fair enough."

I think maybe this is when May also starts to realize how weird it is that I'm sitting at her kitchen table and drinking her hot chocolate, because all of a sudden, she stands up and washes the saucepan.

"I can do that," I say.

"It's fine, it's done." She scrubs for a minute, then puts the pan on a drying rack next to the sink.

It's very quiet.

"How about some music?"

"Yes, perfect," I say, too quickly.

"It's gonna be Christmas music. And you're not arguing with me about how that makes me a bad Jew," she says. "It's the second-to-last day of the season in which it's socially acceptable to listen to Christmas music and you're *not* taking this away from me."

As she scrolls through her phone to find what she wants to play, I say, "I actually like Christmas music?"

She stops scrolling and looks up at me. "I'm sorry, did I just hear you say that Shani 'Fuck Christmas'— Wait, oh my god. I have no idea what your last name is."

"It's Levine. And 'Fuck Christmas' isn't my middle name. That one's Adeline."

"All right, let me try again: you're saying that you, Shani Adeline 'Fuck Christmas' Levine—"

"Well, if you're gonna do it right, my full first name's Shoshana."

"Jesus, okay." She shakes her arms and resets. "Blah blah blah that you, Shoshana Adeline 'Fuck Christmas' Levine, like Christmas music?"

"Yes, fine, whatever."

"This is excellent news."

"It's really not."

"I'm gonna play Sufjan Stevens's entire Christmas discography and you're gonna *love* it because you *love* Christmas. This is unreal."

I put my head in my hands as May makes good on her promise and puts on one of Sufjan's Christmas albums. The worst part is I am of course familiar with it and of course enjoy it. Whatever.

It's an upbeat song, and it sounds folksy and homemade. May bobs her head a little and gives me a thumbs-up and a look that says, *At least I'm* trying *to make things less weird*.

I stifle a laugh.

"All right, then," she says when she sees my face. "If you think it's so funny, let's see you dance."

"No, that's all right."

She rolls her eyes. "You can just bob your head." She demonstrates. "Come on, Shoshana Adeline 'Fuck Christmas' Levine. It won't kill you."

I sigh. "Fine, I'll bob. But I won't enjoy it."

"Of course."

I stand up and move the upper half of my body side to side, awkwardly at first, then with slightly more conviction as the song crescendos and May bobs, too.

Somehow, the bobbing does manage to make things feel a little less awkward.

"All right, so do *you* have a middle name?" I ask to fill the silence when the song's over, before the next one picks up.

"Yeah, it's Ilana. But I hate it because it's impossible to say my full name without slurring it together." She demonstrates: "MayIlana."

"Maybe your parents were drunk when they named you."

She snorts. "Maybe."

"MayIlana," I say, testing it out.

"See?"

"They do flow together nicely."

"That's a kind way of putting it," May says. "I would say it sounds more like someone having a ministroke."

I shake my head at her. She grabs our mugs from the table and starts washing them, like she did with the saucepan: methodically, scrubbing each part with a worn yellow sponge.

But she stops when a new song comes on. It's bright and mellow and slow. She bobs to this one, too, but with more feeling. Then she turns to face me.

"Come on," she says as Sufjan starts singing. "No head-bobbing rest for the wicked."

"I'm not doing this again," I say. "There's no beat. You can't bob to no beat."

"Sure you can." She walks to an open area of the kitchen and lets out a long breath. "Just . . . come here."

I follow her command, and stop a few feet away, standing in front of her.

She bites her lip. "Closer."

The slow chords continue. My heart speeds up. I take another step toward her.

She puts her head in her hands, then looks at the ceiling. She nods to herself and asks, in a slightly pained voice, "Dance with me?" while holding out a hand.

I nod and swallow and take it as Sufjan sings in his high, sweet voice about what the people of old have sung.

Now that she's grasping my hand she stares hard at the floor. So do I.

But the song is sweet, and May is calm, and as much as I've fought it, I want to be near her.

I spin her around under my arm slowly and she laughs, then does the same for me. I get caught under her arm, and we twist too hard and trip over each other.

And that becomes an easy excuse to dance closer.

I'm taller than her, and she holds on to one of my hands as I press the other to the small of her back. We sway, together. She's tense, and so am I, but feeling that she's tense too makes it better. Before I can think about what I'm doing, I rub her back in slow circles in time to the chords, and she leans into me, putting her chin in the hollow of my collarbone.

But the song is short, and after no time at all it's over and then there's a fast song about putting the lights on the tree. We break apart.

I can still feel where her chin fit just right into my shoulder.

May clears her throat, walks over to the sink, and turns on the water even though there's nothing left to wash.

"Should we watch TV?" she asks, her voice higher than normal.

"Uh, yeah," I say, not quite sure what's going on.

But it seems we've mutually agreed not to mention our slow dance—or whatever the hell that was—as we sit down in the living room.

She turns on the TV and we watch for a while—not the

weather, thank god, just a holiday baking show—but I'm having trouble paying attention. I'm hyperaware of my body and hers and of the way they were connected just minutes before. Raphael would've been the perfect buffer between us on the couch, but he hopped down onto the rug and ran in restless circles for a minute before falling asleep.

Traitor.

I curl my legs under me, careful not to touch May. I think she's doing the same, because her legs are scrunched up, and I caught her staring at me while a small child was reprimanded for putting too much fondant on a Rice Krispies sculpture of Rudolph. Of course, that means I was staring at her, too . . . but, like, obviously I was staring at her. How could I not?

The baking show turns out to be ridiculously addictive, and at midnight we're both yelling at the screen because one of the judges sent Fondant Kid home over a slightly underbaked bûche de Noël.

"He was robbed!" May shouts, standing up.

"I'm afraid this is goodbye," the judge says after announcing that Fondant Kid will be going home. "Time to hang up your apron."

"*YOU* HANG UP YOUR APRON, YOU PIECE OF SHIT!" I scream at the judge.

May laughs, which turns into a yawn as she says, "I feel like if we're yelling at the TV, it might be time to call it a night." She pauses the show. "You can stay in my room and I'll sleep in my dad's."

My heart sinks, even though there would be no reason whatsoever for us to sleep in the same room.

"He's not coming home tonight?"

"He just texted," She holds up her phone. "They're keeping him overnight so he can be on TV to greet the early Christmas morning audience."

"That sucks."

"Yeah, but people will be expecting *Greg Stern* to be there when they wake up on Christmas morning. Especially after a blizzard."

"It's wild that your dad has bus ads here."

"I know. I hate it."

We get up from the couch as Raphael stretches and stands on his stubby legs. We let him outside onto the porch for about half a second to do his foul deed into the unsoiled snow, and when he trots inside May slams the door.

Things feel normal again, which is a funny way of describing any part of sleeping over at the house of a girl who I met less than two weeks ago by way of hitting her with my car. But still, it's normal. It's all normal.

Once we're upstairs, May walks me to her room. It's sterile and generic, not at all what I'd expect from her.

She must see my face, because she says, "My room at my mom's house in Ithaca is much nicer. There's stuff on the walls, for starters."

"Yeah, it's pretty bleak in here," I say, glancing at the blank white walls.

"I refused to decorate it when my dad first moved in however many years ago, and now I just don't feel like it." She goes over to the bed and pulls the comforter off, then opens the closet and grabs another blanket. "I didn't think you'd want to sleep on my used sheets."

"Oh, thanks," I say, but that wasn't what I had been thinking about.

"There are towels in that closet if you wanna take a shower, but I'm pretty tired, so I think I'm gonna head off to bed."

"All right," I say, feeling weird, like I fell asleep on a train and missed my stop.

I sit on the bed, on the unused comforter, but May doesn't leave. She lingers by the door, leaning against the frame.

It's very, very quiet. Not a creature is stirring.

Does she want me to say something? Does *she* want to say something? I have no idea, but I can feel my body start to shake, even though I've been warm for hours now.

After a minute of nothing, she says, "Good night, Shoshana Adeline Levine."

I smile, take a breath. "Good night, MayIlana Stern."

She smiles back, but still doesn't move. I think she might say something else, but after a few seconds she puts her hand up in an awkward wave. Then she closes the door.

Try as I might, I can't fall asleep. It's been at least half an hour since May left me in her room, but I just keep thinking about how she's on the other side of the wall. It would be so easy for something to happen. I could barge into her dad's room and say, "What are we even doing here?" and then . . . who knows?

We might kiss.

We would probably kiss.

I could kiss her, if she wanted me to. And I think she does.

Maybe she's thinking the same thing. Maybe she's hoping I'll sneak out of this room and into her dad's.

But really, I *don't* know what she's thinking.

And that's gotten me into trouble before.

So, I don't do anything at all.

And eventually, I fall asleep.

Thinking of her.

You're Ho Ho Hopeless

I wake up to the sun on my face, and keep my eyes closed as I stretch out, preparing to spend the day avoiding Beatrice and human contact in general.

But then I remember two very important facts.

1) I am not in Beatrice's bed.
2) I am, in fact, in May's bed.

I spring out of it, feeling self-conscious, as if the bed might know about my crush. My clothes from yesterday are elsewhere, maybe the dryer, so I walk out of May's room in her Cornell sweats. I figure I'll go downstairs, change into my clothes, go back to Beatrice's, and do my best to forget about the aberration that was last night.

But before I can say anything about grabbing my clothes and leaving, I find May in the kitchen, and whatever happened between us last night feels suddenly, immensely real.

"There's coffee in the French press," she says without looking up from her newspaper. Her hair is sleep-rumpled, and her face is puffy: her eyes, her lips, her cheeks, her lips, her forehead, her lips.

What?

Don't worry about it.

"Thanks," I say, but it comes out first-words-of-the-morning scratchy, so I clear my throat and say again, in a deeper voice, "Thank you."

She looks up then, and smiles. "If you don't want a mug with my dad's face on it, there're some plain red ones in the cabinet above the French press."

I rub my eyes and grab a non-Greg mug, then pour myself a cup of coffee.

"There's also oat milk and creamer," she says.

I trip on Raphael's empty bowl on my way to the fridge and catch myself on the counter.

"Fuck, wait, did you feed the dog?" I ask.

"Fed and watered. He's napping over here."

"Watered? I'm sorry, is he a ficus?"

May rolls her eyes and I look to where she's pointing, just beyond the kitchen table. Raphael's dozing in the sun, making little sniffles and huffs as he dreams. He's on his back, his white paws resting on his chunky torso.

I gently scratch behind his ears, and he howls sleepily but doesn't wake up.

"That's a good boy," I tell him, just because he's a very good boy.

He's in the best spot in the kitchen, with the warm morning light covering his whole body. The sun is reflecting over piles of fresh snow, making it so dazzlingly bright that it's almost hard to look outside.

"It's amazing that you've kept this dog alive without any help," I say as I get up from Raphael's nap spot.

"You think I'm gonna murder a dog?"

"Not on purpose. Just from, like, negligence."

"Shut up and drink your coffee," May says, shaking her head and smiling. "It would take more than a day for my negligence to have an effect."

"Ha ha." I pour a bit of oat milk into the cup and sit down at the table, lifting my legs onto the chair and crossing one under me.

I watch May for a minute, the way she's reading the paper and holding her mug for warmth.

The whole scene is so domestic. Sitting in her kitchen, drinking coffee, a sleeping corgi beside us. It tugs at my heart in a way that feels weirdly nostalgic, like I've been here before. Like we're back in *Snails Space*. Like I've spent a whole lifetime at this table on a snowy morning.

I have no idea where we stand after last night. I'm back to thinking that it was all a snow-covered dream. I'm, like, 80 percent sure we didn't actually slow dance—that part seems particularly unbelievable.

The only way I know it wasn't entirely a dream is that I'm still wearing her Cornell sweats.

But the rest of it could be, everything from last night. Now that it's a new day, we're back to our usual banter.

"Do you want a section?" May asks after a minute. She folds the part of the newspaper she was reading to its original state.

"Sure."

"Which one?"

"Any of them." Then, as she starts to pull out a section: "Wait, do you have Arts and Leisure?" She nods and hands it to me. "I like doing the crossword," I explain.

"Are you any good at it?"

"Well, I'm asking for the Saturday puzzle, aren't I?"

"I have no idea what that means."

I open the paper to the crossword puzzle and fold it over. May scoots her chair closer to me so she can see it, too.

I put my leg down from the chair to make sure it doesn't touch hers.

"They get harder every day, from Monday to Saturday. Saturday is like god-level difficult. I've only finished it by myself once." I scan the clues, looking for one to start with. "My bubbe was a crossword genius, though. She could get through the Saturday in half an hour, sometimes less. She'd always call me if there was a clue she didn't know, though. A 'young person's clue' she'd say. Usually about texting abbreviations."

"I love that," she says. "Let's start."

"You wanna do the crossword?"

"What else are we doing right now?"

She said "we," which makes my heart flop out of my chest and directly onto the newspaper.

"Nothing, I guess. But isn't your dad coming back soon? I should probably go in a minute." But I don't get up from the table. I don't move at all.

"He texted earlier. He's not coming home till after the morning show, so he'll be back later this afternoon."

I stare her down. "If we do the puzzle, you have to follow my rules. You can't jump around from clue to clue until you find something you can fill in."

May puts one hand to her chest and one in the air. "I swear to abide by your pedantic puzzle rules."

"Shut up," I say, shaking my head.

"Let me grab a pen."

She gets up and opens a drawer by the coffee maker. I study her. She's in her pajamas: a long-sleeve shirt that says "Ithaca" on the back in blocky white letters and fleece pants with penguins skiing and participating in various other winter sports.

Sadie never let me see her in the morning. I only slept over in her room a few times, but she'd always be up before me, getting dressed, putting on makeup. It stressed me out, but I thought it was normal. I thought that if you really like someone, you shouldn't see them before they're ready to be seen.

May drops the pen in front of me and begins reading the clues to herself. "I don't think I can get a single one of these."

"Okay, well, not true," I say. "Let's find an easy one." I scan the clues. "All right, this one's just a fact. Those are easier. 'Whites of an egg, scientifically speaking.'"

"You think I know that? I'm an atmospheric science major."

I laugh and write in *albumin*.

Then I tell her about how if a clue ends in a question mark, the answer will be something more irreverent and fun; you have to think outside the box. That helps May a little but not much. I scan the puzzle and fill in a few more words, and then May finally fills in a clue herself.

"My brain hurts."

"You got that last one!"

"If I didn't, I'd be worried about myself." (The clue was "Banjo-playing Muppet": Kermit.)

After we (I) fill in a few more words, we're able to figure out some of the big clues. There are a bunch that end with question marks and are about Christmas, and we figure out that all of them contain the words *ho ho ho*.

"There are usually a few clues that are related to each

other in a puzzle," I explain to May. "And if you can get one it helps you figure out the rest. Let's try this." I read out a clue: "'What did Mrs. Claus say when her husband forgot to put down the toilet seat?'"

"Well, we know there's 'ho ho ho' in there somewhere," May says, staring down at the puzzle with intense concentration.

I count the boxes for the answer. It's long, but there are a few letters filled in, which helps. Even so, I can't quite get it.

"HOLY SHIT!" May shouts after a minute. "I GOT IT I GOT IT I GOT IT." I hand her the pen, and she frantically writes down the answer. "'You're ho ho hopeless.' That's what Mrs. Claus said!"

I look, and it fits. Plus, it's confirmed by a number of other clues we've already answered going in the other direction.

"Oh my god," I say. "I'm deeply impressed."

She stands up and starts jumping around saying, "I GOT IT I GOT IT I GOT IT. SUCK ON THAT. I FUCKING GOT IT!" And then Raphael springs up from his nap spot and starts barking and I get swept up in the crossword spirit and stand up too and jump a little bit, and I reach a hand out to give May a high five and she pulls me in for a hug and I don't fight it, and she keeps jumping for a moment while she grabs on to me and all I can do is laugh and hold on and try not to freak out.

Then we stop jumping, and we're still holding on to each other.

And May lets go. And I let go.

And I don't know what to do because it's the closest I've come to last night's feeling. When we were dancing. When I was falling asleep thinking about how something might happen.

"I'm making you an egg," May says from out of nowhere, rubbing her hands on her pajama pants. "The 'whites of an egg' clue made me hungry." She doesn't look at me.

I sit back down at the table. "You don't wanna finish the puzzle?"

Something's over. The domestic, quiet morning feeling is gone. Poof. Just like that.

"The excitement's too much for me."

"The *puzzle* is too much excitement?" I ask. "Are you one hundred years old? Also, wait, why are you making an egg? How do you know I even like eggs?" I try to bring our antagonistic banter back, in the hopes that it'll make the awkwardness go away, but it feels stilted. That doesn't stop me from trying. "What if I'm deathly allergic?"

She grabs a pan. "*Are* you deathly allergic?"

"No," I say. "I fucking love eggs."

"As you should." She puts butter in the pan and lights the stove.

I try to fill in more of the crossword, but I'm distracted

by May. By the sizzle of the pan, the way she leans on one leg and cranes her neck to check on the eggs.

After a minute she puts a fried egg in front of me, perfectly cooked, covered in salt and pepper. Then she brings one over for herself, and reads another article while I alternate between looking at her and the crossword puzzle.

I can't concentrate.

When May finishes her egg, she gets up and starts washing the dishes. I like that she cleans them right away, but I don't like that she's doing it to get away from me.

I stand up, too. "Is there a dish towel I can use to dry?"

"You don't have to do that."

"But I want to."

She looks at me, hands in the sink, and nods toward the oven. "Just use the one on the handle."

I grab it and dry the dishes after May washes them. We don't speak, but we get a good system going.

When we're done, I rub my hands on the Cornell sweatpants I'm wearing and ask, "Are we partaking in Jewish Christmas today?"

"What?"

"Jewmas, if you will."

"The fact that it was two separate words wasn't the source of my confusion," May says as she flops back down at the table.

I flop, too. "Now I'm confused—don't you usually celebrate Jewish Christmas with your mom?"

"I mean, we watch movies and eat Chinese food, but—"

I let out a huge melodramatic sigh. "Oh, thank goodness. I thought for a second you didn't know what I was talking about."

"I still don't!"

"Well, a Jewmas by any other name—"

"Can you stop saying 'Jewmas'? It sounds bad."

"Never." I lean toward her with my elbows on the table. "Especially because that's what we're gonna do today: watch a movie and eat Chinese food while the goyim are inside exchanging presents or plotting world domination or whatever it is they do."

"So we're talking about the same thing?"

"Yeah, but mine's called Jewmas."

"You know that it's fully impossible to have a conversation with you, right?" She shakes her head and glances down at her phone, then gets up from the table. "Speaking of which, I need to call my mom. I'm just gonna do that super fast and then maybe we can look up movie times?"

"Sounds good." I go back to the crossword puzzle, which has somehow not become magically more filled in since we started working on it.

"Are you gonna call your mom, too? Wish her a happy 'Jewmas' or whatever?" May says as she walks into the living room. "Ask her what her body count is up to now vis-à-vis running people over with her car?"

"Ha ha," I say, staring at the floor. "I'm just gonna text her later."

"She's not forcing you to call? What kind of a Jewish mother is she?"

"She's not forcing me to call, no." Then I add, "It's fine," and she doesn't press further.

May goes into the living room, and I pretend to focus on the crossword, but really I'm listening to the call. I can't make out too many of the words, but the tone is clear. May is speaking to her mom gently, with so much love. It's the opposite of how I've heard her speak to her dad. Her voice is higher, sweeter.

I start to feel pretty bad about the level of communication my mom and I have (and whose fault is that, Shani?), so I take out my phone and text her.

ME: merry jewmas

That's one thing my mom has going for her: she'll know what I mean when I say that. Because it's her word.

A minute later, she writes back.

MOM: Merry Jewmas, Sweet<3

I smile down at my phone, then quickly wipe the expression away as May comes back into the kitchen.

"How's your mom?" I ask, because that feels like

something nice, courteous people do, and I'm trying my best to imitate those people.

"She's good, she's good." May sits down and turns the crossword toward her. I guess she's back in. She scrunches her eyebrows when she sees that I haven't filled out any more of it.

She bites her lip, picks up the pen, and hovers over a blank space on the crossword. "She was just asking me how I'm gonna celebrate Christmas. And also, like, how I'm gonna celebrate my birthday," she says the last part casually as she pushes the crossword back toward me.

"Wait, it's your birthday?"

"Wednesday," she says. "The twenty-ninth. Not for a few days." She takes her bun out and bunches her hair up on top of her head, then lets it fall around her face.

The fight I overheard plays in my mind, the one where her dad argued that she was still a kid, that she didn't have a choice about staying with him.

"Well, happy almost birthday," I say. I don't press the issue, even though I'm guessing she wouldn't have brought it up if she didn't want me to know. "Should we see what's playing?"

"Yeah." May grabs her phone and types something out. "There's an art house theater down the street. With the rest of the theaters we'd have to take the Metro, and between yesterday's blizzard and today being Christmas I'd rather avoid it, if that's okay with you."

"Yeah, sounds good."

She stares at her phone for another second and then says, "Well, there's only one movie playing at the theater, so I guess we're seeing that."

"Anything I would've heard of?"

"Definitely not. It's called *Grandma's Boyfriend* and it literally has *one* review. The *Northern Virginia Daily* gave it three out of five American Foxhounds."

"Can't beat that," I say. "Except with four or five American Foxhounds, I guess." May snorts. "Yeah, let's do it."

"Do you need to borrow other clothes?" she asks. "We have to leave in like twenty minutes."

"I can just wear the ones I wore yesterday."

"Well, the thing is," May says, rubbing the back of her neck, "I didn't put them in the dryer."

"That's fine," I tell her. "They're probably dry by now, right?"

"You can check, they're in the laundry room."

I do, and they're not. If possible, they're even more damp than yesterday.

I slink back over to May, who smirks. "Need to borrow clothes?"

"Yes, fine, whatever."

She looks me up and down, and I have to stop myself from smiling.

"I think we're about the same size," she says. "You can borrow more clothes. On one condition."

"What?"

"I'm choosing the outfit."

I roll my eyes. "Fine. But don't you have, like, a T-shirt and jeans I can wear?"

"I do."

"But I'm not wearing them, am I?"

"Nope!"

And with that she runs upstairs. I hear her rummaging frantically through her drawers, which can't be a good sign.

She comes down a few minutes later, and like last night, there's a neatly folded pile of clothes in her hands.

"It's not bad," she says. When she sees the look on my face she adds, "I promise."

I grab the clothes, not really believing her, and slam the door to the hallway bathroom.

In a shocking turn of events, she's right: it's not bad. It's just nothing I would ever wear. I'd probably describe my style as understated to the point of fading directly into the background. And nothing about this outfit—high-waisted, green-blue-and-red-striped twill pants, and a big red cable-knit sweater to tuck into them—is fading anywhere.

The pants are a little short, so I cuff them, and then stand in front of the mirror with my hands in the very large pockets.

It's an exceedingly gay fit.

But maybe that wasn't on purpose. Maybe May isn't queer and I've been misreading the entire situation.

But maybe it was.

And maybe she is.

"That looks good on you," May says casually when I walk out of the bathroom, as if that's a normal thing to say to someone.

Which, like, it might be. I don't know. My brain is broken.

"We should probably head out."

"Yup," May says, pulling on her boots. "Let me just put the gate up so Raphael doesn't escape."

"You think he's gonna try to make his big break from the kitchen?"

"Honestly? Yes. That dog has plans."

She puts up the gate and places a hand on his head like she's an alien who's been told it's a human custom to pet dogs. In response, he goes cross-eyed and tries to eat the wooden gate.

"Clearly an evil mastermind," I say, pointing to Raphael, who's still happily attacking the bars.

When we get outside it's sunny and mild, but it's almost impossible to leave the house; there's over a foot of snow piled up in front of the door. We dig ourselves out, then trudge through the slush until we reach a part of the sidewalk that some Good Samaritan shoveled earlier this morning.

It should've taken only a few minutes to get to the theater, but the thick layer of snow turns it into a full-on hike.

Even so, it's nice to be outside and not almost dead, like last night. Nothing can dampen my spirits on my day of Jewish freedom. It's not even cheapened by the fact that it's Saturday. I say this to May, how I feel free.

She turns to me as we cross the street and takes a breath. "I do too."

The building is a small classic-looking movie theater, with an art deco sculpture coming out of the awning, which is advertising "Grandma's Boyfriend" and "Happy Birthday, Axel!"

When we get inside everyone's milling around in the lobby, waiting for the doors to open to the single theater. As I glance around, something occurs to me. I lean over to May and whisper, "Are we the youngest people here?"

She surveys the crowd and stifles a laugh. "By about fifty years, I think."

The clientele is made up entirely of what appear to be elderly Jewish couples. Truly, 100 percent of the people in the building, save for me, May, and the ticket/snack person, are over the age of seventy.

When we walk up to the ticket counter, the employee looks mildly surprised to see us. "You know we're just showing *Grandma's Boyfriend*, right?" they ask. "Like, just checking."

"Oh, we know," May answers. "Two tickets?"

"Uh, sure," the person says.

"I'm buying," May tells me as the employee prints out a

pair of tickets. I start to argue, but she cuts me off. "Don't fight me. My dad gave me money for today, and I'm going to spend every fucking penny." She pulls out a hundred dollar bill. "Seriously, don't fight me."

I don't, and a few minutes later the theater doors open and we find our seats.

The movie is about a little kid who takes a road trip to Tucson with her grandma to visit her grandma's new boyfriend. It's not supposed to be funny, I don't think, but May and I can't stop laughing, to the point where the other people in the theater give us dirty looks.

After the movie, there's a mass exodus of theater-goers to a nearby Chinese restaurant, and May and I head there, too. We order egg rolls and vegetable lo mein and brown rice and sweet and sour tofu and it's hot and perfect, and by the end of the meal I feel satisfied that I've had a proper Jewmas.

"We still have a bit of time before my dad gets home," May says as we zip our coats and leave the restaurant. "Wanna take the dog for a walk?

"*You* want to take Raphael for a walk?" I ask.

"'Want' is a strong word. 'Feel obligated' is probably better."

"Either way, that's a huge step. First comes a sense of obligation, and after that, love. You're gonna looooooove Raphael."

"Never."

“You will,” I say in a singsong voice.

“Shut up.” She pushes me lightly with her shoulder as we walk, hands in our pockets, back to her house.

I go inside and grab Raphael’s leash. The second he hears the slightest hint of the metal carabiner, the dog goes out of his mind. He hops into the air on all fours. Like, he doesn’t even jump up on his back legs. He’s so excited he soars, not a single tiny paw on the ground. It’s astonishing.

“Oh, shit,” May says right before we leave.

I’m worried it’s something serious, maybe about her dad, but then she says, “We need his booties.”

“His what?”

“His snow booties.”

She reaches into a basket near Raphael’s bed and pulls out a pair of red-and-black puffy boots and a matching jacket. “He needs to wear them in the snow. That’s an order from Greg. And the coat, too.”

May rolls her eyes, and I reach down and put the booties on one at a time. It’s an incredibly difficult task, because Raphael is too excited and keeps trying to run away. Then I pick him up, wrap my arms around his belly, and stretch the coat over his giant ears. I pull his bootie-clad paws through the limb-holes and put the hood—complete with two slits for his ears—over his head.

When he’s all geared up, we head out.

“Fuck, that’s cute,” I say as we watch Raphael try to navigate the snow in his coat and booties. He keeps stretching his hind legs behind him and lifting his front legs as high as they can go, like a person walking in flippers.

"Unfortunately, I have to agree," May says.

"Where to?"

"How about that tiny park a few blocks over?"

Raphael acclimates a bit to the booties as we walk there but not much. The hood slips over his eyes, and he starts howling, so I pull it down for a more casual look. The whole thing remains adorable for the duration of our journey.

But May and I are pretty quiet. Something's off.

"How long do you think it took to put up those decorations?" I ask to fill the silence as we pass by a house covered in lights and candy canes and inflatable snowmen and just about every other winter or Christmas symbol imaginable.

"A long time," May says.

I take a breath. "I think today is the best day of the year to be a Jew."

"If you say 'Jewmas' one more time—"

"Well, yes, Jewmas is part of it. But it's more than that. Don't you think Christmas is super stressful for people who celebrate it? Like, you have to make it perfect for your family. You have to hide hard truths about Santa from your kids; you have to do so much prep. We don't have to deal with any of that."

"But that's part of the fun, don't you think? That it's such a big deal?"

"I'd rather not be stressed out for two months of the

year. I don't think it's worth it for one day."

"I don't know, it's kind of nice."

"I think that's the miracle of Judaism—the fact that we don't have to deal with it."

"I don't think I hate Christmas as much as you do."

"I don't hate Christmas," I say, shoving her gently as we arrive at the park. "I hate that it's such a big production."

And then something collides with my face. Something cold and wet and round.

"ARE YOU KIDDING ME?" I yell at May, who's laughing and packing another snowball.

I tie Raphael's leash to the bench and run at May, picking up snow as I go. There's no one around and we're far from the road, so I don't even try to be careful. "That was a LOW BLOW," I yell as I chuck a snowball at May and miss.

"No, this is," she says, and throws a snowball at my knees.

I shriek, and she runs toward me. I try to run away, but the snow is too deep and I fall into it. She trips over me and falls too.

It's freezing, but we're both breathing hard and not moving from where we've sunk into the snow. She looks over at me, her whole face covered in ice.

I start laughing and can't stop, which makes her laugh, too.

"Are—you—laughing—at—me?"

"Yes," I say, a stitch forming in my side.

She shoves my shoulder, and I shove her back. We're sinking deeper and deeper, our clothes getting more and more soaked.

And suddenly her face is near mine. So, so close.

We both stop laughing.

She glances down at my lips, her face half submerged in snow.

I glance down at hers, too.

She looks at mine again.

I look at hers.

I don't know what to do. I'm broken.

I'm going to die here in the snow because I don't know if this girl wants me to kiss her or not.

And then, she leans in.

She kisses me chastely at first. Just a peck. Then she pulls away.

And we're back to staring at each other.

Fuck it.

I grab her cheeks in my ice-cold hands and kiss her. Her lips are freezing, and mine are numb, so it's a slow start. But after a minute we're thawing and kissing and she's so warm and soft, and I put my hand into the snow to reach behind her back and I pull her to me and there's snow everywhere and Raphael is barking, and we don't stop kissing until neither of us can breathe.

Then we break apart.

We're grinning at each other, and I start to sit up but she drags me back into the snow and I wrap my arms around her as best I can and we kiss again and Raphael barks even louder and we both yell at him to shut up.

May scrambles to her feet and I follow. She shoves snow down my neck and I scream and shove snow down hers.

Then she pushes me up against a tree, facing away from the road.

"Shit," she says, catching her breath, staring at me with wide eyes.

"Fuck," I agree.

And she kisses me, hard, with tongue and teeth and feeling.

So, uh.

I guess that answers one question: there seems to be a strong likelihood that May is queer.

My Stalwart Prepubescent Barista

It took everything in my power not to text May the moment I got out of bed. But now that's it's been a few hours and I've given myself permission to message her, I try to make it incredibly blasé.

ME: wanna walk Raphael with me today?

MAY: yes yes
but my dad is hocking me about spending time with him so maybe come later?

ME: absolutely

Huh, not super flirty. But fine, obviously, because I'm nervous and she's nervous and the whole world is nervous and these nerves are manifesting in our texts.

So I wait as long as I can, hanging out in the kitchen with Beatrice and Tasha. I'm having a hard time focusing on the conversation until Beatrice asks me what I did for Christmas.

Oh, you know, just slept at a girl's house and then made out with her in a large pile of snow at the park down the road.

"Nothing much."

"Well, that's a damn shame," Beatrice says with a tsk. "I yelled at my boy all day for not letting you come over. I don't know who raised him—wolves, probably!" She throws her head back and laughs. "Were you trapped here in that blizzard? That was the worst one I've seen since 'ninety-six—you remember that one, doll: 'Blizzard Ninety-six' I think they called it."

"Oh, uh . . ."

I don't think it's necessary to mention that I was negative years old in 1996, or that I was, in fact, trapped in the Christmas Eve blizzard—just not here.

Luckily, Tasha saves me by telling us that Moscow has snow cover from November to April and that the blizzard yesterday was nothing, to which Beatrice replies that it isn't a competition, doll, and Tasha says sure, but if it was, I'd win. This earns her a gentle slap on the arm.

The minute hand of the Italian flag clock is ticking forward so slowly that I'm sure it's all some cosmic prank. I arbitrarily decided on five o'clock as the time I would allow myself to go to May's, so when 4:59 turns to 5:00, I tell Beatrice and Tasha that I have to go walk Raphael, grab the clothes May lent me, and leave for her house.

But it's not May who comes to the door—it's Greg. I hide May's clothes behind my back.

"Thanks for walking Raphael in the snow the other day," he says. "Sorry about making you work on Christmas, but well, weather never has a day off."

I want to say that I should be the one thanking him, seeing as the walk led to one of the hottest make-outs of my entire life. But obviously I don't say that because that would be the wildest thing any human has ever said.

Thankfully, May comes to the door then.

"I'm gonna go out for a bit," she tells her dad as she runs outside to meet me.

I have a goofy grin on my face as Greg closes the door, leaving me, May, and Raphael alone.

"Hey," I say, smiling at her and handing back the clothes she lent me.

"Hey." She smiles back at me. "Thanks."

Even Raphael seems happier than usual in his snow booties and coat, wagging his nub of a tail and panting. He makes little grunts and whines until he finally poops, and then I have to remove him from the scene of the crime to stop him from eating it (which wouldn't be the first time).

We're back at the same park that we went to on Christmas day, but walking here now, the vibe is different. I can't bring myself to say much, and May's quieter, too. Raphael barely even wiggles his butt in the snow. We're all hesitant, like we're walking on hallowed ground.

I think briefly about kissing May, of course. But it doesn't feel right. And anyway, I'm happy just to be next to her, out in the snow.

The walk is uneventful. (And by that I mean no snow make-out—whatever, it's fine.) When it's time to say goodbye, I linger on May's porch for a bit too long.

"Bye, Shani," she says finally, and gently closes the door.

Back at Beatrice's, I'm heating up some leftover rice when the front door swings open, and Lauren bursts through, throwing her arms around Beatrice.

Just like that, Raphael's rightful dog walker has returned.

"How'd it go?" Lauren asks as she drops her giant suitcase off in the kitchen. "I hope Raphael didn't give you too much trouble. Or Greg's daughter. I don't really know her but I get such weird vibes every time she stays at her dad's."

"Not at all," I say in a high-pitched voice, my face getting hot.

Then I excuse myself.

♥

After I get home from work on Monday—which is mostly a day of, yes, thinking about May while cleaning fragile millions-of-years-old fossils—I get a text from her.

MAY: so you're not walking raphael anymore??

ME: i guess my duty is done
farewell, sweet pup

MAY: you should've told me!!
i thought it was you coming to the door
i even put on nice clothes

I almost throw my phone directly across Beatrice's room. I don't even know what to say, but luckily, I don't have to reply, because there's more.

MAY: and the other girl is cute
but . . .

Because May's being stupidly courageous, I decide I should be, too. So I ask the question that her last text seems to demand.

ME: but what?

MAY: but she's not a 5' 9" (that's close, right?) girl

who looks amazing in my clothes
and is really fucking good at the crossword puzzle

I'm about to fly through the ceiling and burst into flames and then be reborn, like a phoenix. Where is May's courage coming from?

ME: too bad that girl doesn't exist
i'm only 5' 8"

MAY: shit well
i guess i'll ask that other girl if she wants to get hot chocolate
and not you
:(

ME: right now?

MAY: yeah
meet at the bookstore?
the cafe's open till 10

After some light panicking and jumping around the room shaking my hands and legs, I put on my best jeans, my cleanest T-shirt, and my one jacket.

There's a bookstore-café near The Big Blue Dog, and I know that's the one she's talking about. When I get there,

May's sitting at a corner table, under a string of multicolored Christmas lights, two hot chocolates in front of her.

"I almost didn't sit here," she says as I walk up to the table. "I thought you might be morally opposed to the Christmas lights."

"They're fine." I sit down. "They're good, I mean."

I'm losing it. I have no idea what to say or how to say it.

We're out in public, together.

I put my hands in my lap, and we sip our hot chocolates, not saying much.

"Yours was much better," I say, and when she gives me a funny look I add, "Your hot chocolate."

She leans in toward me, and the back of my neck prickles as she says, "They use a mix."

"Tastes like it." I lean away.

I'm pathetic—eighteen years old, and in this moment my biggest fear is the girl sitting across from me.

"So, how was work?" she asks after I'm quiet for too long.

"Uh, good." I accidentally bump her leg, then move my own away like I touched a hot pan.

She puts her thigh back and smiles at me, eyebrows raised. It's a challenge.

So I smile back.

And something changes.

We both take a few more sips of hot chocolate, staring at each other the whole time.

"Actually, I think I'm done with this," she says, not even a little bit done with her drink. "Do you think you're done with yours, maybe?" Her eyes are wide.

"Yup, I think so."

I get up as quickly as I can, scraping my metal chair against the floor in the process so that everyone in the café glares at us.

I'm pretty sure there's a sweat stain forming in every possible location on my body. All I want to do is kiss her, and at the same time the thought of kissing her makes me want to bury myself in the snow.

We hurry outside, into the dark parking lot near the back entrance of the café.

The second the door closes behind us, May drags me over to the brick wall next to the window. I flatten myself against it so no one inside can see us.

I know what's coming. I want it.

She bites her lip and stares at me, and I pull her in by the bottom of her coat. We kiss frantically, holding on to whatever we can, and when we break apart, she pushes my scarf down and kisses my neck. I let out a small breath, and she bites me. Not hard, but hard enough.

"Ow, jeez." I laugh and push her off me, then yank up my scarf. But I'm so deeply relieved, because the seal is broken.

"Sorry," she says. "Was that okay? I couldn't help it."

I nod and bring her back to me, by the waist this time. I

put one of my legs between hers, pulling off her red beanie and running my hands through her hair.

Then I put the hat on my own head, and she laughs and tries to take it back. But before she can I grab her wrists, wrap them around my waist, and kiss her, hard.

It's like I'm a different person, and I like whoever she is.

"I have to go home," she says breathlessly after a minute. "My dad doesn't even know I'm out."

"Don't," I tell her, and she kisses me again, on the corner of my mouth, then softly on my lips, then on the other corner, to even it out.

She starts walking away, backward, still looking at me.

"Bye, Shani."

A shiver runs down my spine at the sound of her saying my name aloud.

She leaves me there, leaning against the wall.

Wearing her hat.

It's Wednesday now, the twenty-ninth. May's birthday.

I haven't heard from her since Monday evening, since the parking lot behind the bookstore. Not a text, nothing. I know it's not that weird. Like, it's normal to not hear from someone for one full business day. It's totally fine.

I texted her yesterday, but it was just a silly video of a TikTok-famous corgi in snow booties, so it's not like it even really warranted a response.

Okay, fine, I also texted her an hour ago to wish her a happy birthday. But still no answer to that either. Which is, of course, totally chill. She's probably being inundated with birthday messages. Mine must've gotten lost in the fray.

But I'm jumpy and on edge as I head to work. I stop in The Big Blue Dog before hopping on the Metro, and thankfully, my stalwart prepubescent barista is there.

"Shani!" Luke says when I walk in.

His greeting makes me feel slightly reckless.

"Where were you the other day?" I ask as I pretend to grab my wallet, even though I know I won't need it.

"What day?" He leans both his arms against the counter and his pimply face is alarmingly close to mine.

I try to put on a semi-sultry voice as I say, "Just . . . the other day," but it comes out sounding like I have a blob of mucus stuck in my throat.

"Thinking about you, probably," he says, and he, honest to god, purrs.

He purrs at me. I want to vomit.

But I don't. I just nod and smile.

Then he says, "I'll *whip* you up something special," with so much emphasis that I feel actively worried.

He hops from the espresso machine to the fridge to the sink and back again. I contemplate running away, just sprinting to the Metro and letting it carry me directly to Hell on the red line.

But then he turns around and I slap on a smile as he

bows and says, "A macchiato for your troubles, milady."

He hands me the coffee cup and I start to bow my head back at him, then stop myself.

"If you open the lid, you'll see I've replaced the foam with whipped cream."

"Wow," I say, removing the lid and finding that, yes, most of the coffee cup is filled with poorly sprayed whipped cream. And at the very top there's a maraschino cherry. Because of course. "This looks great," I say, trying to suppress a grimace.

"On the house." As if I would've ever paid for this drink.

But I thank him and walk to the Metro, worrying about what drink he'll make me next time.

When I get to the lab, Mandira's already there, filling out paperwork. I think that's a big part of her fellowship, punching numbers into forms.

"Graham's not here today, so we're gonna go absolutely wild," she says without looking up from her spot on the stainless-steel bench. "Kidding, kidding," she adds. "We're just gonna do our jobs."

"Dr. Graham's not here?" I ask. "Is he dead?"

Mandira laughs. "Nope, he's sick, which is almost as surprising. Earlier in the year he came into work with a fractured ankle. He tripped on ice and his ankle was as big as a balloon, but he waited until six to go to the hospital."

"Jesus."

"I know," she agrees. "So, I was thinking . . . do you want to help me do some coelacanth prep?"

Holy shit.

Of course, Mandira picks today to let me do the coolest task. The day I'm completely distracted by May.

I told myself at the beginning of this internship that I wasn't going to get sidetracked, and now I'm about to help prepare a coelacanth fossil. It's not the time to think about girls who push you up against walls and kiss the corners of your mouth.

"Yes, of course," I tell Mandira. "That would be amazing."

She smiles and pats the stool next to her.

I gape at the table. "Oh my god."

"I know."

Because sitting directly in front of me and Mandira is what appears to be an entire school of juvenile coelacanth fossils, each lying on their own plaster cast. The specimen I saw on the first day is there, too, now surrounded by all these other fish. I force my mouth closed.

"Where was the dig site?" I ask, still marveling.

"Good question." Mandira pulls out a box of gloves. "The Waterloo Farm locality in South Africa."

"Wasn't that an estuary in the Devonian?" I've read a few papers on Waterloo Farm. It's a pretty famous dig site for paleoichthyologists.

These fish are celebrities.

"It was," Mandira says, smiling now. "Why do you ask?"

"They were probably using the estuary as a nursery, right? If all these juveniles were found together?"

"Hell yeah," she says. "Well, that's what we think, at least."

My heart's racing, because even though I wasn't the first to figure this out, it feels like a discovery. It's the high of piecing ancient clues together.

And yet I still don't know why May isn't texting me back.

It's a foolish thought, but it's there, and I can't shake it.

Mandira gives me a few brushes and we start ever so gently cleaning the fossils, but even with baby coelacanths sitting directly in front of me, I can't stop thinking about May.

Which then makes me think about how I haven't even told Taylor everything that happened yet. I was still processing on Sunday, and then I was going to tell her Monday night, but I was kind of . . . busy.

But I'm going to tell her. I *need* to tell her. It's not like with Sadie, where I thought our relationship wouldn't mean as much if I told other people about it, people from my precollege life.

I'm going to tell Taylor everything about May, because she's my best friend and she deserves to know. I could text her, but I'd rather do it over FaceTime. Some things are too big for a text.

So all my thoughts and feelings and angst about May have been trapped in my head, ready to burst out at any moment. Which is why, after a few minutes of cleaning in silence, when Mandira asks me, "What's new?" I immediately tell her everything.

She already knew about the car crash and the dog walking and the portrait gallery, so it's easy to fill her in about the Christmas Eve blizzard sleepover and the kiss. I leave out the details, obviously, and I don't tell her about making out on the brick wall behind the bookstore café. I try to keep it PG.

"That's unbelievably romantic," Mandira says. "And I don't want to say I told you so, but I told you so."

"Told me what?"

"That it's like a Hallmark movie! Because it kind of is!" I shake my head, but she continues. "Listen, I've watched every single Christmas movie in existence in the past few weeks with my girlfriend, and I could basically plot one out right now. Maybe the baby coelacanths are your fun-loving coworkers who you gossip to once your supervisor—me—leaves the room."

I laugh a little at that. "I would absolutely gossip with the baby coelacanths."

"Very much same," Mandira says. "But honestly, if this was really a Hallmark movie, we'd both be the quirky sidekicks for the WASPish main character who returned to DC to work on her family's hot chocolate farm or whatever."

"Hot chocolate farm?" I ask, grinning. "Why does that make it sound like an algorithm wrote the script?"

"I'm gonna take that as a compliment," Mandira says. "Because an algorithm wouldn't put a queer Jew or—heaven forbid—a queer brown Hindu in a Christmas movie."

"You're not wrong."

I've tried before to map my life into the plot of a rom-com, tried to make it fit into the formula, squeezing it into a place where it doesn't quite belong.

"At this point I wish things were *more* like a classic WASPy, feel-good, Christmas, hot-chocolate-farm Hallmark movie," I tell Mandira, who gives me a questioning look. "Because I honestly don't know what's happening with us now. I'm so stressed. She hasn't texted me back in thirty-six hours."

"That's not that long," Mandira says. "And didn't you say it was her birthday today? She's probably busy with friends or something."

"Yeah," I say. But I don't know. I don't think May has any friends in DC. She's told me as much.

"She's probably figuring out how she feels too," she adds, clearly trying to make me feel better.

It doesn't.

Work goes by quickly after that (we make sure to avoid

any additional relationship discussions), and when I get out of lab, I try to call Taylor, but she doesn't pick up.

TAY: call later!

family catan night

if I don't get longest road I'll die

ME: lol sorry to distract

have fun

Of course, Taylor can't talk, and I don't feel like going directly home, so I walk around a little. And when that doesn't distract me from thoughts of May, I do something wild.

I call my mom.

She picks up on the first ring. "Hi, hon."

"Hi," I say, and somehow my voice sounds annoyed even though I'm not. Yet.

"What's going on? How was Jewmas? Are you getting ready for New Year's Eve?"

"What would I need to do to get ready?" I snap, then immediately want a do-over, to try again with a gentler tone.

"Reflect on your year, maybe. Think about your resolutions."

"I'm not doing that."

I stop walking and put a hand to my forehead, feeling

furious at myself. Because this is the second time in the past month that I've been a bitch to my mom because of a girl, and it's also the second time that I can't tell her about it.

So I steel myself and try to be nice.

"Did you see a movie on Saturday?" I ask.

"Of course," she says, and she's clearly so pleased about the minimal effort I put in that I feel even worse. "Just the newest superhero movie. It was loud."

"Sounds great."

There's a pause. "Are you eating enough?"

"What? Yes, I'm eating fine."

"Do you need me to send anything?"

"No."

"I'm cooking dinner now," she says. "Was there anything else?"

"Uh, no," I say, slightly taken aback. I'm usually the one to end our conversations.

"I can call you back after it's done, but I need to chop a few things right now."

"No, it's fine."

I think about my mom eating dinner alone. Chopping for one. I don't know what else to say.

"Take care of yourself, Shani."

"I will." And right before she hangs up, I add, "Love you."

"Love you, too."

Even though the conversation was a solid D-minus, I

feel a little better. Good enough that I hop on the Metro. For the first time all day, I'm not panicked about May's lack of communication.

And then, because my brain's a hot mess, my thoughts drift to Sadie. If I hadn't responded to *her* all day, if I hadn't told her where I was, she'd be mad. She wanted to know my whereabouts at all times, and I was happy to tell her. But fuck that. It took her breaking up with me to realize that's not healthy. That's not love.

I don't want to be like that with May. If she's not answering, so be it. I don't need to know where she is. I'd *like* to—fine, sure, yes—but I don't *need* to. I'm not entitled to that information.

Mostly, I'm mad at myself. I opened up. I made out with a girl who is not Sadie. I made out with her *twice*, actually. And now she's not texting me back.

This is what I get for being vulnerable.

When I make it home, I run upstairs to avoid Beatrice and Tasha and Lauren. I don't even try calling Taylor back. I can't right now.

I turn off my phone and read for a while, but my eyes keep closing and I'm not taking in any of the words, so I brush my teeth and get ready for bed.

Before I fall asleep, I turn my phone back on to set an alarm and check my texts, one last time.

I open up my conversation with May.

The happy birthday message didn't even deliver.

I don't know what that means. Maybe she's somewhere without service?

I can't think about it right now.

So I put my phone on airplane mode so that I don't get any texts either.

I throw myself into work wholeheartedly the next day, the 364th of the year. I'm gentle but thorough with the fossils, removing every speck of dirt. The day goes by quickly that way, scrubbing and asking Mandira a million questions about the juvenile coelacanths I'm cleaning, and I'm learning, really *learning*. I can tell she's happy to talk about fish and not my relationship drama. It feels good to do what I came to DC to do and do it well. I hardly think of May at all. I remind myself that I *shouldn't* be thinking about her.

Leaving work is the worst part of my day, the loneliest, when I say goodbye to Mandira and head home to spend the evening alone.

Still no response from May.

And I don't even get to console myself by seeing Raphael, with his little doggy smile and his tiny, bouncy legs. That's Lauren's job again. It was never really mine in the first place.

I once again head straight to my room when I get home, as if I've been given a time-out—except it's self-inflicted.

Like yesterday, I can't concentrate on reading or watching TV or anything. So, of course, I look at my texts with May.

The message *still* hasn't delivered. I press on the blue bubble and choose to send it as a text. So now it's green, and there's no way of knowing if she got it, and I'm starting to think that maybe I should just go over to her house to make sure she's okay. She can't fault me for checking in.

I decide it's a good idea—or maybe delude myself into thinking it is—but it still takes me a little while to work up the courage to walk the few blocks to May's house.

I knock on the door, and Raphael starts barking inside. It's a comfortable sound, and it makes me feel better about coming; his bark seems to confirm that this was a good idea.

But when the door opens, it's Greg who answers, like last time. He looks at me like he's not quite sure who I am. He's more haggard than I've ever seen him: not in his usual suit but in a stained T-shirt and sweatpants. He clearly hasn't shaved in days.

"Lauren already walked the dog," he says, and starts to shut the door.

"No!" I shout. Then, in a more level voice: "No, wait." He pushes the door back open. I take a deep breath. "Sorry, but I was just wondering if May's here?"

He looks almost angry for a moment before his face goes back to its neutral expression. "No, she's not," he says, and shuts the door.

He doesn't even wait for a response. Just . . . slam. Closed in my face.

I turn to stare out onto the street, wondering what on earth just happened. Wondering if May's okay. Where she is. And why, why, *why* she's not responding.

I don't even walk off the porch before I try to FaceTime Taylor. She texts saying she doesn't have Wi-Fi and I should just call her instead, so I do that.

When she picks up, I'm so relieved I almost start crying. "I have so much to tell you," I say. "Shit really hit the fan over here."

"Can you wait to tell me in person?" she asks.

"What? No. Are you kidding? I feel like I'm gonna explode."

There's some background noise from Taylor's end, and she says, "Uh, can you wait for, like, two seconds?"

I start to feel angry. I need Taylor right now, and she's putting me on hold. I thought we weren't doing this anymore, that we learned something from our first semester apart.

Well, fuck that. "I'm just gonna hang up," I say as I turn onto Beatrice's street. "I'll call you back when you have time to talk."

"No, really," Taylor says. "You can tell me in person."

I'm about to smash my phone on the ground. "Why are you being like this?"

Then Taylor laughs, but I don't hear it through the phone.

"Hi," Taylor says, hanging up and running to hug me.

"WHAT THE FUCK?" I scream, hugging her, then pushing her, then hugging her again. "I was about to not talk to you for a solid month. Maybe two."

She wraps her arm around my shoulders. "Are you surprised?"

We've been the same height for the past few years, but she used to be way shorter than me. It's nice to be able to stand eye-to-eye with her, especially right now.

"Fucking obviously, yes." She laughs, but it's true. My body's in shock. "I hate you."

"Of course," she says as we head inside. "Now tell me everything."

Amy From Model UN's Ex-Boyfriend

I drag Taylor inside, clinging to her like a best friend leech. I want to alternate between telling her everything about May and then just sort of crying and letting her pet my hair. Then we can switch and she'll cry about anything she wants to and I'll pet *her* hair.

But before I can get her upstairs, Beatrice is there, standing in front of us. She has a sixth sense for knowing when I most want to be left alone and appearing out of nowhere, like a Victorian ghost-child.

"Now, who's this gorgeous young thing?" Beatrice asks in the way old women do, where it sounds like they're flirting but really they're just admiring a younger woman. (Or maybe they *are* flirting. Who knows?)

"This is my best friend, Taylor. Taylor, this is my . . . Beatrice." I realize as I'm introducing Beatrice that I have no idea what to call her. My landlady? My roommate? The latter makes it sound like we're staying up all night eating Takis and watching bad reality TV. What it doesn't communicate are the facts that she's a ninety-six-year-old woman and I'm staying in her sex bed.

"It's so important to have a best girlfriend," Beatrice says after my failed introduction, and I cringe. One of my biggest pet peeves is when people describe friends who are girls as "girlfriends." But Beatrice gets a pass.

"Did this doll here"—Beatrice speaks to Taylor but points to me—"tell you that her mom and I were best friends?"

Taylor gives me a questioning look, and I shake my head and mouth, *Great-grandma,* as Beatrice reminisces about Sandy.

"Everyone at school loved her," Beatrice says, putting one hand to her heart and clamping the other on Taylor's arm. "She had this swagger, and the girls would almost swoon over her, like they did with the fellas!"

I can tell Taylor's about to lose circulation in her arm, so I say, "This, uh, *doll* had a long trip, so she should probably rest."

"Okay, angels," Beatrice says as I drag Taylor upstairs, "have a nice little nap."

"Was your great-grandma queer?" Taylor whispers at the top of the steps as she massages her forearm.

"Honestly? The more Beatrice tells me about her, the more it seems like she might've been."

I imagine the possibility of having a queer ancestor—though, in all likelihood, I had many—as we settle into Beatrice's room.

I hope they're proud of me and the gay chaos I've created.

I ask Taylor how she got here (bus) and *why* she's here (didn't want me to be alone on New Year's Eve—that gets a big ol' hug), and then the whole May story spills out of me. Even the behind-the-bookstore make-out that I didn't tell Mandira about for obvious reasons. Taylor and I sit cross-legged on my bed, facing each other. She's a great listener: she'll gasp when something shocking happens and laugh at the funny parts.

When I'm done, Taylor pushes me over so that my legs are still folded but sticking up in the air, and we both laugh as she says, "Why the fuck didn't you tell me about the kiss the moment it happened?"

"I don't know! I was overwhelmed."

She reaches out her hand and I grab it so that she can pull me back to an upright position. "And she still hasn't texted?"

"The message hasn't even delivered." I pull out my

phone to show her what I mean. "I'm worried she's in trouble or something."

But when I navigate over to my texts with May, the message is now blue.

It delivered.

"What's going on?" Taylor asks when I don't show her the texts.

"It went through," I say, slightly stunned. "So now I can't even use her not getting the message as an excuse. She's just not texting back."

"Maybe she will, though. She doesn't have read receipts, right?"

"No."

"Then you don't even know if she's seen it!"

"She's obviously seen it," I say. "Everyone looks at their fucking texts. They just don't respond to them when they make out with a girl twice and regret it a day later." I throw my phone to the end of the bed. "Sorry," I say. "I'm just frustrated."

"Which *totally* makes sense." Then Taylor tries to distract me by talking about the latest boy who's obsessed with her and who she doesn't feel like dating, and I tell her she's too good for men as a whole and she tells *me* that obviously she'd stop dating them if she could.

Since it's a work night, we decide to go to bed fairly early. Taylor's an excellent guest, because she's happy to be on my schedule, and I love her for that.

"We're waking up at seven, okay?" I call to Taylor as she brushes her teeth.

"Yeah, that's fine," she says back through a mouthful of toothpaste.

I grab my phone to set the alarm, and my heart almost stops.

There's a text from May.

I scramble to open the phone. My hands are shaking so badly that I can barely type my code.

But I do.

Deep breath.

MAY: thanks!

Nothing else. Just "thanks."

ME: are you okay??
where are you??

It delivers, and there are bubbles right away. Maybe I shouldn't have asked where she is. Maybe it was too much of a controlling, panicked, Sadie-ish thing to do. But I'm genuinely worried about her, even if I shouldn't be.

MAY: i'm fine
can't really talk rn
at my mom's house

I read the last text over and over. Her mom's house? In Ithaca?

I think about the conversation I overheard with her dad, where she said that the second she turned eighteen, she'd leave DC.

It's silly, but I thought that maybe, because of me, or whatever, she wouldn't. That she'd want to stay.

I'm a grade A fool.

Fuck.

Then I see *more* bubbles, and my crush-addled heart soars into my throat.

MAY: we'll talk soon though?

I can't rn but soon

ok?

I just thumbs-up that text—I don't want to seem too eager—and Taylor shuts off the bathroom light and climbs into bed. I groan.

"What's wrong?"

I hold out my phone and cover my eyes. "She texted back."

Taylor grabs it and reads the messages. "I don't think this is a bad thing," she says. "A little weird, maybe. But it sounds like she really wants to tell you what's happening?"

"Yeah," I say. "Maybe."

But what if she never comes back? What if the "talk

soon" is her telling me we had our fun but she's staying in Ithaca forever and cutting off contact with her dad and it's all over, everything?

I try to remind myself that this was my goal, that I was going to be a Jewish nun and focus on the lab and go to sleep at eight pm and return to the uncomplicated, paleoichthyology-driven life I had pre-Sadie.

But as hard as I work to convince myself that this is true, I don't quite believe it.

I feel slightly less weird in the morning, knowing I'll be at work with Mandira and then spending New Year's Eve with my best friend.

I set Taylor free in the natural history museum and tell her to meet me out by the food trucks at noon.

"Sounds good," she says. "But I'm gonna get into some *Night at the Museum*–style mischief while you're at work, just so you know."

"Yup, makes sense!" I shout to her through the cavernous atrium as I open the staff door. "Have fun, stay safe."

"I will, and I won't."

When I get to the lab, Mandira's back to playing Christmas music.

"You're legally allowed to play it until New Year's Day," she says before I can ask why Michael Bublé's smooth, jazzy voice is serenading us with "Have Yourself a Merry Little Christmas."

"I didn't know there was a law," I say, laughing.

"It's almost more than a law," she tells me. "It's, like, part of our social fabric."

We talk about the legality of playing Christmas music after Christmas (and before Thanksgiving) as we clean up the benches. We're going to start on some fossil-coelacanth habitat analysis in the new year, which'll be super cool.

At noon, I text Taylor to meet me outside the main museum entrance for my lunch break. Luckily, she's still intact, and even more luckily, the grilled cheese truck is here. We walk there as I explain that Smithsonian employees go out of their minds when grilled cheese is available to them.

"And rightly so," she says as we get in line.

We sit on the museum steps, sandwiches in hand, and after a minute of shoving perfectly melted cheese and perfectly grilled bread into our faces, Taylor says, "How would you feel about going to a party tonight?"

I pause mid-grilled-cheese bite. "I mean, fine I guess, but that might be a problem since I don't know anyone who's having a party."

"Well, duh," Taylor says, and I make a face at her. "But I do."

Of course.

Taylor somehow knows exactly when and where things are happening on any given night. And when she walks through a door, everyone shouts, "Taylor!" like she's their long-lost cousin or cult leader. Meanwhile, I'm lucky if one person other than Taylor knows my name. That's a *good* party for me.

"You know Amy?" she asks.

"From Debate?"

"No, no, Amy from Model UN. Fuck Amy from Debate."

"She's the worst," I agree.

"Yeah, well, Amy from Model UN is *not* the worst. And you remember her ex-boyfriend?"

"No? Literally, why would I remember Amy from Model UN's ex-boyfriend?"

"Well, his name's Teddy," she says, as if that'll jog my memory. "We respond to each other's IG stories every once in a while, and the other day he was telling me about this party his friend from Georgetown's having tonight. They both stayed in DC for winter break."

And then it clicks. "Are you trying to hook up with Amy's ex-boyfriend?" That's the only logical explanation for this convoluted story about a girl we vaguely knew in high school.

"What? No," she says, but she's a terrible actor, and when I lift my eyebrows, she relents. "Fine, yes. I'm trying to hook up with Amy from Model UN's ex-boyfriend. But, okay, his friend is this superrich Georgetown kid, and apparently, he has this amazing house right by campus, and Teddy's saying this party's gonna be huge, and we have to go."

Taylor's out of breath after telling me all that, and I let her rest for a moment before I say, "Whatever, fine, yes. Let's go." Because the alternative is sitting in Beatrice's kitchen and, like, listening to the countdown on the radio or something.

After lunch I head back to work and set Taylor free in DC once again, but at three Mandira tells me I should go home for the day.

"Are you sure?"

"Yeah, of course," she says, skipping "Do They Know It's Christmas?" in favor of "I Saw Mommy Kissing Santa Claus."

"Thank you so much, Mandira." I put on my jacket. "See you next year."

"See you next year, Shani. Good work this week."

I grin.

God, I love positive reinforcement.

"What's the vibe of this party?" I ask Taylor when we're back in my room at Beatrice's, getting ready. "Like, what should I wear?"

"I'm wearing *this*." She pulls a sparkly gold dress out of her backpack.

"I don't have a single piece of clothing that fits that vibe," I tell her as I open and close my drawers, hoping for something fun and party-appropriate simply to appear.

"Ooh," Taylor says, and I can see the gears turning in her head. "Did you bring that pinstriped blazer I got you?"

One of Taylor's many talents is knowing the contents of my entire wardrobe. It helps that she's bought me most of the non-T-shirt clothes I own.

I dig through the drawers, looking for the blazer she's talking about.

"You didn't hang it up?" she asks, horrified. "This is truly why you can't have nice things."

I don't listen to her and keep rummaging until I find it in a rumpled pile of nice clothes that I haven't even tried to wear in the past three weeks.

"Yes, excellent," Taylor says. "You're wearing that. And you can even wear it with jeans, but not if they're stained."

"You don't need to tell me not to wear stained jeans." She raises her eyebrows at me, and I add, "Fine, fine. I'll wear my clean pair."

She grins. "What would you do without me?"

I know she doesn't mean it seriously, but I kind of had to find out this past semester. When the only person in the world I thought I cared about was Sadie.

I don't meet her gaze as I say, "Taylor?"

"Yeah?"

"I'm a piece of shit."

"What?" She walks over to me. "Why would you say that?"

"I didn't talk to you for a whole semester and now you're being so *good* to me." I look at her then. "Why? I'd never talk to me again."

She shakes her head. "First of all, because that's just, like, what best friends do." I smile, but now it's her turn to not meet my eyes. "And it's not like I tried to talk to you, either."

"Why didn't you, though?"

She sighs. "I guess it's because I wanted to just be, like, *Taylor* for a while, you know?" I furrow my eyebrows, confused. She takes a breath and looks up at the ceiling, like she's trying to think of how to explain it. "We were 'Taylor and Shani' for all of high school, and I didn't want it to be like that at college. I didn't want people to see me as half of a whole."

Tears well in my eyes, and I wipe them away. Because, yeah.

I messed up. Not just our friendship, but, like, my life.

She went to college and tried to become her own person, and I lost myself. I went from being "Taylor and Shani" to "Sadie and Shani." My name always seems to have another one before it.

"I get it," I tell Taylor through tears, because I do. We need to be *Taylor*, full stop, and *Shani,* full stop. Best friends but separate.

Not dependent on someone else for a sense of self.

"I'm sorry, Tay."

"I'm sorry, too," she says, but since she's not one for sentimentality, she clears her throat, wipes her eyes, and declares that it's time for us to get changed.

I go to the bathroom to get dressed and let Taylor have the bedroom.

Honestly, I look pretty good. I stare at myself in the mirror for a bit too long, running my hands through my hair and posing.

"You look *hot*," Taylor says when I come out of the bathroom.

I smile a little and say, "Thanks," but don't add anything else.

She's always been way more comfortable complimenting me than I've been complimenting her. I think it's because she can look at the clothes I'm wearing and say objectively that, yes, this outfit is hot. But even though I know Taylor looks beautiful, I don't say it, because I don't want to seem creepy. (Thanks, internalized homophobia!)

Taylor and I leave at around ten to catch the bus over to Georgetown, but not before Beatrice reminds us to stay safe and to come home right after the clock strikes midnight. We humor her and say, sure, absolutely, no problem.

When the bus lets us off in Georgetown, Taylor pulls her phone out and directs us to Teddy's friend's place.

It's a beautiful town house, with big bay windows and

an ornate front door—which Taylor opens without so much as a knock or a steeling breath.

And of course, right on cue, someone shouts, "Taylor!"

"Teddy!" She runs up to a tall guy with bright blond hair and skin that's too tan for a white person during an East Coast winter, then goes in for a hug. She wraps her arms around his neck and his hands get way too close to her butt for me to want to continue watching this interaction.

I use this as an opportunity to inspect the party. The house is packed with people around our age and maybe a little older, all of them looking more put-together than I'll ever be. They're not even holding plastic cups. They're using actual *glasses*. It's unreal.

The house is dim and full of dark wood and neutral-colored, expensive-looking furniture. Taylor's talking to Teddy on a leather couch, and I would be very, very surprised if they don't hook up later.

I leave them alone to flirt, and I go look for a drink. My search leads me to the kitchen. It's the brightest place in the house, and people are hanging out, chatting, sitting on counters (mostly in pairs) and flirting just as shamelessly as Taylor and Teddy. The counters are black marble, and there's an island with a glass pitcher of something that someone's unhelpfully labeled "Gluten Free ;)."

It doesn't look anything like the jungle juice Sadie and I would drink at Binghamton parties, the kind that was definitely dangerous and was served in the plastic Gatorade barrel that gets dumped on champion football players' heads. This one is pink and sparkly and has mint leaves and blueberries and pomegranate seeds floating at the surface, and may or may not contain gluten.

I grab a fancy glass from the counter and pour myself a drink. It's unbelievably delicious and barely tastes like alcohol, which might be more dangerous than jungle juice but in a subtle way.

"It's good, right?" a girl asks me as she walks up to the kitchen island to pour herself some punch.

I nod and take a sip. "Yeah, definitely."

"How do you know Josh?" she asks, and I'm assuming she means the host.

"Oh, you know," I say, hoping that'll be enough.

"Totally." She smiles at me, then reaches out to touch my shoulder. "I like your blazer."

Instinctively, I pull my arm back, and her face goes from a gentle smile to abject horror.

"Shit," she says. "Sorry. I thought you might be—" she starts. "Are you not? I'm new at this. I thought maybe—for a New Year's kiss—ah, fuck me, then." She puts her head in her hands.

"No, I *am* queer, if that's what you're asking," I tell her, and she removes her head from her hands to look at me. "I'm just not . . ." I trail off.

What was I even going to say? Single?

Because I very, very much am.

Mostly.

"Sorry," she says again.

"Please don't apologize."

"I can't help it."

"Fair enough," I say, and walk out of the kitchen.

I feel a number of things in that moment: bad for the girl, good that she was flirting with me. But mostly, foolishly, I find myself wishing that May was here.

I can't help thinking what it would be like to kiss her at midnight. To grab on to each other and to know that we were entering a new year, together.

I've never had a New Year's kiss.

Oh my god—wait.

Should I send her a New Year's text? I know she said she couldn't talk, but this wouldn't be talking, per se. This would just be me wishing her a happy new year. That's something people do. Right?

I push through the throng of people and find Taylor sitting on Teddy's lap, which doesn't deter me from grabbing her hand and asking her what I asked myself: "Should I send her a New Year's text?"

"Oh," Taylor says, jumping up from Teddy's lap and putting on her planning face. "That's not a bad idea."

I love that, even though we essentially came to this party

so that she could hook up with Amy from Model UN's ex-boyfriend, she's still entertaining my panicked flirting questions.

"I'll bring her back soon," I tell Teddy as I drag Taylor away.

We find a quiet staircase and walk toward the top, then sit shoulder-to-shoulder on a step. I open my Notes app so I can write down options for a text to send to May but can't think of a single message.

"This is a terrible idea, right?" I ask Taylor.

"No, no, this is good. What if the text is like an inside joke or something? That way it's cute but not too much."

"I've known her for three weeks," I snap, feeling the panic and nausea bubble through my intestines. "We don't have any inside jokes. She didn't even fucking tell me when she left for her mom's house."

Taylor raises her eyebrows and puts her hands up. "I'm just trying to help."

"I know, I know. Sorry, I'm stressed."

But then again, maybe we *do* have inside jokes, or at least inside-ish. There has to be something from the portrait gallery, or the movie we saw on Christmas day.

"What if you just say, 'Wish you were here'?" Taylor suggests.

"This isn't a postcard! It's a text to a girl I've kissed twice and ideally would like to kiss again if she ever returns to DC."

"Okay, how about that?" Taylor asks. "'Liked the first two kisses. Down for a third? Happy New Year.'"

"That's your worst suggestion yet."

"I don't hear you coming up with anything!"

I look down at my notes app. I jotted a couple things down after Taylor's inside-joke comment, but all I have so far is *midnight kiss?* on one line and the words *dog booties* on another, which looks dirty, somehow.

"Maybe I shouldn't text her."

"No!" Taylor shouts, which causes some of the people milling around the bottom of the stairs to scowl up at us. "No," she says, quieter this time. "A New Year's text is the perfect thing for a budding romance. Especially if you're worried she might not come back to DC. We just need to brainstorm."

"Well, we only have like twenty minutes till midnight." I bury my face in my hands. "Also, I don't think anything I say is gonna convince her to come back if she doesn't want to." I put my phone down and bounce my legs as fast as they'll go. "This is pointless."

Taylor ignores my panicking and instead checks her phone and says, "Shit, it's that late?"

I sit up. "Time flies when you're crafting a text to your best friend's crush."

"Who said that? Churchill?"

"I think it was Nixon."

"Right, right."

I put my head in my hands. "Fuck," I say, desperation turning to panic.

We're both quiet for a minute as the party gains momentum downstairs, everyone anticipating midnight, a new year.

"OH, OH!" Taylor shouts, jumping up and almost banging her head on the handrail. She sits back down, grabs my phone, and starts typing. My whole body clenches.

"Type it in Notes! Don't put it in Messages yet," I yell back at her, leaning over to try to see what she's writing.

"Obviously I'm putting it in Notes," Taylor says, tongue out, concentrating on the message that could make or break whatever's going on between me and May. *If* there's anything going on.

When she's done, Taylor hands me the phone. *Wish you were here, but how about a rain check on a midnight kiss?*

It's bolder than any message I've ever sent, but I don't hate it.

"This actually isn't bad."

"See?" she says, knocking my knee with hers. "I think it's good. It's flirty, it implies that she'll come back to DC, and that, if she wants to smooch in the future, your tongue is available."

"Ew." I read the text again. "All right, fine." Then I read it a few more times, and copy it into Messages. "I'm gonna send it. I should send it now, right? Or should I wait till midnight?"

"No, send it now," Taylor says. "That way at midnight she'll be thinking about how she could've stayed in DC and had you as her New Year's kiss."

I look up at her. "I can't do it."

She grabs the phone from me and I let her. "On your count." She hovers her thumb over the up arrow that will send this message to May.

"Fuck." I fold my torso over my knees. "Three," I say, trembling.

"You got this."

"Two." I'm going to melt into a puddle on the stairs.

"This is a good text," Taylor says. "Now let's get this puppy sent."

I groan, bang my head against my knees, then groan again. "One."

I sit up in time to catch Taylor's thumb pressing down on my phone. To watch the message catapulted into the ether, forever out of my reach.

"Perfect," Taylor says. "Now let's get a drink." She leads me into the kitchen, where she refills my glass with the fancy punch.

I down it in one gulp, then check my phone, knowing there won't be anything but desperately hoping anyway.

"Ten minutes, sluts!" an incredibly drunk girl shouts as she tries to stand on the countertop.

Everyone cheers, and fuck it, so do I.

11:50, and still no response.

I get more punch, and then follow Taylor back into the living room, where she returns to Teddy's lap.

11:52. Nothing.

11:53. I don't think I've ever been less excited for a new year to arrive.

11:55. Everyone's gathering in the living room. It's an almost fishlike instinct: school together, be near other members of your species as you jump forward an hour, a day, a year.

11:58. Someone turns on the TV, and we watch people going wild in Times Square.

11:59. Everyone in the room is paired like Noah's fucking ark.

I check my phone and check my phone and check my phone and there's nothing and the room is hazy, but I feel so weirdly good and my body is buzzing, and now I don't even want this year to be over and I'll just stop time and it'll be great, and I check my phone again and obviously there's nothing and there will never be anything because having a crush is pointless and now it's—

"FIFTEEN, FOURTEEN, THIRTEEN—" seconds to go and everyone's shouting, smiling, screaming their way into the new year. And I'm staring at my phone. "TWELVE, ELEVEN—" If she doesn't text back, I'll throw my phone into a toilet and start fresh on another continent. "TEN, NINE, EIGHT—" I wonder what Sadie's doing right now.

The last time I was at a house party I was with her. It was the night everything went wrong, and I was even drunker than this. Waaaay drunker. Drunker is a funny word. Drunker drunker. And Sadie was drunker-er. And then—

Noooo. No, brain. Stop. Sadie's not gonna be the last fucking person I think about before the new year. "SEVEN, SIX—" I spot the girl who was hitting on me before. We lock eyes. "FIVE, FOUR—" She walks over and stands so close I can smell the punch on her. Or maybe that's me. "THREE, TWO—" She wraps her arms around my neck. I grab her waist.

"ONE! HAPPY NEW YEAR!"

We kiss, and it's sloppy and wet and her tongue feels like a dead eel inside my mouth, but at least I'm not checking my phone.

"THAT'S HOT!" some guy shouts, and he tries to wrap his arm around my shoulders. I duck under his grasp and stumble away, into the bathroom.

I grab the counter and check my phone and holy shit there's a text and everything's hazy and the contact starts with M and has three letters and I pull my phone close to my face and it's . . .

MOM: happy new year, sweet<3!

stay safe!

luv u

I slide down onto the tile floor, and of fucking course the tiles are heated like the ones in May's upstairs bathroom where Raphael slept the night of the blizzard and I'm just . . .

I'm scared of losing her. May. Even though we just met. Even though she maybe ran away. I'm scared and now everything's ruined and the only person other than Taylor who cares about me is my mom and I don't even deserve her.

There's a knock on the door. "Shani? You in there?"

I bury my head in my knees. "No."

Taylor comes in and sits down next to me, resting her head on my shoulder. "You okay?"

"She didn't text back."

"Well, fuck her, then."

We sit there for a while, even though Taylor could definitely be sucking face with Amy-from-Model-UN's ex right now.

And yet we're both here, on a stranger's bathroom floor, ringing in the first minutes of the new year with each other.

"I love you, Tay."

"You're drunk."

"I still love you."

She sighs. "I know."

I rub Taylor's hair, grateful that she's here, that she's solid, when everything else in my life seems to be slipping under layers of silt, fossilizing before my eyes.

Maybe it'll all be excavated in one hundred million years, alongside my heart.

You're Blocking the Escalator

I'm not 100 percent sure how Taylor and I got home, but we did. I think maybe Teddy's rich friend called us a car?

It's not even that I was too drunk to remember—though, fine, I was pretty drunk—it's more that I was entirely distracted by thoughts of May.

Even so, it felt like a gift to fall into bed with Taylor snoring next to me. Plus, I slept between the sheets, which was a win for my frankly unhealthy fixation with the sex bed.

Taylor's gone now, though. She woke me up before the sun to say goodbye, and in a groggy haze, I did my best to convince her not to leave. But she had to catch an early bus so she could be home in time for her mom's birthday dinner.

I slept a while longer after that, but now the sounds of conversation and laughter downstairs seep into my bedroom. And for the first time in a number of days, the idea of being around people isn't the worst thing in the world.

Beatrice smiles and gets up from the table when she sees me walk through the kitchen archway.

"Happy new year, doll," she says, and yanks me down to mouth height so she can plant a kiss on my cheek.

"Happy new year," I say to her and to Lauren and Tasha, who are both sitting in pajamas around the kitchen table, nursing mugs of coffee.

I pour myself a cup and breathe in the steam.

"We were just talking about our resolutions," Lauren says as I pull over a chair.

"What are yours?" I ask, trying to avoid having to list off my own nonexistent ones.

"Well, I wanna get more sleep, like at least three hours a night—kidding! Like seven hours, ideally. And I'm going to read fifty books," Lauren says.

"And I told her that's a silly goal, because fifty books is too many!" Beatrice cuts in, smacking Lauren's shoulder with a folded newspaper. "What's she doing, reading fifty books? Watch some damn TV. That's what I say. Doctor's orders."

"What's your resolution?" I ask Beatrice.

She laughs. "Doll, I'm too old for resolutions. If I haven't changed in the past ten thousand years, I'm certainly not going to now."

"I want to meditate more," Tasha tells me. "That's my resolution. I'm very stressed all the time."

"That one I agree with," Beatrice says.

Lauren snorts, and Tasha rolls her eyes, but a smile creeps onto her face.

"What about you, Shani?"

They all look at me.

Honestly, I think New Year's resolutions are pointless. If you want to improve, you should be able to start at any time. It's too much pressure to slog through the holidays and then immediately have to better yourself the moment the calendar turns to January.

Maybe I *should* have one this year, though. I can think of innumerable ways that I can improve. Being nicer to my mom, for starters.

But I don't want to tell them that, so I just say, "I think I'll try to eat more vegetables."

They nod like this is a fascinating answer, even though it's the most basic possible resolution.

But even if I *do* eat so many carrots that I'm able to see in the dark, it won't make me a better person. It'll just mean that I might live longer as a shitty one. I pour myself a bowl of cereal and another cup of coffee, then listen as Beatrice gushes about the "beautiful young man" who was the substitute teacher at her aquacise class the other day.

After a while, I excuse myself and go upstairs to get dressed. Maybe I'll do some more DC wandering today. Now that Taylor's gone, I have nothing else to do.

I grab my phone to check the weather and see two texts.

From May.

Sent twenty minutes ago.

MAY: meet at snails space in an hour?

we need to talk

A fleet of emotions passes through me in the time it takes to read her messages. The first, and most powerful, is a strong desire to shit myself.

And when that's gone, I'm left only with shock. I honestly didn't think she was ever coming back to DC. But now she's here, and she wants me to meet her at *Snails Space*. In an hour. Well, forty minutes.

Fuck.

ME: yes

i'll be there

I throw on my good jeans and a jacket and run out of my room, ready to sprint all the way to the museum.

But then I remember that I still have May's beanie, the one I stole off her head when we kissed behind the bookstore. I grab it and shove it in my jacket pocket.

I jog all the way to the Metro, and by the time I get on the platform my chest feels like it's going to explode, partly from nerves, but mostly because I'm unbelievably out of shape.

After that, I don't sit down for the whole ride. I stumble and shake as the train starts and stops. I pace the length of the car, and the few families who are on the train on New Year's Day give me weird looks. But I don't care.

Because May needs to talk to me.

What could be so urgent that she needs to talk to me *right now*? Like, I want her to tell me why she left, what's going on, anything. But I don't even know if I deserve those answers. It's not like we're a *thing*.

When the prerecorded voice announces that we're at Gallery Place-Chinatown, I step off the train and bend over, rubbing my hands over my jeans and trying to suck in as much air as possible.

"Are you all right?" a woman with a baby strapped to her chest asks me.

"Yeah," I say, not moving. "I'm fine."

"That's good, hon," she says. "But you're blocking the escalator."

"Oh, sorry." I let her go in front of me. Maybe I should take the Metro back to Beatrice's house. Now seems like a good time to give up, cut my losses, shave my head, join a hermitage—

No.

May wants to talk to me.

I wish I could stop comparing what's happening with May to what happened with Sadie, but I can't. And in this case that might be a good thing. Because Sadie and I didn't talk about how we felt. We talked about stupid shit, and when it finally mattered, when I *needed* to speak up, I didn't.

And everything fell apart.

No nope no no. Not thinking about *that* right now. May is *not* Sadie and I'm going to get up this escalator if it kills me.

I step on, and it carries me to the street.

My body goes on autopilot as I walk into the museum and trace the steps I took with May last week, up the spiral staircase, through the grand hallway.

Into the modern art exhibit.

I take a deep breath. I'm freezing cold and sweaty and so tense that I think my throat might close up.

I walk past the cylinder of light, which is now telling me that, "You can watch people align themselves when trouble is in the air." I don't know what it means, but at least it distracts me for a moment.

Then I see her.

Sitting on one side of the bench in *Snails Space*, alone. Wearing the sweater she lent me on Christmas day.

I didn't realize how relieved I'd be to see May, to know that she's in the same physical space as me. To not be panicking about what to text her or worried something happened.

I have no idea what she's going to tell me.

But I know I can't delay it any longer.

I walk over to the bench and sit down, slowly, quietly. I'm on the opposite edge of the cushion from her, one leg tucked under me, trying to make myself small.

For a moment, I'm worried she doesn't see me. The lights in the space turn from green to purple. Shapes appear and disappear.

And then, without looking over at me, she says, "Just let me talk. Don't, like, say anything. Okay?"

I nod, hoping that she'll see the movement in her peripheral vision. She must, because after another minute of watching the lights change, she takes a deep breath and begins.

"I made a New Year's resolution," she says. Of course she did. "It was that I'm not gonna be so fucking scared anymore, you know?"

I hold my breath, worried that if I make any sudden movement she'll disappear into a cloud of smoke.

"Like, I hate how scared I was last year. Of going to college, of staying with my dad, of realizing I'm a lesbian."

The whole room is red now. For the first time, I glance at May's face. It's red, too.

"I just hopped on a bus," she continues, and I'm not sure what she means until she says, "I got into another huge fight with my dad so I got on a bus that left at midnight, the second I turned eighteen. I needed to see my mom, so I went. Didn't even bring anything with me.

"And I felt like shit the whole bus ride. I was sure I'd ruined everything with my dad." She takes a breath. "And with you."

The red light is fading, and a new, green light rises to illuminate a corner of the piece. It's not enough to reach our faces, but it's there, changing the painting, revealing shapes where there was only darkness.

"So, this is my resolution—part of it, anyway. I want to make things better with my dad. And I don't want to be scared." For the first time, *she* turns to look at *me*. I look at her, too. "You scare me, Shani." She must see the confusion flash over my face because she turns back to the painting and shakes her head, smiling a little. "You scare the shit out of me."

I still don't say anything, because I have no clue how to respond to that.

"The thing is, though . . . I really like you."

My heart speeds up like it's trying to fly up and out of my throat.

"And it's fucking hard for me to say that." May sort of grunts in frustration, as if to prove her point. "This is gonna sound like such a gross cliché, but I don't know if I've ever felt this way before." She shakes her legs and the bench shakes along with her. "I can't even look over at you right now because, like . . . yeah. I know we've only known each other for a couple of weeks, and that I was a bitch when we first met. Maybe I still am.

"Like, I ran away, which sucks. But I'm back." She shrugs and takes a breath. "And I guess it's just that I've never really done this before. Whatever *this* is." She motions between the two of us. "And it might be a stupid assumption, but I feel like whatever it is, it could be something— Jesus, okay, I'm just gonna say it." She takes a jagged breath. "Okay. You should know that I've never dated anyone before—not that I think we're gonna start dating or whatever, but . . . *fuck*."

She sounds so freaked out, so un-May-like, that it freaks me out, too. And before I think about whether I should, I reach my hand out and put it on her shoulder. It's the most awkward thing in the entire world, especially because now I can tell that we're both shaking. It's like there's a current traveling from her shoulder into my hand and back into me.

Then she says, "It's not just that I've never dated anyone before. I've never done, like, *anything*." She bends forward so quickly that my hand falls from her shoulder. She buries her face in her legs.

I know I need to say something now, so I start with the truth. "I like you, too."

It takes a second, but May must've registered what I said because she slowly sits up, then turns on the bench so that she's facing me.

I'm worried I said the wrong thing. That somehow, even after she ran away and then came back and bared her soul to me, I went and ruined everything with four words.

But her face breaks into a smile.

I smile back, so relieved I could cry.

"So, I guess this is happening, then?" May asks so quietly that I have to lean closer to hear her. "Are we gonna try something? With us?"

"I guess so," I say, matching her volume.

She smiles, but her eyebrows knit together. "But I wanna take things slow, okay? Like, really slow?"

I nod fervently. "Yes. Yeah. Absolutely."

In that moment, I briefly consider telling her about Sadie. Telling her that I'm so completely okay with taking things slow, because I just got out of a relationship where my heart was shattered into a million pieces and slow is the only speed I'm capable of.

But if I tell her about Sadie, she'll think I'm more experienced, when that couldn't be further from the truth.

"Shani?" May asks, shaking me out of those thoughts.

Those actively harmful thoughts that have no place in this exhibit, where a cute girl who I somehow had the good luck of hitting with my car is telling me she has a crush on me and wants to try *this*.

I lean in on the bench and whisper to her, "How would you feel about me kissing you here?" I don't think this is something straight people worry about, but I want to make sure she's okay with kissing in this semi-public exhibit.

"I would feel very good about that," she whispers back.

She scoots closer to me on the bench, puts her hand on the back of my neck, and kisses me, right inside *Snails Space.*

Our cold noses touch. I lean into her more, our legs pressing together. I don't want the kiss to end.

Without taking my mouth off hers, I zip open my jacket pocket and pull out the red beanie.

We break apart slowly, but when I lean back, she pulls me forward and rests her forehead against mine.

I awkwardly lift my hands from where they are on her waist and try to put the beanie on her.

She laughs and helps me, until it's back on her head where it belongs.

"I was hoping you'd give that back," she says, smiling, our faces still pressed together.

"I thought I'd have to keep it forever," I tell her. "I thought you weren't coming back."

"Well, I needed to get the beanie," she says with a wink, standing up from the bench, "didn't I?"

She grabs my hand and pulls me up, and we walk out of *Snails Space* together, hands laced, just for a moment, as the green and red and purple lights crescendo and the whole painting is illuminated.

Not a Literal Cougar

After our talk in *Snails Space*, May and I spent most of the day together. We didn't kiss or hold hands or anything, but neither of us could stop smiling.

It was kind of amazing.

It's Sunday now, and after all of yesterday's excitement, I slept in a bit, and now I'm wondering if it's still too early to text May. Like, not just too early in the morning but too *early.*

Because what if yesterday counted as a date? And if it *did*, aren't you supposed to wait two days or three days or a week or something before you go on another one?

Maybe our situation's different, though.

Or . . . maybe it's not. I should probably just spend the day minding my own business and preparing for the juvenile coelacanth analysis that we're doing in lab tomorrow. I could read a few articles, put in the work.

Or what if I text her anyway?

But that might make me seem desperate.

And just as I'm about to descend into a never-ending thought spiral about whether or not it's too early to text May, something wonderful happens: *she* texts *me*.

MAY: remember when you said we should go to the natural history museum?

Remember? I've been agonizing about it for the past week. About when I told her that we'd have to go to the museum together sometime. When there was no "we" to speak of.

But instead, I text back

ME: yeah!
are you thinking of going or something?

MAY: well yeah I'm thinking of going
but with u silly
:0

I smile at my phone like a fool.

ME: today?

MAY: mhm

like right now maybe?

unless ur busy

i thought we could meet at the coffee shop by the metro

Oh no. The coffee shop by the Metro . . .

ME: u mean the big blue dog?

MAY: that's the one

they have decent coffee

have you been yet?

ME: a couple times, yeah

but I don't really need coffee rn

MAY: lol but I do

meet there in 30 mins?

ME: sounds good

I bury my face in my pillow and try not to laugh. It's horrible, but it's also hilarious.

My actual crush and my . . . flirty teen barista are about to be in the same place at the same time.

My one saving grace is that Luke might not be working today. I think DC schools start up again tomorrow, so hopefully he's preparing for his first day back after winter break.

Oy.

I get dressed and go downstairs, not rushing to get outside like I did yesterday. I'm running a few minutes late, which hopefully means that May already got a cup of coffee and is waiting for me at the entrance to the Metro.

This is, of course, wishful thinking. When I get to The Big Blue Dog, May's inside, talking to a barista who isn't Luke, thank goodness.

I sneak in as the bell above the door rings and stand in a corner that's slightly obscured from the counter.

ME: look to your left lol

May checks her phone, then looks up and smiles, shaking her head at me. "What are you doing, Shani? Come here."

And maybe it's hearing my name, or maybe it's a sixth sense, but at that moment Luke steps out of the kitchen.

"Shan Shan!" he shouts, because of course he's picked right now to test out a new nickname.

"Hey, Luke," I mutter.

I glance at May, hoping she's checking her phone or something, anything to distract her from what's about to happen here. But no. She's looking directly at me. Her eyebrows shoot up to the top of her forehead, and I can hear the unspoken question: *Shan Shan?*

May pays the barista and walks to the end of the counter to put milk and sugar in her coffee.

"What can I get for you?" Luke asks, looking somehow both younger and more eager than I've ever seen him.

"Nothing for me, thanks." I walk over to May, trying to usher her out of the café.

"What?" Luke asks. "No, come on. How about another macchiato? I'll make you a 'Shani.'"

I don't fight him because I know it'll be worse if I do. I keep my head down as he prepares the drink, and I try as hard as I can not to look at May.

When I hear whipped cream spraying from behind the counter, I want to sink into the floor.

"On the house," Luke says as he hands me the drink, "of course."

"Thanks," I mumble, then walk quickly past May out of the café.

When we're on the sidewalk, she bursts out laughing.

"Holy shit," she says, tears forming in her eyes from

laughing so hard. "I didn't realize you were already in a committed relationship."

I rub my face with my non-macchiato hand.

"I can't believe you're a literal cougar," she says.

"Well, not a *literal* cougar," I say.

"Are you gonna get him something nice for his bar mitzvah? Maybe a promise ring or Nats tickets or . . ."

"Well, first of all, he's not Jewish—"

"*That's* what you took from that? He's not Jewish? Not that he's thirteen years old?" May starts laughing again as we get on the Metro escalator.

"He's gotta be at least fourteen."

"I can't believe you're letting a child flirt with you for free coffee. And he *named a drink* after you. This is hilarious."

"Well, I'm never going in there again, so . . . problem solved."

We're on the platform now, waiting for the Metro to come.

"No! You'll break his heart!"

"He'll survive."

It's pretty crowded on the train, so we stand and hold on to a pole by the door. We take the path I've been taking to the museum for the past two weeks, but it's different doing my commute with May.

It's nice.

"We're going directly to Deep Time," I say when we get inside the museum. It's my favorite exhibit, and one of the only ones worth seeing. Even with their attempts at reckoning with their past, most natural history museums are still strongholds of colonialism and stolen artifacts, and this one is no exception.

But there *are* rad fossils, so that's . . . something.

"What about the geodes?" she asks, reading the large sign that says, "GEODES!"

"Geodes are for after Deep Time. I can't believe you'd even suggest geodes."

"The audacity," May says. "What was I thinking?" I roll my eyes and she grins at me. "Fine, let's go."

The Deep Time exhibit is the museum's newish fossil hall, but it's way more than that, because it's also about evolution and life on Earth more generally, and about how humans have screwed everything up. I tell May this, and she seems excited about the humans-screwing-everything-up part.

It's unbelievably crowded near the entrance, partially because it's still sort of the holidays and partially because, well, there are dinosaurs.

"Okay, listen," I tell May as we walk in, turning to block her view of what's inside. "The exhibit's gonna try to suck you in by showing you a supercool T. rex absolutely demolishing a triceratops."

"I'm sucked in just by that description."

"Well, too bad," I say, "because that's not where we're starting. The whole exhibit is chronological, so we have to start at the beginning. Shield your eyes if you have to. Whatever it takes."

"Aye aye, Captain."

"Promise me you won't look at the T. rex ripping the triceratops to shreds."

"But you're making it sound so cool," she whines.

"That's honestly on me," I tell her, and we walk in.

May plays along and makes a big show of covering her eyes as we hurry past the dinosaurs and toward the actual beginning of the exhibit.

Which happens to be the beginning of everything. Well, not *everything*, but the beginning of life on Earth, 3.7 billion years ago.

We zoom past the origins of life and the first three billion or so years, because it was pretty much just microbes and shit.

I run up to an interactive-game-screen thingy, and May comes up next to me so we can play together. I know I'm moving through this exhibit like a hyper child, but I can't help it. It's exciting to have someone to explain everything to.

The game is about the ancient origins of modern bodies, and you get to examine different body parts on an animated person to see how they evolved.

The person is mostly featureless and completely gender neutral. They're wearing a black bodysuit and have spiky brown hair and light brown skin, and they jump around the screen as you press different parts of their body.

"I love them?" May says as she presses the person's hand to learn about how our opposable thumbs evolved.

"A nonbinary icon," I agree as I press their ear to learn about the evolution of hearing in mammals.

"Is this maybe a little violating for them?" May asks as she presses the person's feet and they jump into the air.

"Yeah, let's let them rest."

We wave goodbye to our new screen-friend and walk to the next exhibit just as a small child runs up to the screen and slaps their whole palm against the avatar's torso to make them dance.

The next thing we see is a sign that reads, "It's Not Easy to Live on Land."

"You're telling me," May says.

"No, but it seriously is so tough," I say.

And then I want to launch into my thoughts on how fish are superior to all other creatures and how land is overrated. I want to tell May all my fish knowledge, to transmit it to her so she knows more about why I am the way I am.

But.

I don't want to fall into the "well, actually" mode of speaking that people—usually boys who think they know more than me about fish evolution just because they've caught a coelacanth in Animal Crossing—have used on me. It sucks to have someone make you feel inadequate when you're learning something new.

So instead of launching into some monologue about fish, which I would gladly do, I try to start a conversation. "That first dumbass fish that crawled onto land fucked us all over. Like, he should've just stayed in the water. The ocean is literally one thousand times better than any square inch of dry land."

"Wasn't it good for those little guys to be the first things there, though?" May asks. "That way there was no competition for food or shelter or whatever else an animal needs."

"Yeah, but you have to deal with things like gravity and the sun. In the ocean you can float. Fish have it so easy—they're just vibing."

"That's what this says"—May points to the exhibit copy below the sign—"that animals who moved out of the ocean had to get all these weird adaptations."

I wish I wasn't this predictable, but I find it so hot to hear May talk about terrestrial adaptations.

And, more than that, May reading the sign and explaining it to me is what I love best about museums: that people can discover things for themselves. They can make this difficult concept *theirs*, one they can explain to family and friends and girls they are maybe ambiguously dating.

Finally, we reach the part of the exhibit that I had forced May to shield her eyes from at the beginning: the T. rex eating the triceratops.

"It *is* pretty cool," May says.

"How dare you."

She bumps my shoulder. It's the first time we've touched all day—I know because it's also the first time that my body's felt like it's been set on fire. We didn't even press into each other on the crowded Metro. I tightened every muscle in my body to ensure that we'd stay at least an inch apart.

I'm a mess.

We keep walking through time as mammals become the dominant group of animals on Earth, but my brain is stuck in my shoulder, with May's touch.

Next, we make it to the recent ice ages. Not, like, *recent* recent. Recent geologically—they started tens of thousands of years ago.

"Oh, this is the good part," May says as we get to the point where humans are starting to evolve, and as is our nature, ruin everything.

The exhibit talks about how life changes as the Earth changes. The continents move, oceans rise and fall, global climate fluctuates. And life adapts. Or tries to, anyway.

One of the final parts of the exhibit is a wall of animals that have either been driven by humans to extinction or to the brink of extinction. It's essentially the "we fucked up" wall.

May and I take a moment of silence for the moa, a giant flightless bird that lived in New Zealand until it was hunted to extinction by humans. Though, to be fair, it was an incredibly silly-looking bird.

This part of the exhibit is pretty bleak, because it's about the role humans have played in what is now a new global extinction event.

"And climate change is a huge factor in this, you know," May says. "Part of what was interesting about those exhibits about extinctions that happened millions of years ago was that temperature had some factor in all of them. And now we have higher carbon dioxide levels than we've had since, like, before humans existed, and that's part of what's driving all these extinctions."

I love hearing May talk about weather and climate. The subject matter is horrifying, but she's so passionate.

It's the same way I felt back on Christmas Eve when she first told me about how she loves weather.

I must've been staring too intensely, because her eyebrows knit together and she asks, "What?"

"Nothing," I say.

Now I feel shy. We weren't super touchy or flirty today. Which makes sense because it would've been weird to, like, make out while we were lamenting the extinct moa.

But now I want to. I want to so badly it hurts.

"No, seriously. What?"

And that's when I realize: this isn't like when I was sleeping in May's bed on Christmas Eve while she slept in her dad's room, when I fantasized about what might happen if I worked up the courage to make a move.

"Come in here," I say, and she's closer than she's been all day as we walk into a small dark, empty room showing a movie about climate change.

We sit down, still next to each other, still touching, still as close as we can be without . . .

And then she kisses me.

I lean into her, and my whole body feels like my shoulder did earlier.

The movie's British narrator explains that our ecological footprint today is written through stories of the past, and we keep kissing. We kiss so hard that I know, I *know* she's been thinking about this, too.

I wrap my arms around her waist. She pulls even closer, and reaches her hands under my sweater. Her skin is soft and cold and so, so human. I can feel the millions of years of evolution that have brought us to this moment. I want to go out to the area of the exhibit with the gender-neutral avatar and tell everyone who passes by that the interactive screen is wrong. That we evolved opposable thumbs so that May could touch me like this, her hand grasping at my waist, her thumb gently brushing my rib cage.

And then there's stomping.

We pull apart so fast I almost get whiplash. We both sit still, facing forward and breathing heavily.

From behind us, a little kid shouts, "It's just a stupid movie."

I turn around, less worried and more annoyed, and see that it's the touchy kid who's been following us through the exhibit.

"DON'T SAY THE S WORD!" an adult yells from outside the dark movie room, and the kid stomps out, leaving us alone again.

We pick up where we left off. We kiss until the narrator

tells us that the world is doomed unless we take action.

And even though this probably isn't the action he was talking about, it still feels like something.

The next day in lab, we spend the first part of the morning preparing fossils from the juvenile coelacanth site for isotopic analysis, and I can't stop thinking about May.

But I try my best, because I'm excited to learn about the technique, to participate in something I've only read scientific articles about.

Dr. Graham emerges from his closet a few minutes after I arrive, carrying an oversized filing box with more specimen.

"Devonian shells," he says, with no additional context.

I look into the box. and sure enough, there are hundreds, maybe thousands of unsorted fossil shells, mineralized and beautiful.

"We collected these at the dig site where we found the juvenile coelacanths," Dr. Graham says. "We can spare a few of them, but we can't spare any of the coelacanth specimens."

The thing about using isotope analysis is that, to learn anything useful about the sample, you need to destroy it. But once you do the isotope analysis of a mineral sample (like the shells), you can start to reconstruct the aquatic environment of fish found at the same dig site.

"This could be a *huge* breakthrough in Devonian

juvenile coelacanth pupping grounds," Dr. Graham says with as much excitement as an astronomer talking about somehow finding sentient life on another planet. "So let's get powdering!"

We work for a while on crushing the shells, and it becomes just as monotonous as cleaning fossils. Not boring, just monotonous.

Dr. Graham goes back to his office to work, which leaves me and Mandira alone in the main lab area.

I want to tell her about what's going on with May, but I know I've been monopolizing the conversation with my relationship drama. And the worst part is, I still want to keep talking about it. So I decide to get there the roundabout way.

"What'd you do this weekend?" I ask, trying to sound casual, to hide my ulterior motives. "Anything fun?"

Mandira snorts. "Um, nothing much. Same as usual." She gives me a curious look. "Why the sudden interest? Not that—I just mean, you haven't asked me much about myself before."

I'm deeply embarrassed when she says this, because she's right. I've been using her as an older-queer sounding board. But to have it called out like this is . . . rough.

"I'm sorry," I tell her. "I really do want to know about you. Like, I'm so, so—"

"Shani, it's fine," she says. "I love talking about relationship stuff, and I can tell that's what you're gearing up to tell me." I stare down at the bench as she says this, but she's right. "I wish I had someone to give me advice when I was in my first year of college," she adds.

She pulls a new shell out of the box, then there's a beat. A moment where neither of us says anything.

"All right," Mandira says, laughing a little, "tell me what happened with *you* this weekend."

She looks at me with her eyebrows raised, and I apologize once more before launching into this edition of the May Story Hour. I finish with, "So, I guess that's why I'm kind of distracted today."

"No offense, but I think you've been kind of distracted every day—not that you've been doing bad work," she adds. "But you've definitely been distracted."

"That's fair," I say, but I'm not *super* paying attention because I check my phone and see a text from May. It's an illustration of a moa with the caption "RIP." The bird has freakishly long legs and a round, potato-like body.

I text back:

ME: omg leg goals
gone too soon :'(

"Let me guess," Mandira says. "You're texting her right now."

"What?" I say, too quickly, putting my phone away. "No."

"Why don't you take lunch now?" she asks. "And when

you come back, you'll put your phone away for the rest of the day, if that's all right." When she sees the useless tears prickling at the corner of my eyes, she adds, "This isn't even me saying this to you as a supervisor. Sometimes it's good to unplug from a new relationship for a little while. Even if it's just for a few hours."

"Okay," I say, nodding and holding back tears, my face hot with shame.

I walk out of the lab and let myself cry. The worst part is she's right. I'm in DC for dead fish, not some girl.

But at the same time . . .

I take a breath and look for the grilled cheese truck. Of course, when I need it most, it's not there. So instead of searching for a subpar, non-grilled-cheese lunch, I sit on the museum steps and text Taylor.

ME: i have news

The bubbles pop up so soon after I send the message that I'm almost convinced Taylor's been waiting for me to text.

TAY: wait don't say anything
let me guess

ME: go ahead

TAY: may came back
things went well
that's pretty much the whole guess
but it's right
no?

ME: lol yes
but literally how did you know???

TAY: you haven't texted me in two days
i figured it was your superstition thing
or that you were pulling a Sadie
and I was never gonna hear from you again

The superstition she's referencing is that, if something good happens to me, I can't tell her about it for a few days because I'm worried the good thing will go away. Which is part of the reason I didn't tell her about Sadie at all. But I know I need to do better now, or at least try.

ME: not pulling a Sadie I promise
but like yeah may and I are kind of dating??

TAY: !!!
like officially??

ME: i mean
we didn't say it super officially

TAY: oh you didn't sign a contract?

ME: lol no
but yeah things are good i think??
also this is perfect
wanna know why

TAY: can i guess this one too

ME: no
it's perfect bc i'm kind of in a relationship
and it's going well so far
which means that maybe in a few weeks
when it's more official
i can finally tell my mom i'm queer

TAY: you know you can tell her when you're NOT in a relationship, right?

ME: oops sorry lunch break's over gotta go

TAY: ur a piece of shit

ME: <3 <3 <3 <3 <3 <3 <3

And with that, my conversation with Taylor is over. For the past couple of years, I've refused to listen to her perfectly reasonable advice about coming out to my mom. I don't want her to argue with me about it, because if we do, she'll win.

But I can't tell my mom. Even though I'm sure it'll be fine. Even though it might actually bring us closer. I think everyone on the planet knows that I'm queer, except for her. Part of me hopes she'll figure it out on her own, and then we'll never have to talk about it, because talking about it would be mortifying. I don't want her to know that I've had romantic or sexual feelings for anyone, ever.

I still have a few minutes left of my lunch break, so before I have to go back inside and turn off my phone, I text May.

ME: what are you doing later?

MAY: my dad wants me to have dinner w him
like at a table
save me from that plz

ME: lmao let's hang out ?
wanna come downtown ? since i'm here for work

MAY: ooh yes wait
let's go to the train show

ME: the what?

MAY: at the botanic gardens
it's not like incredible
but it's fun

ME: no that sounds amazing
i love trains
beep beep

MAY: i'm sorry
is that the noise you think a train makes???

ME: what sound does it make??

MAY: choo choo!!!!!!!!!!!!!
get your head in the game, levine

ME: sorry it's been a long time since preschool

MAY: shameful
see you later

And, smiling down at my phone—of course—I head back to lab, with both isotope prep and botanic gardens to look forward to.

Thomas the Tank Engine Has Emerged From His Slumber

It's pouring rain when I get out of work. There aren't any windows in the lab, so I never know what the weather will be like when I'm done for the day.

There's no Metro stop to get from the museum to the botanic gardens, and it's too far to walk in the freezing rain, so I steel myself and run to a bus filled with soggy tourists.

The botanic gardens are a beacon in the dark. The building is made of glass and metal and in the center there's a giant dome that's emanating multicolored lights.

Inside, the climate is entirely different: it's warm and humid and the plants must have no idea it's winter. Lucky them.

The entrance hall is long and narrow and filled to the brim with poinsettias, but the main attractions are the long fountain pools that stretch the length of the hall, with their deep turquoise tiles and yellow-tinted underwater lights.

I spot May sitting on a bench, right by a model of the botanic gardens made from what looks like sticks and leaves and other natural materials, illuminated from the inside in the same way the real one is tonight.

She's sitting with her eyes closed, and I'm hesitant to disturb her peace in this warm oasis.

But, after a few seconds, the part of me that wants to run around the botanic gardens with May while flirting about trains wins out.

"Boo," I say, nudging her leg with my foot.

She doesn't move. "I'm not sleeping. Just resting with my eyes closed."

"Well, up and at 'em." I hold out my hand.

She rolls her eyes, but grabs it, and a current flows between us. I wonder if she feels it, too.

"Train time?" she asks, letting go of my hand.

"Beep beep," I reply.

"Truly horrible." She snort-laughs. "Follow me."

We walk through the main conservatory, a huge room that's even warmer than the entrance hall. Above us, giant tropical plants flap lazily in the wind of the ceiling fans.

We follow the crowd into the main showroom. It's filled to the brim with trains and trees and plants and bridges and model buildings and people. Despite what May texted earlier, it's pretty incredible.

Trains chug through tree groves while kids screech with delight, which is annoying but understandable because the whole room is covered with miniature intersecting tracks. It feels like we're giants controlling the rails.

"They should do this year-round," I say as we walk under a wooden bridge and a model train speeds over us.

"But then it wouldn't be special."

"I guess," I say, but she's probably right. There's something spectacular about a warm, cozy room packed with people who are getting their once-a-year fill of model trains.

Some kids behind us scream so loudly that my first instinct is to run, only to turn around and find that Thomas the Tank Engine has emerged from his slumber to do a grand tour of the room. Toddlers chase him, shouting, "Thomas!" because it's fun to identify things.

After a few minutes of staring at the trains in awe, May says, "I lied about where I was going. To my dad."

I look at her, confused. I'm not sure why she's telling me this, so I say, "I get it. It's hard to come out to a parent." Which is completely hypocritical, considering I haven't come out to mine.

May laughs a little. "No, no, it's not that." We stop by a miniature windmill that keeps bumping into a fern as its blades spin. "I don't think he'd care."

"Then why'd you lie to him?"

"I didn't—" She sighs, then turns to me. "It's because I don't want him to know about you. Or, us."

There's a pang in my chest, and not the good kind. Why would she tell me this at the holiday train show?

May must see it in my face because she adds, "No, listen. You're too important to me, that's why." Thomas the Tank Engine whirs past and a group of kids bump into us, almost knocking me off balance. May grabs my arm to steady me as she says, "My dad and I don't get along so well, which I know you know. And I guess I just don't want him to know about *us*, is what I'm trying to say."

Her hair falls into her face as she explains this, and all I want to do is reach up and push it behind her ears and tell her it's okay. So that's what I do.

"It's okay," I say as I tuck a thick strand of her hair away as best I can. "It's actually, like, really sweet."

She seems so relieved, and we're standing so close, but I don't want to kiss her in front of this crowd of people. So, I pull her to me, and we cling to each other in the midst of the train-show chaos.

"Wanna go back to my place for tea or something?" I ask after we walk aimlessly around the gardens for a while longer.

I don't want her to have to go back to her dad's house. I want her with me.

"Sounds great," she says, and we say goodbye to the trains and hop on the Metro.

“I’m home!” I shout as we walk into the house. I don’t usually announce myself, but doing so now means that we’ll have to sit and talk to Beatrice for a while.

And then maybe May won’t ask me why I’m not taking her up to my room.

“Come to the kitchen, doll!”

We walk through the living room, and before we’re even through the kitchen archway, Beatrice stands up from the table, reaches her arms out, and says, “A new angel! And she’s gorgeous!” She hugs May, who looks surprised but not upset.

I wave to Tasha and Lauren, who are sitting next to each other eating microwave pizza. “This is May,” I say, more for their benefit than Beatrice’s. “She’s my friend.”

I feel silly after I say that last part, because it probably makes our relationship seem more suspicious than if I hadn’t said anything at all.

But Beatrice doesn’t seem to catch on. She grabs May around the waist and stares up at her.

“We know each other,” Lauren says in response to my introduction. She nods to May.

“Oh, right, duh.”

I almost forgot that Lauren is the one who usually walks Raphael. And not only that, she also apparently gets a “weird vibe” from May. Which could be a good thing right now, because maybe it'll conceal the other weird vibe—the flirty weird vibe—that is almost definitely emanating off me and May. I wonder if everyone else can see it. If the vibe is so powerful that it's coming off us in visible waves.

We sit down for a slightly awkward cup of tea and a slice of microwave pizza, and after a few minutes May asks Lauren, "Have you walked the dog yet?"

Lauren looks at her in an *Are you kidding me?* sort of way. "Uh, no. I was gonna go after dinner."

"No, sorry, I was just asking because if you haven't you don't need to worry about it. Shani and I can walk him."

Now Lauren tries to give *me* a look, a *Why are you spending time alone with weird-vibe girl?* look, but I turn away so she can't hold my gaze.

"Uh, okay," Lauren says, "that's fine."

We hadn't discussed walking Raphael beforehand, but I'm suddenly ready to be alone with May again and see the pup, so after we finish our tea and pizza and stilted conversation, we head out.

"Don't come back too late," Beatrice says before we go.

"I'll be home soon," I tell her. "Within the hour, probably."

"Well, stay out later than that." She chuckles, and May and I walk outside.

"I'm just gonna run in and grab Raphael," she says when we get to her house.

"*You're* going in to get Raphael?"

She shakes her head. “I’ll grab him quickly so my dad doesn’t bother us.”

I nod and stay where I am. I really don’t want to have a run-in with Greg after the last time, and it’s turned into a pretty mild night now that the rain’s stopped.

After a minute, Raphael comes outside, pulling May along with him. He runs right up to me and jumps onto my legs. I bend to pet him as he wags his tail and moves his tiny little paws back and forth over my jeans. He howls, and I tell him to shush, but I’m honored that he’s making such a ruckus for me.

“He missed you,” May says. “He’s never greeted me like this.”

“He would if you loved him,” I say as I grab the leash from her.

Even in the dim streetlight I can see May roll her eyes, but then she laughs, and I laugh too, and Raphael howls again.

I imagine this being my life forever: going to museums and gardens with May, walking a dog that she vaguely tolerates and I adore, talking, just being together.

But this isn’t real life. It’s winter break.

And, for the first time since Saturday—since May and I got together—a thought pops into my head: What happens next?

We’re both going back to school soon. And when we do, I’ll be busy studying and avoiding Sadie and applying for a job in the paleo lab at Binghamton and whatever else I need to do.

What happens then?

I try to shake the thought out of my head, to enjoy the brisk walk with May and Raphael. But now that it's in there, I don't know if it's coming out.

It's day two of preparing the fossil shells for isotope analysis, and I'm having an even harder time concentrating than I was yesterday. Mandira told me to put my phone away—out of love, she said—but May keeps texting me silly things and I keep responding to them with silly things of my own.

But at the back of my mind, I wonder if Mandira's right. I can't stop thinking about how May and I really only have a few days left together in the same place and we *just* started dating and everything is terrible.

In the afternoon, Mandira has me switch to cleaning fossils, so I grab a toothbrush and get to work, looking down at my crotch every few minutes to see if May texted. After an hour or so of cleaning and crotch-checking, my toothbrush is frayed. I toss it in the trash as I check my phone. I clean off the rest of the bench, too, as a courtesy to Mandira.

I sweep the dust and rocks and stuff into the garbage, simultaneously reading May's text where she tells me that according to the Thomas Wiki, Thomas the Tank Engine's top speed is only forty miles per hour.

> **ME:** our slow boy!
> taking his time
> a king!

I wipe the remaining dust off the bench with a paper towel, grab another fossil, and start scrubbing it with the new toothbrush, which is doing a much better job.

Mandira and I work in silence, one that's only punctuated by a custodian coming in and taking out the trash.

Toward the end of the day, Mandira goes into Dr. Graham's closet to do her afternoon check-in, and when she comes out, she asks, "Can you bring Dr. Graham the fossils you were working on earlier?"

"Which ones?" I ask. "The coelacanth? Or the shells?"

"Both," she says, coming over to my bench. "And the other ones too. I think there were a bunch of microfossils from Waterloo Farm."

"Uh . . ." I look around my workstation, a horrible feeling rising in my chest, one I felt in high school when the teacher would ask us to take out our homework and I didn't realize we had any. "I don't think I cleaned those? I'm really sorry."

"That's fine," Mandira says, sounding a little annoyed.

"But do you have them? They were in the same box as the shells."

I look inside the box.

Nothing.

Oh.

Fuck.

Panic bubbles up inside of me.

I dumped out the contents of the box on the table.

And swept it into the trash.

Which was removed.

Hours ago.

"Shit," I say under my breath. "Shit, shit, shit, shit, shit, shit, shit. Shit."

"Shani," Mandira says. "Where are the fossils?"

"Um, I kind of maybe . . . threw them out—but not on purpose," I add. "I was trying to clean up. *Shit.*" I'm starting to hyperventilate, which is actually great because it means I might pass out from lack of oxygen and then I won't have to look at Mandira.

"The trash that was taken out earlier today?" she asks, speaking so slowly that it freaks me out.

I nod.

Mandira runs her hands through her hair. "Shani, Graham wanted to look at those fossils later this evening."

I'm the worst intern in the history of interns. I *promised* myself this wouldn't happen. That I wouldn't be distracted by anything. That I'd focus all my time on the lab.

And then I met a girl.

"I'll fix it," I say. "I will. I'll fix everything. I'll get them back."

The first thing I do is go to the security desk and ask where the building's trash goes.

The guard gives me a weird look but then says, "You can check with facilities management."

She tells me they're located in the main Smithsonian castle, so I run out of the museum and sprint the few blocks to their office. I'm wearing only a T-shirt, but the cold doesn't register.

Because I'm fucked. I threw *fossils* into the garbage because I was texting May.

I get to the facilities management office, and I'm out of breath and in an inconsolable state of panic.

"Are you okay?" the person behind the front desk asks as I bend over, trying to catch my breath.

"Oh yeah," I wheeze.

"Great," she says. "What can I do for you?"

I stand up and ask, "Where's the trash?"

"Excuse me?"

"The trash," I say, as if repeating myself will help. "The trash that gets taken from the museums. Does it go here?"

"Oh," she says with dawning comprehension on her face. "Yeah, that's here. But why are you asking?"

"I work at the natural history museum, and I accidentally threw something out that's really important."

“Is it jewelry?” she asks. “We get a lot of people trying to steal jewelry, so I have to check.”

“No,” I tell her, not even hiding the annoyance in my voice. “It’s a fossil. Or a bunch of fossils, actually.”

“Like a dinosaur?”

“Um, kind of,” I say, tapping my fingers against my legs, anxious to find the trash before it gets dumped in a landfill or something. “It’s fish.”

“Like, salmon?”

“Uh, not really. But is it here? Can I look through it?”

“ID?”

“What?”

“Your Smithsonian ID? I need to scan it.”

Holy shit, did this work?

I hand her my ID.

“You should get a new picture,” she says. “This looks nothing like you.”

“I know.”

“Maybe the worst I’ve ever seen.”

“Thank you,” I say, too loudly.

She stares up at me with her glasses on the bridge of her nose, then shakes her head. “The dumpster’s out back. Don’t steal any jewelry.”

“I won’t,” I say, but now I kind of want to.

Also, if it’s already in the trash, is it really stealing?

But I don’t think about the ethics of trash jewelry theft

for too long, because soon enough I'm face-to-face with a giant orange dumpster proudly displaying the Smithsonian logo on its side. It's at least eight feet tall and twenty feet wide, filled to the brim with trash bags.

This is my penance. It's what I deserve.

I climb the ladder and jump in.

The first thing I hear is a squelch, followed by a low oozing sound that I don't investigate further. The smells of rotting food and lord knows what else overwhelm my nose to the point where I don't know if I'll ever be able to smell anything again.

There are hundreds upon hundreds of plastic bags. I figure I only need to look on the top layer since someone just took the trash out earlier today, which is the one positive in a literal dumpster-full of negatives.

The winter sun isn't strong, but it's there, making the black garbage bags absorb heat and attracting bugs I didn't even know existed at this time of year.

I breathe through my mouth, apologize to the bugs and the universe, and open the first bag. The custodian emptied the lab's trash into a larger container, so now I won't even be able to recognize it by sight.

This bag is mostly half-eaten french fries and napkins, probably from a food court at one of the museums. I try not to think about all the saliva and snot and hair and whatever else is in here. I try not to think at all.

I lose track of time this way, opening bags, sifting through them, throwing them aside when I don't find any fossils (or jewelry, for that matter).

I'm ready to give up, to throw in the towel, climb down the ladder, and resign from my internship.

And that's when I pick up a bag, one that's heavier than the others I've been sorting through.

I've already been tricked a number of times into thinking a bag was filled with fossils when it was actually filled with, like, bricks and car seats and other weird shit that people must've chucked into the dumpster. Sorting through the trash has been like an anthropological study of the worst parts of human existence.

I open the bag, preparing for more random crap, but there's something in there that makes me want to jump for joy (but I won't because my shoes are trapped in a sticky substance near the bottom of the dumpster): dirt.

I shove my hand in the bag and sort through it, and sure enough, it's the garbage from my lab. I even see a receipt for the coffee Mandira got this afternoon.

"YES!" I scream, and pump my fist in the air.

I delude myself for a second into thinking that I'm the best employee in the world, until I remember that I got myself into this mess in the first place by throwing out the fossils.

I somehow lug both the trash bag and my body out of the dumpster and past the front desk woman ("Your last chance to return any jewelry!"), then clutch the trash to my chest the entire way back to lab. Everyone I pass shoots me nasty looks, both on the street and in the atrium of the museum, but it doesn't matter.

I did it. I found the fossils.

Sure, I was the one who lost them. But still.

I heave the bag through the door, sweaty and smelly and a little too proud of myself.

"Holy shit," Mandira says, getting up from her stool and walking over to me. "Is this what I think it is?"

"Yup," I say, placing the trash bag full of fossils onto an unused corner of the lab bench. "This is it."

"Jesus Christ, Shani." She tentatively looks inside. "Okay, I have to be honest, I was pretty mad when you left but—how did you find this?" She puts on rubber gloves (shit, why didn't I think of that?) and sorts through the bag.

"The Smithsonian dumpster."

"Well, you're definitely the first intern who's ever dug through the trash to find a fossil." She pulls a handful of dirt out of the bag. "But you're also the first intern who's ever thrown a fossil in the trash, so . . ."

I clear my throat. "I'm really sorry," I say. "Like, so, so unimaginably sorry."

She sighs. "I know. And I think digging through trash was punishment enough, so I'm not gonna tell Dr. Graham. But you *need* to be more careful." She says this last part meaningfully, looking right at me. I stare at the floor. "Okay?"

I avoid her gaze. "Of course."

I spend what's left of the workday being a model employee: cleaning the fossils and the bench and even getting Mandira more coffee, all while smelling like actual shit. Mandira offered me her hoodie, but I didn't want to stink it up.

I don't even check my phone until I leave the museum, and when I do I see a text from May.

MAY: what are you doing tn?

I'm tempted not to answer. To ignore her texts or to call and tell her she's distracting me from my job. To end things with her entirely.

But the problem is, I'd rather sort through the dumpster again—I'd rather sort through all of DC's trash—than break things off with May. And, like, I got the fossils back. Everything worked out.

ME: absolutely nothing

MAY: come over?
my dad's working a little late tn
so it'll just be us and the dog

She had me at Raphael and no Greg, but I can't go over smelling the way I do right now.

ME: i just have to go home and shower first

MAY: can you wait till later?

my dad's not gonna be at work THAT long

and I still wanna hang out

ME: not really

it's a long story but I spent most of my day in a dumpster

MAY: lmao what??

are you oscar the grouch

ME: yes

MAY: knew it

but can you still just come over?

I'm sure it's not that bad

ME: it literally is

MAY: I'll be the judge of that

I sigh, because I know what I'm going to say before I even type out the message.

ME: fine

but you'll regret it

I'm weak, and I want to see May. And also possibly make out with her.

So I hop on the Metro and walk straight to her house.

"Oh my god," she says when I walk in. "You weren't kidding."

"I tried to warn you!"

I stick to the entrance area so I don't get my stench on everything. Raphael doesn't care, though; he jumps all over me.

"Don't stink up my dog!"

"Oh, when I'm stinking him up suddenly he's *your* dog?"

"Yes," May says. She pulls Raphael away by the collar, holding her nose. "You really do smell like shit," she adds.

"If I'm lucky." There was so much unidentifiable garbage in that dumpster that the source of my smell could be anything.

"You were right," May says, "you need a shower."

"Yeah, I know."

"You can take one here, if you want? In my bathroom upstairs?"

I blush at the thought of using May's shower, because it feels so personal, so private.

And then I blush at the maximum possible level when she adds, "Not, like, with me. Just in my bathroom." She slams her hand on her forehead. "I don't know why I said that. I literally don't know why I said that. I'm so sorry that was so dumb, obviously it wouldn't be with me."

I take a beat to let my breath steady, and then, because the thought of showering with May is in my head and it's so, so appealing, I let my mouth speak before my brain can think: "Why not?"

May pulls her head out of her hands and looks up at me. Her face is beet red, and I'm worried I said the wrong thing and that she'll think this is too fast after we specifically said to take it slow—not that showering together is the same thing as sex, or that it means we'll have sex or anything or—

Fuck. Does it? No. No?

No.

But I can't worry about that for much longer because May walks up to me and wraps her arms around my waist and kisses me.

"Aren't you worried you'll smell?"

She smirks. "It'll wash off."

I bite my lips to stop myself from smiling too much but release them so that I can kiss the outline of May's neck. I reach my hands under her shirt, getting as close as I dare to her bra.

But then I start to get in my head about the whole thing.

May's going to see me naked.

And I don't know how much I love the thought of that.

But I love the thought of seeing her naked; I love the idea that she's thinking the same thing about me.

And then I'm embarrassed for even having any of those thoughts.

I stop thinking so much as May's hands migrate down to the pockets of my jeans. She wraps me into her, and even though she's smaller than me, I feel safe, protected.

After a minute of kissing, she pulls away and buries her head into my shoulder, laughing.

"What?"

"You smell *so* bad."

"Oh my god," I say, laughing too, and feeling embarrassed but hugging her closer, since she's not letting go.

"Let's go take a shower."

I take a deep breath. "Okay."

She grabs my hand and leads me upstairs and down the hall.

"I'll, um, let you get in first," she says quietly as she grabs a towel from the linen closet.

My heart's beating into my throat and blocking words from coming out, so I just nod and walk into the bathroom and close the door. I watch myself in the mirror as I take off my T-shirt, then my jeans. I look at my body in my sports bra and underwear.

Maybe this is a terrible idea. The first and only person to see me naked was Sadie, and that was in a dark bedroom when we weren't—

No. Nope.

I watch mirror-Shani wipe away the tears that managed to fall less than a millisecond after thinking about Sadie.

Then I watch her take a deep breath and pull off the rest of her clothes.

I face away from the mirror and turn the shower on as hot as it'll go, then step in and rub every available soap and shampoo product onto my body.

"I'm coming in, okay?" May calls through the door after a minute.

"Okay." I stand directly under the nozzle and let the water flow over my nose and into my mouth.

The room is now filled with so much steam that I can barely see May through the glass shower doors. It feels impolite to look as she takes her towel off, so I don't. I close my eyes, and don't open them again until May's lips are on mine.

But opening your eyes directly under the shower nozzle is a terrible idea, and the shampoo trickles into my eyes, water and suds clogging my vision.

"Ow ow ow ow ow," I say through the stinging, bending down to grab the edge of the tub. But I can't see anything and I don't get a hold on it and I slip down to the floor and bang my knee. "Fuck."

May laughs, and puts her hands on my waist, steadying me.

"Are you laughing at me?" I ask, but it comes out with a slight gurgle from all the water pouring into my mouth.

"No," May says, still laughing. "Come here."

We're both on our knees, and she drags me to the other end of the tub, where she rubs my eyes with a washcloth.

"Better?" she asks as I open my eyes to find her silently laughing.

"This is going well," I say, trying not to look down, trying to just look at her face.

"Shut up," she says, and while we're both on our knees facing each other, she kisses me and it's wet and squelchy but everything is warm and it's so, so nice.

I keep my eyes closed as I press her closer to me, so that as much of our bodies are touching as possible. We explore parts of each other we haven't before. I kiss down her neck to her chest, marveling at the fact that I get to touch her like this.

But after a few minutes, the hot water runs out, and my knees hurt, and now we're kneeling in cold water.

"Can we get out?" May asks.

"Yes please," I say, relieved.

She reaches over me to turn off the shower, then jumps up and grabs her towel, throwing mine over as she does.

I cover up quickly as the steam dissipates, and when the towel's securely on, May comes up to me and rests her head on my shoulder. "You smell nice."

I rest my chin on her head. "I smell like you."

She snorts. "I'm getting you clothes. Wait here."

"If it's the Cornell sweats I'd rather be naked," I shout after her, but she's already gone.

I made a fool of myself; you'd think I'd never taken a shower before in my life.

And yet.

May didn't run away. She pulled me to her and gave me a towel when the water turned cold.

But there are still echoes of laughter in my head. And it's not from May.

Because as hard as I try not to, I hear Sadie. Sadie, who brought me to my dorm, both of us laughing, stumbling through the halls. Sadie, who ended things because—

I stop these thoughts as May comes back into the bathroom dressed in non-Cornell pajamas. She hands me a folded pile of clothes with—of course—the aforementioned sweats.

She leaves me in the bathroom to get dressed, and as I'm pulling on the sweatshirt, she calls through the door. "There's still a bit of time before my dad gets home. Wanna watch TV or something?"

"Sure," I call back, because oh boy do I wanna watch some TV with May and not worry about whether or not I've accidentally done something so, so wrong.

We go downstairs and sit on the couch, and it somehow happens that May's head rests on my chest, and my arm wraps around her. Like it's the most natural thing. Like this is how our bodies were meant to be.

Then Raphael jumps onto the couch, and burrows

himself into May's lap. She recoils, but I reach over and pat his head and he settles down and closes his eyes. May relaxes, though she still doesn't touch Raphael.

Now it's the three of us, together, my arm around May, my hand on Raphael's head.

May turns on a cooking show where children sabotage each other to win college scholarships, because we live in a broken country where our kids need to compete to afford higher education. We get extremely sucked in, booing when a kid we don't like steals aged cheddar from a kid we do.

But the whole time we're watching, I'm trying to convince myself that everything's fine. That it's okay that I'm so into May. That it's okay that I was so distracted in lab today I threw out precious microfossils. That because I fixed it, there's nothing wrong.

And maybe there isn't. Maybe I can have both things: May and the lab. May and anything.

May and everything.

But it also doesn't matter whether or not I can have both. Because as I look down at May and kiss the top of her freshly showered head, I know one thing for sure: I'm already past the point of no return.

The point where I can back out gracefully and tell her, "Eh, this isn't really working out." Because I know, I know, I know—I'm falling for her.

Spiders and Fascism

At work the next day, I take Mandira's advice and turn off my phone. I'm still thinking about May the entire time, but at least I'm not texting her.

I *do* turn my phone on at lunch, though, and I have a text from May asking if six is a good time to meet tonight. I tell her it's perfect.

Because we're going on a date.

A *real* date. At a restaurant.

We planned it last night right before her dad got home and she had me sneak out the sliding doors in the back of her house. I was more than happy to oblige.

I'm nervous as hell, even though I've hung out with her one-on-one so many times. I guess it's just the official *date* designation that's making my stomach hurt and my palms sweat.

I got her a gift, too, which makes the whole thing feel like an even bigger deal. To be fair, I bought it more than a week ago and it's a tiny thing, but I've been waiting for the right time to give it to her.

I think this is the right time.

It's unseasonably warm today, so I stay outside and text Taylor before going back to lab. The best thing about it being winter break is that she's doing almost nothing, so there's always a good chance she'll be free to talk.

ME: heyo
what's up?

TAY: LITERALLY NOTHING
so bored
i even texted teddy

ME: lol you mean amy's ex bf?

TAY: obvs
the thing is he has the personality of a sack of bricks

ME: love that for him

TAY: yeah he'll do fine in life

he's hot and gives great head

ME: TRULY TMI

didn't need to know that

TAY: sorry!!!!

but it's true ;)

anyway

how's your love life going???

ME: pretty good

TAY: just pretty good??

not . . . AMAZING??!!

ME: idk

i guess i'm just worried

TAY: about what??

ME: falling into old habits

TAY: ah

ME: yup

TAY: like u mean . . .

old Sadie habits?

ME: mhm

like I was in a dumpster yesterday

a L I T E R A L dumpster

so I'd say that's about how things are going

TAY: bestie . . . .

ur gonna have to say more about that

plz

ME: maybe later

but suffice it to say

i clearly have REASON to be worried

DUMPsTER 😭

TAY: ok that's fair

u WERE a piece of shit while you were dating sadie

I mean I assume u were . . .

since we . . . didn't talk

ME: lord

how many times do I have to apologize for that???

TAY: once more couldn't hurt

ME: FINE

you're right :(((((

I'm very, exceptionally sorry. Please forgive me, my perfect best friend. Love, Shani.

TAY: excellent

but seriously I don't think you have to worry

may doesn't sound anything like sadie

The thing is, even when I started talking to Taylor again, I didn't tell her everything about Sadie. But I told her enough. Right after Sadie dumped me, I FaceTimed Taylor, sobbing and screaming about how controlling and shitty and whatever else Sadie was, even if I didn't fully believe it myself. I wanted Taylor to hate her enough for the both of us; she told me I was way too good for Sadie, and she didn't mention anything about how we hadn't talked for three months. She was just there for me.

But I didn't tell Taylor one crucial detail. I didn't tell her *why* Sadie broke up with me, just that she did.

And I can't tell her that now either. I won't.

So instead, I just say:

ME: she's not

Because it's true: May's nothing like Sadie. For starters, she cares about what I have to say. She tells me about the things she loves. She lets me know when she's mad.

But.

ME: I'm worried things are going too fast

TAY: they have to go fast!
this is a winter fling!
like a summer fling but for cuffing szn
you just have to enjoy it

Maybe Taylor's right. Maybe I should just enjoy what's happening, even if "fling" feels like such a trivial word for it. Because if Taylor approves, then everything's fine.

And I'm going to have a good time, damn it.

The restaurant we're going to is in a cool part of downtown, and I feel deeply inadequate when I pass by a group of well-dressed twenty-somethings smoking and chatting on the patio.

May texted a minute ago that she got us a table, so I take a breath and head inside. It's crowded and loud and colorful, with rainbow pom-poms and tassels hanging from the ceiling and the bar.

"Table for one?" the hostess asks.

Is that the vibe I'm giving off?

I try not to sound offended when I say, "I'm actually meeting someone."

I look around to find said someone, and when I do I get very sweaty.

May's sitting at a table near the back, her face glowing softly in the candlelight. She's wearing the softest-looking maroon sweater I've ever seen, with lipstick to match. Her hair's in a bun, and there are two strands loose, framing her face and curling around her lips.

She's so fucking beautiful.

Seeing her makes me wish I'd done something. Like, dressed up more than I have (at least I opted for a turtleneck under my T-shirt). Done my hair. Anything.

But then she looks up from the menu, and our eyes meet across the restaurant. She grins, and I wave, feeling smug as the hostess walks me to the table.

"Hi," I say to May as I sit down.

"Hi."

We look at each other for a beat, and I don't know what to do and I wish I wasn't nervous but also there's a cute girl in front of me so of course I'm nervous. My body is tense and shaky and I wish I could tell it to stop. Relax.

"The food looks really good," May says after I don't speak for what must be a full minute.

"Cool," I say, grabbing the menu but not taking any of it in.

"I heard they do good meats and stuff," she says, eyes on the menu. "But I'm a vegetarian."

"You are?"

She smiles. "Is that a deal breaker?"

"No," I tell her. "I am too."

We both laugh at that, and the tension in my body eases a bit.

"How have we not talked about this?" she asks.

"I don't know!" I say. "I honestly forget most of the time. I've been a vegetarian since I was little."

"Isn't it a stereotype that like every queer person is a vegetarian?"

"Oh, for sure," I say. "We're fully stereotypes."

"Of course we are."

I smile down at my menu, actually reading it this time. The restaurant is pretty fancy, so the menu is small and highly curated. I order the tahdig and May gets the cucumber curry, and we get a squash-based appetizer to split, and then the waiter takes our menus.

Without the crutch of the menu for talking points, there's another lull in the conversation. Why is it that the one time I'm on a date and need to be talking and flirting, my brain refuses to come up with discussion topics?

So, I figure now's as good a time as any to give May her gift. "I got you something," I tell her.

She tilts her head, surprised. "Like, a present?"

"Yeah, exactly like that, one might say." I ignore her eye roll. "It's sort of a belated-birthday-slash-holiday gift."

As I pull the rolled-up poster out of my bag, May gasps melodramatically. "This is wild."

"What is?"

"It's confirmation that you're not a total Scrooge."

"Well, Scrooge is an antisemitic caricature, so . . ."

"Jesus, are you trying to ruin *A Christmas Carol* right now?"

"I'm just saying, he's a moneylender who doesn't celebrate Christmas. . . ."

"I hate you," she says, but she's laughing.

It's comfortable to talk to her like this, to bicker.

"Here." I hand her the poster.

She pulls off the rubber band and unravels it.

"It's a Hockney print," I say, "for your wall."

"And it's the famous gay one," she says after a moment of staring at the poster with a hand pressed to her cheek.

"It's absolutely the famous gay one." It's a print of Hockney's best-known painting, *Pool with Two Figures*. "You know, with the blank walls in your room—I just thought maybe you'd want to spruce them up."

"Thank you," she says, and her eyes get all watery. "I love it."

"You're so welcome."

Before another lull can set in, the waiter comes by with our squash. The poster's still unfurled, so May furls it and we eat, attacking the appetizer from opposite ends.

"This is so good," I say. "I didn't know squash could taste like this. It's, like, unreal."

"I'm sorry, is this a commercial for squash?"

"I wish it was. I'd come up with such good taglines."

"All right," she says. "Let's hear some."

"Well, for starters, 'Squash: Very Gourd.'"

May snorts. "Is that supposed to be a play on 'very good'?"

"Obviously."

"Try again."

I clear my throat. "How about 'Squash: Because Pumpkin's Days are Numbered'?"

"That makes it sound like squash is going to murder pumpkin."

"I mean . . ."

We come up with a few more taglines, and then the squash is gone and the gift is given and we once again run out of things to say.

That is until May clears her throat. "So, remember when we were in *Snails Space* that first time?"

"Of course," I say, because . . . of course.

"And I told you I had seen it before with a friend from Ithaca?" I nod, not sure where this is going. "The thing is, she wasn't just my friend. Or, well, she *was* just my friend. But I wanted her to be more." May looks down. "She was the first girl I ever really had a crush on."

I would've thought May telling me about another girl she had feelings for would make me jealous, but I want to know more. "What happened?"

"*Nothing*," she says. "Except she found out I had a

crush on her and told me she didn't feel the same way. We haven't talked much since then."

"I'm sorry."

Well, shit.

May just told me about a girl she had feelings for. The *first* girl she had feelings for. Which means that now would be the perfect time to tell her about Sadie. Not everything, of course, but just that she exists. That I came to DC heartbroken, and that, even though I like May—*really* like her—in many ways I'm still a hollow shell of a person.

But then our food comes, and I'm thankful for the distraction because telling May about Sadie feels like an earth-shatteringly horrible idea, even if now would be the best time to do it.

And anyway, Sadie's over. To quote the most famous lesbian of all time, Elsa of Arendelle, "The past is in the past."

So, I'm letting it go, and I stuff rice into my mouth and listen as May tells me about how there might be a cold front coming in, which doesn't sound particularly interesting, but it is when she talks about it.

"Were you always into weather?" I ask May after a few minutes of her describing how a cold front can rapidly change the forecast. It's super hot—her, not the weather.

She gives me a questioning look. "Were *you* always into fish?"

"Pretty much, yeah," I tell her.

"Well, same for me."

"But what about your dad?" I ask.

I want to take it back immediately, since he's probably not the best person to bring up on our date. But isn't that what this is for anyway? To learn more about each other? To talk about our lives and our hopes and our dreams and then make out?

"What about him?"

"He's a weatherman, right?"

She must sense the other question that's on the tip of my tongue—something along the lines of *Don't you hate that you're following in his footsteps?*—because she brushes her hair back from her face and puts her elbows on the table.

"Back when we got along really well, I wanted to be exactly like him. I would follow him around at work and watch him create the day's forecast, and it seemed magical. Like he was predicting the future." She smiles a little. "I know now that it's a science, but that's what I thought then. And I just love it. I've learned about climate change and oceanography and the moon and tsunamis and how people behave differently when it rains."

My heart almost bursts as she tells me this. I could listen to her talk about weather for hours.

For the rest of my life.

"That's so cool," I say, and I mean it.

May rolls her eyes, but the blush across her cheeks is evident even in the candlelight.

I move my foot to cross it over my leg, but I accidentally

bump into May. She bumps me back. She smiles as she does it, so I know it's on purpose.

So I bump her again. And she bumps me. And soon our ankles are twisted around each other and we're playing footsie and it's much easier than talking.

My body relaxes. It's not even the touching May part that relaxes me, exactly. In fact, I think it's the opposite: she puts my whole body on edge. It's more that the hardest part is over, the one where I didn't know when or if or how I could touch her.

So I don't pull my foot away. It feels grounded against her, like rubber in a lightning storm.

When the waiter asks if we want dessert, May says, "I think we need a minute," so they nod and go check on another table.

May meets my eyes in a way that makes me ask, before I can think about what I'm saying, "Do you want to come home with me?"

To which May immediately responds, "Yes."

When the waiter comes by again, May asks for the check, our feet still intertwined. She insists on paying, for which I profusely thank her, then I insist on getting us a rideshare because it's late and the way she's looking at me makes me want to do things to her that most Metro riders probably wouldn't want to see.

We start making out the moment we hop into the car. It feels somehow more urgent than the other times, like we're trying to tell each other something. Like our bodies are operating separately from our minds.

I tip the driver very well.

When we get to Beatrice's house, I run in first to check that the coast is clear, and when I don't hear anyone in the kitchen I usher May upstairs.

In the back of my mind, I hear Lauren telling me the rules on my first day in DC. *"No boys allowed in your room, ever."* I think about how I changed the rule so it applied to me, how I wouldn't bring anyone into my room, period.

But . . . I'm not *technically* breaking a rule by having May in my room. In fact, by bringing her there, I'm fighting the heteronormative edict head-on.

So it's fine—more than fine, really—to take May upstairs.

We make it undetected and pick up right where we left off. We stumble over to Beatrice's bed, and then fall into it, tangled together.

"Hey," she says, looking up at me. "Is this—do you think this counts as slow?"

I think back to the conversation we had on Saturday. Less than a week ago, in *Snails Space.*

I meet her eyes. "Do you?"

She takes a deep breath, then bites her lip. "I don't care."

And right now, neither do I.

I wrap my arms around her waist and kiss her to convey this fact, and when we break apart, she looks relieved.

May reaches under my T-shirt and tugs it a bit. "Is this okay?"

I nod, and she pulls it off, along with the turtleneck underneath. It's cold in the room, and with my skin exposed I feel an even stronger urge to press into her as hard as I can.

I reach under her sweater, and before I can ask if it's okay, she pulls it off herself. Next comes my sports bra, which is easy enough because it can slip over my head.

I kiss May's neck, then her chest, redistributing the maroon lipstick she transferred earlier from her face to mine. I push her bra strap down and kiss the piece of shoulder that was under it.

"You can take it off," she says.

I pull the second strap down and kiss her other shoulder, then reach behind her to try to unhook the bra. I try and try and try.

But May just sits up, pulls it off in one smooth motion, and flops back onto the pillow.

Making out now is different than in the shower. There was something about the water and the steam and the slipperiness of the tub that made it clear nothing more than kissing was going to happen.

But now we're in a *bed*.

And my body knows what's about to happen and it *definitely* wants it.

But my brain isn't so sure. In fact, it's telling me to get

out of here while we can. It's saying that I have no idea what I'm doing. It's reminding me that I've never done *this* sober. That I'm just going to make a fool of myself.

My skin starts to feel tight, and May's mouth stops being perfect and soft and everything turns, becomes suddenly harsher. Like we're making out under surgery lights.

I don't know what to do. I'm worried it's too late. That I can't stop what's about to happen. Especially because May's hand drifts down toward my jeans. "Is *this* okay?" I nod. I don't stop her as she fumbles with the button, then the zipper. Because I should want this. I *do* want this.

But if I want this, then why does my mind keep yelling at me to stop? Why does it keep drifting to Sadie? Why does it keep replaying the moment that led to the downfall of our relationship?

Why?

And then there's a bloodcurdling scream.

Beatrice is screaming.

I shoot up to a standing position, and a new sort of dread is forming inside me, but the other one is receding as I zip my jeans up and pull my shirt back on.

I run out of the room, slamming the door behind me so that if anyone's out on the main landing they won't see May in my room, half-naked.

Lauren got to Beatrice first, and she's helping her down the attic stairs.

"Are you okay?" I ask, reaching out a hand to help Beatrice the rest of the way.

"She's fine," Lauren says, sounding slightly annoyed. "She saw a spider."

"If you saw the way it was looking at me you would've screamed too!"

Tasha comes out of her room then, balancing a laptop on her forearm. "What's going on?"

"Beatrice saw a spider," Lauren repeats, and Tasha rolls her eyes and retreats to her bed.

"That's it?" I thought Beatrice was on the verge of death. She's ninety-six years old. It wasn't that wild of an assumption.

"Doll," Beatrice begins seriously, holding on to my arm as she reaches the landing. "I'm only afraid of two things in this world: spiders and fascism."

"So, you're okay?" I ask.

"Fine, angel." She waves her arm. "Don't worry about me."

With that, Lauren takes Beatrice downstairs for a cup of tea.

And I have to go back into Beatrice's old room.

Where May is.

Where she's half-naked, and I'm fully clothed, and she probably expects me to have sex with her, even though she said she wanted to take things slow.

I can't go back in there, and I don't know what to do, and I know it's horrible but I wish something *had* happened to Beatrice—not anything bad, just bad *enough*—so that I didn't have to face May again.

I push the heels of my palms against my eyes until there are spots and colors, then take a breath, fighting the urge to vomit.

I open the door, and May's under the sheets, looking anxious.

"Is Beatrice okay?"

"She's fine," I say, not moving toward the bed.

"That's good, right?"

"Yeah."

May sighs with relief and pats the pillow beside her. "Come back?" she asks, biting her bottom lip. "We can keep going. Pick up where we left off. . . ."

But the idea of picking up where we left off makes me want to die and I don't know how to tell May that or how to tell her that maybe her definition of slow isn't the same as mine. I don't know how to tell her how scared I am, and that I don't want a repeat of what happened with Sadie.

So instead of telling her any of that, I just say, "I'm kind of tired."

"That's okay," May says. "We can just go to sleep." She pats the bed next to her again and lifts the covers.

But that's just delaying the inevitable. Now that we've almost had sex, it's going to happen any day now. And I want it, but at the same time I'd rather jump out of a plane without a parachute.

I've done a lot of research, and I know I'm not asexual.

But I'm so fucking scared.

My body clenches.

"Uh, Beatrice really doesn't like people sleeping over."

"She doesn't have to know," May says in a voice that would probably sound sexy to any other human being but is currently filling me with dread.

I hate that I don't want to get back into bed with May. I *should* want to, but I can't.

"I don't know," I say, still standing by the door. "She's pretty freaked out. And I'm worried she'll see you leave and it'll freak her out even more." This is mostly a lie, but I don't know what else to say.

May sits up, looking confused. "Do you not want me to stay?" The air in the room goes still, and when I don't respond May frowns and says, "I'm gonna go."

I nod, then look away as she gets dressed. I walk toward the bed as she walks to the door.

"Bye, I guess," she says as she leaves.

"Make sure Beatrice doesn't see you on the way out," I say, still not looking at her.

She slams the bedroom door, and after a few seconds the front door slams, too.

I put my head in my hands and try to cry, to sob, to weep, but nothing comes out.

Everything is messed up, every single thing.

I wish I had the courage to run after her. To explain everything.

But I can't embarrass myself like that.

I just chased a girl away, a girl I like *so much*, because I'm afraid to have sex with her.

Because of fucking Sadie.

Fuck.

I have to end things with May. There's no coming back from this.

I climb onto the bed and feel something papery crunch under me.

I lift the sheets to find the Hockney print, crumpled beyond repair.

Homo Fuckup

I don't sleep at all that night. I don't even lie down. The thought of sitting on Beatrice's bed—the one where she conceived her kids, the one where I almost had sex with May—is too much.

Instead, I pace from one end of the room to the other, trying to stop my heart from pounding and my body from shaking.

I draft a text to May in my head as I pace, writing and rewriting each word until it's a jumbled mess of ideas and feelings.

I can't text Taylor about this, because then she'll try to find out what happened, and I won't be able to tell her because if I did my skeleton would leave my body. And then she'd just think I'm once again acting like I did with Sadie.

But here's something I could tell *May*: that I came to DC to focus on paleoichthyology, and that focus is gone. And it's because of her.

At least that would be truth-adjacent.

The problem is, I'm not sure what the real truth is.

That I'm scared? Sure, that's part of it. I'm terrified all the time: of coming on too strong, of loving someone only to push them away.

Of sex.

If I told her that last thing, that I'm scared of sex, it might sound like an excuse. Maybe she'd be like, *Yeah, sure, okay*, and in her head, she'd think it meant I just didn't want to have sex with *her*.

Something else I could tell her: I'm still getting over a breakup; this is too soon.

That wouldn't be wrong either.

But none of these sort-of-truths add up to a text I can send May. Or one I want to send.

What I *want* to do is slam my fist into the wall. To punish myself for not telling May about Sadie, even in broad strokes.

Now she's probably in bed at her dad's house, lying under an empty wall, thinking about how the girl she thought liked her just kicked her out of bed mid-hookup. Embarrassed her.

Fuck.

So I decide to keep it simple, to get it over with.

My hands shake violently as I type out a text.

ME: I don't think we should see each other anymore

I stare at my phone. One part of me is screaming, *DON'T SEND THIS! DON'T YOU DARE!* and another part is goading me on, whispering, *Tap the little blue arrow. Come on, do it.*

I listen to the goader.

Then I run to the en suite and try to vomit, but nothing comes out.

So I go back to pacing.

I don't know what I expect her to say in response to that message.

Well, no, that's not quite true. What I *want* her to say, no matter how deluded it is, is this: "No, we're not ending things with a text. Tell me what's wrong. Tell me why you kicked me out. We'll take things even slower. It'll all be okay."

I get a response after an hour, when it's so late—or maybe so early—that the sky is beginning to turn from black to dark blue to gray, like a bruise.

MAY: I think that's for the best.

I read the text over and over. Each time, new tears form in my eyes, blurring my vision. And then I wipe them away so I can read it again.

I think that's for the best.

I think that's for the best.

I think that's for the best.

I read it until it becomes true, until it becomes an inevitable fact of our brief relationship: it's for the best.

But if it is, then why did I expect a different answer? Why do I feel like someone just punched me in the face?

I lie in bed, staring at the ceiling.

Time passes. My alarm goes off.

It's tomorrow.

This is all that's left: the lab. Doing well here. Proving to Mandira and Dr. Graham that they made the right choice in hiring me, even though there are mountains of evidence to the contrary.

I scrub the fossils until they're raw, getting every speck of dirt off.

"Are you trying to revive them or something?" Mandira asks when she sees my vigorous cleaning. She laughs a little, but when I don't respond she says, "Hey—hey, stop that for a second." I look up. "Are you okay?"

"I'm fine," I say. "Just trying to get this done."

"Okay," she says, eyebrows raised. "But you know I'm here to talk."

"Yup."

But what can I tell Mandira now that my personal rom-com has soured? Now that I've ruined everything so profoundly that it's not even a rom-com anymore? Now that it's a horror movie or a thriller or a black-and-white French film about a depressed woman with melancholy eyes who roams the streets of Paris?

After another few minutes Mandira adds, "Well, if you're gonna scrub so efficiently, you might as well glue the pieces together."

She hands me the PaleoBOND and shows me where to reattach the pieces of the fossil I've been working on.

I get started, glad to have a new task.

Except that it allows my mind to wander. And now it's wandering to the fact that May hasn't texted me since *I think that's for the best*. I don't know why she would, but maybe, if I check my phone . . .

No.

It's over. It was going to end when I left next week to go back to school anyway. This was just ending it on *my* terms.

Who cares that she opened up and let me in and made me feel safe?

I certainly don't, that's for sure. I'm not thinking about it even a little bit. I'm definitely not playing every moment of our incredibly short relationship over in my mind, our shitty rom-com in reverse.

And in no universe am I thinking about how she

unbuttoned my pants so gently, how she checked in with me to make sure it was okay.

I'm not thinking about how she was so good to me. And how I was terrible back.

How I kicked her out. How I didn't tell her why. How I was too ashamed.

I glance down at the fossil I've been gluing, only to find it wasn't the fossil at all. My thumb and index finger are stuck together with PaleoBOND.

Honestly, this is fine. Let me fossilize like this. It'll put me out of my misery. Someone can put me on display in the museum and use me as a type specimen for a new subspecies of human that ruins every relationship they touch. *Homo fuckup.*

It might be a bit on the nose, but everyone who walks by will know exactly the type of person I was: the type that doesn't deserve love. A gay screwup.

I don't tell Mandira that I glued my fingers together, but she sees me struggling with the fossil and comes over to help.

"Here," she says, handing me a toothpick. "That's the secret to getting PaleoBOND off your hands. It happens to me all the time."

"Thanks," I tell her, even though I wish she hadn't helped me.

I wish she'd just leave me here to fossilize.

♥

When I get home, I have no idea what to do with myself. My days have been so filled with May that having a free evening feels wrong.

I drop my stuff off in Beatrice's old bedroom, then head down to the kitchen.

Beatrice isn't there, but Tasha and Lauren are. They're laughing and sipping Baileys from tiny glasses. I pop my head into the archway.

"Hey," Lauren says, "glad to see you're finally joining us."

"I told you she would," Tasha tells Lauren. "We just needed to wear her down."

"So did we?" Lauren asks. "Wear you down?"

"Uh—"

"Grab a glass," she says before I can tell them that they didn't, in fact, wear me down. That I'm here because I had nowhere else to be.

I pull a glass out of the cabinet, glad to have someone telling me what to do. Lauren pours me a tiny bit of Baileys, an adult amount, and I down it in one sip. It burns my throat, and I almost convulse from the pain. But when it hits my stomach, I feel warm and tingly.

"Whoa there," Lauren says, as if she's trying to calm a horse.

But then Tasha says, "Nasdrovia," and downs her glass, too, and Lauren shrugs and drinks hers. Then she pours us all another round.

"Let's toast," I say, raising my cup. Tasha and Lauren raise theirs too. "To Beatrice."

"To Beatrice," Lauren adds.

"Beatrice," Tasha says, nodding.

And down the hatch. This one goes smoother than the first.

It feels good to be doing something. To not be wallowing in my room.

"What made you finally decide to join us?" Tasha asks.

Well . . .

I don't want to tell them about May. Lauren hates her or gets weird vibes from her or whatever, and I don't know how sympathetic she'd be if I told her I ruined a relationship she didn't know about with a girl she doesn't like. Plus, Beatrice asked me the other day if I had a *boyfriend*, and I almost spat out my coffee, but I didn't correct her. Maybe Tasha and Lauren think that too.

I can use that.

"Boy troubles, I guess." It sounds so unnatural coming out of my mouth that I don't even fault Lauren when she gives Tasha a skeptical look.

"Well, cheers to that," Lauren says, regardless of her clear incredulity.

"You've been dating the same boy since high school,"

Tasha says. "What kind of boy troubles are you having?

"Plenty," she says, "I just don't tell you about them."

I let Lauren and Tasha's familiar squabbling pass over me.

Then they pour a third glass, and my legs start to feel numb and my head's spinning. After a minute, Lauren pushes the bottle toward the center of the table. "I think that might be enough."

"Sure," I say, glad to have someone making a decision for me. Then I go back to listening to Tasha and Lauren talk about Lauren's grad school applications.

But I can't concentrate. I don't understand how they're going about their normal lives right now when nothing is normal. And yet here they are, at the kitchen table, talking about the world in the future tense.

It's too much, so I excuse myself and go upstairs.

I sit on the floor of Beatrice's room, hunched over my phone. Debating who to text.

I could text Taylor.

But . . . no.

Because if I text her, I'm sure she'll be mad. She'll ask why I didn't let her know what was happening. She'll tell me I'm acting like I did first semester. She might even try to offer rational advice. And I can't have that.

But there *is* one person who definitely won't be offering any advice.

I navigate to Settings.

I press Call Blocking & Identification.

I tap Edit.

I unblock Sadie's number.

I draft a text.

And I ask a question that's been bothering me since we broke up. I ask it even though, deep down, I already know the answer.

But I need to hear her say it.

ME: why'd you do it

A few minutes later, there's a response.

Shit.

Seeing Sadie's name on my screen gives me the same chemical jolt I felt while we were dating. The dangerous, delirious influx of something that could almost be happiness if you tilt your head the right way.

SADIE: Shani don't do this

ME: why though

SADIE: Are you asking why I broke up with you?

ME: well why did you?????

SADIE: Babe, you know why

I shiver, seeing the word *babe* coming from Sadie's contact on the screen.

SADIE: It's like I told you

Sex is a huge part of a relationship

If you didn't want it, we weren't a match

I hate the words I'm seeing. They're so detached, like she's writing a business email.

I shouldn't even answer. I don't want to know any more.

But I can't help myself.

ME: but I DID it

for you!!!!!!!!

I'm feeling desperate now. All I want to do is turn off my phone and throw it out the window. I want to watch it smash to bits.

SADIE: Once.

We only did it once

And then you didn't want it again

You want a real explanation?

No.

ME: yes

SADIE: I need a fulfilling sexual relationship

And I knew you weren't going to give me that

You're supposed to **want** to have sex w your girlfriend

Like, wtf?

I scream. I actually scream in frustration. And then I throw my phone. It flies across the room and lands on the floor with a crash. I don't know why I fucking did this to myself.

Why did I text Sadie?

Because here's the real story.

I don't remember having sex with her.

That Thursday, the day we said, "I love you," we went to a house party and got drunk. Too drunk. Like, so-drunk-I-barely-remember drunk.

Then we went back to my room.

The only memories I have of that night come in flashes: Sadie grabbing my waist, leading me up to my room. Sadie kissing me.

Sadie pulling down my pants, and her own.

Me, copying what she did.

Being excited to do it, to please her.

And then, nothing.

My memory goes dark.

Until we woke up the next morning, both of us naked.

Me with a splitting headache. Sadie grinning.

Sadie, looking so beautiful.

Sadie, telling me how well I did.

At what? I remember thinking.

Until it came back to me.

I was pretty sure the feeling I had in that moment was happiness. It was a bit hollow, sure. A bit tinged with dread. But maybe that was okay. I had gotten it over with. I had had sex with a girl.

And then she wanted to do it again.

But I didn't want to. I asked her not to. I wasn't ready. I wasn't feeling it.

I moved her hands up from my pants. Put them back around my waist.

She asked me why not. Tried again.

But I told her no.

So she left.

And then she broke up with me.

I smack my forehead with my hands.

I can't think about this anymore.

I grab my phone from where I threw it. There's a crack down the middle, but it's working fine.

And there are more texts from Sadie.

SADIE: it's cool if ur ace or whatever

But like regardless

You need to get your shit together

That very last text she sent might be the only true thing she's ever said to me, the part about needing to get my shit together.

And the first step I take in that endeavor is re-blocking her number.

Then I climb into bed and sob. I burrow under the sheets and wail until my throat hurts and my eyes are sore, and a thought pops into my head that I don't think I've had since I was five years old:

I need my mommy.

It's such a primal feeling. I need her. I need her *here*.

I pull out my phone again, sit up, take a breath, and call her.

"Shani?" My mom asks when she picks up, and before I can respond she says, "You haven't called in so long I thought you disowned me or something."

She laughs weakly at her own joke and hearing her voice breaks something in me. I start sobbing, so loudly that I know she hears it too. I try to stop, but I can't. After a second, I finally choke out, "Mom?"

"Honey, are you okay?"

I cry for another minute, trying to pull myself together.

"Shani?"

"I need you here," I say through hot, thick tears.

"In DC?"

I try to say "mhm" while sobbing, but it comes out as

more of a choking sound. I swallow a glob of snot and say, "You were right." Then I start to cry even harder. "You were right," I repeat.

"About what, sweetheart?" she asks so, so gently.

I snort, I cry. "I shouldn't have come here. I should've stayed home."

"No, hon," she says, using her softest voice. "You're so brave. My brave girl."

Another sob comes out, and then a hiccup, and she lets me cry for a minute until I say, "Please come. Please?"

She sighs, but not angrily. "Okay, sweetheart." I hear the sound of typing on a keyboard. "I just have to email my boss, but I can be there early tomorrow morning. Can you wait that long? Will you be okay?"

I grab on to a pillow. "Yeah," I say, the tears clearing up.

"Do you wanna talk about it now? Or later?"

"Later."

"Okay," she says, then repeats it. "Okay." She takes a breath. "I'm leaving soon. Call me if you need anything, all right?"

I nod, even though it's a phone call, even though she can't see me.

"I love you, Shani. I love you so much, always. You know that, right?"

My vision clouds with tears again as I say, "I love you, too."

Then she says, "Stay safe. I'll see you soon," and hangs up.

I'm crying again, but this time from relief. It doesn't matter how badly I fucked up. My mom's coming, and everything's going to be okay.

And with that thought, and after a few more minutes of crying, I fall asleep.

The Big Blue Whatever

It's dark when I wake up, and for a few seconds I don't know where I am or what happened or why my whole body hurts.

I check my phone. It's five in the morning on a Saturday, and I have seven texts from my mom.

> **MOM:** Here
> Waiting outside in the 🚗
> But take ur ⏰
> Im guessing ur asleep
> Let Me Know
> <3 u so much

I don't change out of my PJs. I don't text her back.

I just slip out of bed and run out to the street—my mom's Subaru is parked right out front. I knock on the driver's side window.

My mom was clearly sleeping because, when she hears the knock, she startles and bumps her funny bone on the door and shouts, "FUCK!" But then she sees me, puts a hand to her chest, and scrambles to unlock the car to let me in.

I walk around to the passenger seat. It's warm as I hop in; she has the heat on full blast. When I sit down, she leans over to hug me. I let her, and I don't cry, mostly because I don't have any tears left. But I do bury my face into her sweatshirt as she combs her fingers through my hair that is also hers and holds on to me.

"I was so worried," she says into my head.

"I know."

"I love you so much."

I let her hold me for a few minutes in silence.

After a while I say, "Please don't tell me you knew it."

"Knew what?" she asks, still holding on to me.

"That I couldn't handle the holidays alone."

"I would never say that," she says, "because the holidays are over." I snort into her sweatshirt. Then she adds, "I just knew you couldn't live without your mom."

I know she's joking to try to make me feel better, and it does, but I also start crying again. I guess I wasn't all cried out.

"I'm sorry," I say through tears.

"No. Don't apologize. I would drive a million miles if you needed me."

"Not just for that. For, you know . . ." *Being a total bitch.*

I pull away and look up at her. She waves a hand. "Shan, you were so easy in high school. You were so *good.* I was waiting for you to hit your teenage phase." I laugh and she wipes away the tears streaming down my face. "It came a bit late, but it's fine. It's so fine, sweetheart."

We sit and watch as the sky gets lighter, and after another few minutes she asks, "Breakfast?"

"Yes, please." The anxious knot in my stomach has loosened a bit and now I'm extremely hungry.

"What about that place we went to when I dropped you off? The Big Blue Whatever?"

"No," I say, too forcefully. Then, trying to even out my tone: "Somewhere else, okay?"

She nods, no questions asked, and checks her phone to see if there are any breakfast places open at this hour.

"There's a diner down the road that's open twenty-four-seven."

"Sounds perfect."

She puts the car in drive, and we head over.

The last time I was in this car, we bumped into May. Between then and now, we powered through the full cycle of a relationship: first I hated her, then I had a crush on her, then we started dating, then I ended things.

I had just gotten out of a relationship the last time I was in the car, and I'm recently out of one again. Maybe my life is a never-ending cycle of shitty relationships and Subaru rides.

But then again, maybe not. Things feel different this time. I'm not being a bitch to my mom, for starters.

When we get to the diner, my mom parks directly in front—there's no competition for spots at this hour—and we head inside.

A tired-looking waitress sits us down in a booth and hands us a menu and two glasses of water, then goes to check on the man passed out on a stool by the bar. Other than him, we're the only people here.

"Get anything you want," my mom tells me. "Sky's the limit."

I order coffee and orange juice and chocolate chip pancakes and my mom gets coffee and apple juice and an omelet and we split a whipped-cream-covered waffle.

We eat in a cozy silence, but as we finish up my heart starts pounding. I shift around in the booth, unable to find a comfortable position.

And I know why.

It's so long overdue.

I move an uneaten pancake around on my plate and squeeze my eyes shut. Everything hurts. And I know it'll feel better when it's over, but I can't bring myself to say anything right now.

In high school I always thought, *Oh, I'll just tell her when I'm dating a girl. That way we wouldn't have to talk about my sexuality, really. Just about the girl. It'll be easier that way.*

But that was wrong. Because I'm a lesbian separate and apart from any girl I've dated in the past, from anyone I'll date in the future. And I want my mom to know.

She gives me an opening when she asks, "Do you want to talk about it now?"

I nod slowly but still don't say anything. I take a sip of water. Then a sip of orange juice. Then a sip of coffee. Then a sip of water again to get the orange juice and coffee taste out of my mouth. "Okay," I say, tapping my fingers against the table. "Okay."

"Okay."

"Mom," I say, because I feel like that's the way this sentence has to start, "I'm a lesbian."

She looks at me for a minute, and my heart drops because what if I'm wrong and she's not okay with it?

And then tears form in her eyes and fall down her cheeks.

"Mom," I say again, my heart breaking.

"I just love you so much," she says. "From the moment I saw you."

And just like that, I'm crying, too. "Mom," I say once more, but this time my heart stitches itself back together, growing three sizes, Grinch-style.

"Thank you for telling me," she says after a bit more crying.

I nod, because I can't think of anything to say to that.

Except to tell her the real reason I called her. I owe her that much. Because even though I came out to her, I still need to explain why things were so terrible when I came home for winter break.

So I tell her the story of Sadie. Start to finish. I make it mom-appropriate, but I want her to know as much as possible. I tell her how controlling Sadie was, and how much I loved her anyway.

I don't talk about May. I'll tell her eventually but not right now. It's too raw.

At the end of the story, my mom grabs my hand.

"I feel awful that you didn't think you could talk to me about this," she says. Then she adds, "I hate that girl."

"I'm sorry."

"No more apologizing." She takes a shaky breath, then looks down at my half-finished pancakes. "Eat."

I follow her Jewish-motherly command, and when I'm done with the stack she says, "Are you talking to anyone at school?"

"What?"

"I mean, a therapist? They have those available to you, right?"

"Yeah," I say. "They do. And no, I'm not."

Binghamton's mental health resources are notoriously bad, but at least they exist.

"Can I help you find one? Before I leave tonight? We can make an appointment together."

I'm surprised, but I nod. My mom and I don't talk much about mental health. All I know is that she sees a therapist sometimes.

But maybe this can be the start of something. The start of us talking more freely with each other. The start of us not having any secrets.

As my mom pays the check, I feel lighter than I have in a long, long while.

My mom had to leave later that night, but even so it was one of the best days we've had together. After breakfast, we went back to Beatrice's and kibitzed with her for a while, then my mom had me email the counseling center at Binghamton to schedule an appointment for when school starts back up again. I felt less overwhelmed the minute I hit Send.

Well, I still felt unbelievably sad and anxious, but in a more manageable way. When my mom left late that evening, I hugged her goodbye for as long as she'd let me.

"I'll see you in a few days," she reminded me.

I nodded, but I still cried as she drove away.

Now that she's gone, though, May's been weighing on my mind again.

I didn't tell my mom about her at all. I couldn't. Telling my mom about May felt like an invasion of privacy. Not of mine, really. Hers.

I guess I don't know what I'm saying. I just miss her.

May became such a big part of my life so quickly, and now that she's gone there's a gaping hole in which she had somehow perfectly fit.

But I think that the best thing to do is just forget about her. To acknowledge that I'll do better next time, whatever the next time may be. Even if it's not with her.

The good news about all of this is that I'm much more focused at work. The bad news is that it's now my second-to-last day at lab, so the focus came a bit late.

Dr. Graham comes out of his closet for a little while, and we discuss a paper he's been working on about an extinct species of coelacanth and its vision. It's nerve-racking to talk to him but so, so exciting. Mandira's here too, and she gives me a thumbs-up from behind Dr. Graham's back.

"I think this'll be really big for sclerotic ring research," he says. "You know the sclerotic ring? It's where the eye is located in most reptiles and fish." He explains that his paper is focused on the ring's evolution, and coelacanths are a great organism to study how traits evolved, because they're closely related to early tetrapods. "I'm thinking it might even help scientists who study mammalian eyes."

"Oh, cool," I tell him. "Are the sclerotic rings well-preserved in any of the coelacanth fossils?"

"Great question," he says, and I beam. He speaks even faster as he says, "They're *rarely* preserved in fossils, but the ones in the coelacanths we found on a dig earlier this year *are*, and they could help us learn about sclerotic ring evolution." He grins. "It could be a huge breakthrough."

Listening to him speak is like being in the audience for a personalized TED Talk. It makes me wish I hadn't been as distracted for the first few weeks of my internship. That I'd asked more questions.

At the end of the day, Mandira pulls me aside. "I'm glad to see you're more focused." She lowers her voice and adds, "I think it's something that's so hard to learn—that a relationship doesn't have to be all-consuming. That you should be able to be yourself and live your own lives but together. And it seems like you're already learning that, which is awesome."

My heart's a freight train in my chest. She looks so excited to be giving me queer relationship advice.

"It took me a while to figure that out with my girlfriend," she continues. "I was pretty obsessed with her when we started dating. But now things are calmer. I love her, but I'm not *obsessed* with her. There's a difference."

I nod and thank her, then rush out of lab. I won't be

telling her that the reason I'm no longer obsessed with May or our relationship is that there isn't one.

But as I'm heading home on the Metro, the May-based sadness creeps back in, like it did this morning before lab. My mind drifts to all the good things, which makes me even sadder: Raphael witnessing our first kiss, cuddling on the couch. When she wiped the soap out of my eyes in the shower. It makes me cringe, but it was still good. It was all so, so good.

When I take the escalator up and out of the Metro at my stop, I suddenly feel paranoid. It's a bit irrational, but I'm worried I'll run into May.

I need a distraction while I walk home, so I call Taylor. It's time to come clean to her, anyway. We haven't spoken since before shit went down with May, and she needs to know.

"Long time no talk," she says when she picks up the FaceTime call. She's giving me a look that says, *You'd better not be pulling a Sadie.*

"Yeah," I say. "About that . . ."

And I launch into the story. I start with Sadie, and unlike my mom, Taylor gets *all* the details about how things ended. I tell her everything. Then I apologize for not telling her everything when I called her crying about how Sadie broke up with me. Then I apologize again just because I feel like the first apology wasn't enough.

"Why didn't you tell me this before?" she asks. "I

literally would've driven to Binghamton and given Sadie a piece of my mind."

"That's it? Just a piece of your mind?"

"And a piece of my *fist*."

I shake my head and laugh. I'm taking the long way home, winding through the backstreets of the neighborhood.

"But really, thanks for telling me, Shan," Taylor says. "You know I love you so much, right?"

I nod, a lump forming in my throat.

"And *none* of that was your fault," she says so gently. Then she takes a deep breath. "I also wanted to say that what she did to you really sounds like it was sexual assault."

The lump in my throat disappears and is replaced by a sob.

I nod again but don't say anything.

I knew in my head that what happened with Sadie felt *wrong*, but it's really, really validating to hear Taylor say that out loud.

That it was sexual assault. Because that's what it was.

Taylor lets me cry for a few minutes, a calming presence on the other end of the phone.

When I calm down, I tell her about May. About why I freaked out when things started to, like . . . happen.

"That's so completely understandable," Taylor says, but I miss the next thing as sirens blare in the distance.

"What?"

"I said that I get it if you don't want to try again with May, but I think you should."

"I don't know." I stare down at the sidewalk, which still has the tiniest bit of snow at its edges, the last evidence of the Christmas Eve blizzard. "I doubt she's going to forgive me for ending things without an explanation."

"Then give her an explanation!"

"I don't know. . . . " I repeat.

Because I've been thinking that, even though I miss May, maybe I shouldn't be in a relationship right now. In fact, I almost definitely *shouldn't* be.

Probably.

Taylor lets go of the topic after that, and we switch to talking about Teddy and his lack of personality.

I say goodbye to her as I turn onto my street, but when I look up from my phone, my heart drops.

There's an ambulance and a fire truck, both with lights flashing.

Parked in front of Beatrice's house.

Café and Morgue

I sprint toward the door as Lauren runs outside. She stops in front of the ambulance, shell-shocked, then spots me and walks over.

"What's going on?"

"She fell," Lauren says, out of breath. "Up in the attic. I wouldn't even have known if I hadn't called up and asked if she was coming down for dinner." Her eyes fill with tears, and I'm panicking and it doesn't help that I have no idea how to comfort people in distress. I pat her arm robotically and then pull my hand away.

"Is she still up there?"

"No, they just got her into the ambulance," Lauren tells me.

And then, the question I don't want to ask: "Is she okay?"

"She's alert, but in a lot of pain," Lauren says, shivering. "When she wasn't answering I went upstairs to check on her and she was lying on the floor, trying to crawl to her landline. She said she didn't want to bother me."

I try not to think about that too hard. But I can't keep the image out of my head of Beatrice, who's normally so spry, being so helpless.

It's fucking bleak.

"Shit," I say.

"Yeah."

The ambulance blares its sirens and pulls away from the house.

"Wait!" I shout, trying to chase it until it's too far away. "Why aren't we going with her?"

"I don't know!" Lauren says, sounding more panicked than she did a few seconds ago. "I forgot to ask! I should've asked! And Beatrice is all alone in the ambulance and she probably thinks we abandoned her and she's gonna get sepsis and die in the hospital—I read that somewhere once. That the two main things people die of in the hospital are infection and a broken heart."

I want to tell Lauren to take a deep breath, but it would sound hypocritical since I'd be saying it in an equally panicked voice.

"Is Tasha here?" I ask. "Can we take her car? We need to follow the ambulance."

"No, she has a late meeting today," Lauren says.

Why am I so bad in a crisis? I should've paid more attention when Sparky the Fire Dog came to my fourth-grade class. Granted, he told us only what to do in a fire emergency and this is an old-woman-falling emergency, but who knows? He might've had some good tips.

No.

I need to stop thinking and start *doing*.

Right now, Beatrice is being carted off to the hospital. Alone.

"Did you call her family?"

Lauren shakes her head. "Don't have their numbers, and I can't find Beatrice's address book. She once told me she kept it in a safe in her attic, but I thought that was a joke and it would be sitting on her desk or something." Lauren tries to take a deep breath. "They'll call her family from the hospital, I think. They have ways of contacting people. Like, this has to happen all the time. That they need to contact someone when they don't have their number?"

"I guess, but she'll be alone when she gets there! What if she needs surgery and she's sitting there wondering where her family is?" I feel utterly, completely helpless. And then I feel bad for feeling helpless because Beatrice is the one being rushed to the hospital, without anyone to meet her or hold her hand or tell her she'll be okay.

"We can take the bus over," Lauren says, pulling out her phone. "There's one coming in, like, fifteen minutes."

"Fifteen minutes?" I shout at Lauren, as if she controls the DC bus schedule. "Sorry," I add. "That's just a long time."

"If you have any other way of getting us to the hospital faster, be my guest." She stares at her phone. "Last time I tried to take a rideshare to the hospital they cancelled on me, then called to yell about how they weren't a 'fucking ambulance.' I was just trying to get to my pap smear appointment and—"

Lauren keeps spiraling, and as she does, I realize that I *do* have a way of getting us there faster.

That is, if she's home.

I know she has a car, at least.

But I don't even know if she drives. And she's d*efinitely* not going to want to see me. She would have every right to slam the door in my face.

No. This is for Beatrice.

"Come on," I tell Lauren. "We're going to Greg's house."

"Really?" she asks. "Greg's gonna drive us?"

"No," I say. "May is."

Lauren gives me a skeptical look but reluctantly follows as I run in the direction of May's place. It takes only a couple minutes, but I'm gasping for breath as we walk up to their front path. I'm hopeful my plan will work when I see Greg's car parked out front, but then my heart starts pounding as I think about what I'm about to do.

I walk up to the front door with the determination of someone who's never known fear.

I knock.

A minute later, the door opens, and it's May, in her pajamas even though it's barely six o'clock. The determination seeps out of me, and then, really, I just want to stare at her. Which is the exact wrong impulse at this moment.

She doesn't meet my eyes as she says, "Oh, um, I guess I'll get Raphael," and starts to close the door.

"No! Wait!" I shout, and she reopens it a tiny bit. Deep breaths. "Do you know how to drive?"

After a beat, she turns to me, confused. "Uh, yes?"

I nod, but now that she's finally looking at me, I don't say anything. I *can't* say anything.

Thankfully, Lauren steps in: "Beatrice is in the hospital. Can you get us there?"

May folds her arms over her chest, rocks back and forth, then nods. "Yeah, okay."

A few seconds later she's back outside, wearing a coat over her pajamas and holding a set of keys. She motions us toward her dad's car.

I debate letting Lauren sit in the front, but then I suck it up and hop in the passenger seat, and we're off.

We don't talk for the entire car ride. None of us. Not a single peep. Which allows my brain to contemplate what it means that May's driving me and Lauren to the hospital.

Just that she's a good person, probably. It doesn't mean anything about *us*. But maybe it could?

I start to formulate an idea. About me and May. I'm not sure if it's a good one, but I let myself mull it over until the hospital comes into view.

"Can I drop you two off here?" May asks as she pulls up to the front entrance.

Lauren gets out of the car, but I don't. And then, before I know what I'm saying, I turn to May and ask, "Can you come in, too?"

She puts her hands on top of her head, flattening her hair.

After a moment: "Let me find a parking spot." I exhale for what feels like the first time since I saw the ambulance. "You two should get out here, though."

"Thank you so much," Lauren says from outside the car. I raise my eyebrows—I guess weird vibes can be ignored in a crisis—and follow her as May drives toward the parking garage.

When Lauren and I get inside, we frantically inquire about Beatrice's whereabouts, and a kind orderly walks us to her room.

We step in quietly, in case she's sleeping, but she's speaking with a doctor. I don't catch what they're saying, but Beatrice is waving her hands dismissively and smiling a bit, so it can't be that bad.

Lauren walks over to her bed first.

"Dolls!" she says when she sees us. "Would you believe I'm still alive?"

"No," Lauren says, and Beatrice throws her head back in laughter.

The doctor introduces herself as Dr. Clarke and shakes our hands. "I'll be back in a bit to check on Beatrice, but in the meantime, don't let her eat or drink anything. She can have ice chips if she's thirsty."

"Why?" I ask.

"Well, we can't rule out surgery, and if we need to take her to the operating room her system has to be clear."

"*Her* system is just fine," Beatrice says.

"As I was telling her, the X-rays came back showing a hairline fracture in her hip, and we usually don't like to operate on someone of such an advanced age"—Beatrice barks with laughter at that—"but she's in remarkable condition."

I hate the way Dr. Clarke talks about Beatrice like she's a show dog. There's something about seeing her tiny body in the sterile hospital bed; I feel protective of her.

"All right," the doctor says, clapping her hands together. "I'll be back in a bit."

"Good riddance," Beatrice says when she's gone.

Lauren sits on the edge of the hospital bed, and I fall into a nearby chair.

"Why didn't you call for me?" Lauren asks, holding Beatrice's hand and wiping away tears. "I would've come! I would've helped you!"

"I know that, doll," Beatrice says, "but you do enough. I had it under control."

"Did you?" Lauren asks, eyebrows raised, "because I'm pretty sure being admitted to the hospital doesn't count as having it under control."

Beatrice swats at Lauren, wincing slightly as she does. "You don't need to worry so much about me, doll. If I survived 'fifty-three, I can survive a little spill!"

"What happened in 'fifty-three?" Lauren asks.

"Oh, you know, being accused of having Communist sympathies, that bastard McCarthy, yada yada. Don't want to bore you with the details."

I would love to be bored with the details of Beatrice and her Communist sympathies, but at that moment, May shows up, pausing in the doorframe.

"Is that another angel?" Beatrice asks as she waves May in with no further question.

May seems supremely uncomfortable, and I can't blame her. She looks the way I feel. But, in addition to my discomfort, there's another feeling I get from seeing her: it's warm and soft and tingly and too much for right now.

"All right, but how are you *feeling*?" Lauren asks, turning back to Beatrice, holding her hand.

"Oh, perfectly fine. But you wanna know what I'd really love?" Beatrice motions for Lauren to come closer. "A glass of Baileys with a big scoop of ice cream. Can you do that for me?"

Beatrice grins, and Lauren and I laugh politely, humoring her, while May silently haunts the far corner of the room. She's been alternating between staring down at her phone and up at me, then quickly back down. Which I know only because I've been doing the same.

We're like lesbians in a seaside town–based period drama.

"But since I can't have that, how about you dolls"—she points to me and May—"go get me and this angel"—she points to Lauren—"a cup of coffee? How does that sound?"

"You can't drink anything," I remind her. "The doctor said only ice chips in case you need surgery."

"What's a little coffee going to do?" But Lauren gives her a *look* and Beatrice says, "Okay, just get coffee for the angel, then."

"I can get it myself," Lauren says, glancing over at May.

"They can do it," Beatrice insists, waving a hand. "You stay with me."

If I didn't know better, I'd think Beatrice was giving me an excuse to be alone with May.

I turn to find May, who's once again looking at me. My heart speeds up, and I nod my head toward the hallway. She doesn't react for a moment, then she walks outside.

A confirmation.

Which makes my heart beat even faster. But I know it's necessary; we really do need to talk. No matter what's happening between us, the least I owe her is an explanation.

"We'll be back soon," I tell Beatrice.

"Take your time, angels," she says. "The doll and I can make our own fun."

"That we can," Lauren says. "And a little milk, please? In the coffee. Any milk will do."

I give a thumbs-up and walk out of Beatrice's hospital room, hoping that May is following me. But before I have this talk with May, there's something *else* I need to do.

I draft a text to my mom.

ME: beatrice is in the hospital

she fell

If this had happened last week, I probably wouldn't have texted her. But I'm trying this new thing where I'm open about important things in my life and other people's and—this will come as a shock—not a total bitch to my mom.

No more secrets.

MOM: Holy 💩

Is she OK??

ME: yes

but the doctor's seeing if she needs surgery

MOM: Let me know if there's anything I can do to help!

ME: thanks
will do

I put my phone away. May's standing across the hall from me, next to an empty hospital cot.

If I'm really doing this whole no-more-secrets thing, then there's a lot I need to tell her. Not that I'm expecting anything to come of it. I just need her to know.

I clear my throat. "Should we go to the cafeteria?" It comes out scratchy and half-formed, like the first words of the morning after a particularly restless night.

"Yeah." She puts her phone in her coat pocket. She has the long jacket zipped all the way up, with her pajama bottoms peeking through—they're covered in anthropomorphic suns that are wearing sunglasses.

If May and I were talking to each other, I'd probably say something like, "Isn't it weird that the sun has to wear sunglasses? What's it protecting itself from? Another sun?" And then she'd say something snarky and we'd laugh and laugh and laugh.

But I don't say that. We walk in silence as the hospital beeps and buzzes around us. When the elevator doors open, there's a group of young-looking doctors chatting loudly about this and that and aortas.

"Basement," a serene woman's voice says as we head down. "On this level: café and morgue."

The doors open.

The cafeteria is packed with a mix of hospital staff and patients' loved ones. It would be easy to tell the difference even if one group wasn't wearing scrubs—the loved ones all look overwhelmed and tired. More than a few have obviously just finished crying. Some are *actively* crying; they're given a wide berth.

"Coffee?" I ask May.

"Yeah," she says, eyes on the floor. "Thanks."

I get us both a cup of coffee, and we sit across from each other at an empty table.

I can't delay this conversation any longer. And I don't want to. I need to tell her what I should've told her from the moment we first decided to try this: everything.

I start with a breath, and then say the same words she said to me in *Snails Space*: "Just let me talk, okay?" I close my eyes, take one more deep breath for good measure, and begin. "I know you might not want to speak to me after what happened the other day. And that's fine. It's *so* understandable. But I wanted to offer an explanation so at least you know where I'm coming from."

As painful as it is, I know the first talking point has to be Sadie. "I was dating someone before I came here. Right before, actually. This girl Sadie. Not that it matters what her name is, but sometimes it's annoying when someone's telling a story and they say 'this girl' or whatever and you're thinking, like, 'Use her name!'"

I know I'm rambling. I'm trying to build up a reserve of courage so that when I get to the really hard part, it's not so bad.

May's been staring into her coffee this whole time, putting her face close to the steam.

"So, anyway," I continue, "this girl—Sadie—and I started dating at the very beginning of the semester, and then we broke up right before we left for break." I take a sip of coffee, and it burns my tongue. But I don't stop talking. "Well, that's not true, really. *She* broke up with *me*."

I scan May's face for a reaction, but there's nothing. Only face-to-coffee apathy. And that's fine. Expected, even.

I need to keep going.

"And the thing is, part of the reason she broke up with me was because of something that happened—I guess everything is because something happened but"—*Jesus Christ, spit it out, Shani*—"it had to do with, like, some stuff with *sex*." I lower my voice a bit on the last word so that the people sitting by us who work at the hospital won't hear. Not that the word *sex* would embarrass a medical professional, but still. It's embarrassing to me. And that's part of the problem.

"So, yeah." I raise one of my hands to my cheek and my face is hot to the touch. "My heart was broken when I got here back in December. And I had promised myself I wasn't going to get involved with anyone, like, ever again. Because the thing is, I wasn't just heartbroken. I also felt violated and confused and angry. Because, like . . ." I trail off.

Breathe, Shani.

You know it's bad when you have to remind your body to perform an involuntary function. *Breathe two three, out two three.*

I have to tell May. I *want* to tell her.

"Because I don't exactly remember having sex with her." At that, May looks up from the coffee, eyebrows knit. Now I'm the one who looks down. "I was really, really drunk. And I think maybe she was too but I honestly don't know. And I've kind of always been uncomfortable with the idea of sex, but after that and after she broke up with me, I got even more freaked out and . . . I don't know."

I glance up at her now. For the first time during this whole conversation (can you even call it that if I'm the only one talking?), we're both looking at each other. "The thing I regret most is not telling you all of this sooner. Because it's been eating at me from the inside out and then of course it all came up at the worst possible moment . . ." I trail off again. My face is cook-an-egg-on-it hot. I know May knows what I'm talking about, the night we almost had sex but didn't. "So that's what I wanted to say. And that I'm sorry I didn't tell you. *And* that I'm really sorry about how things went down, and even though whatever we had was short, it meant a lot to me. Is what I wanted to say."

I take a shaky breath, feeling, for the first time since May left my bedroom, that I got something right with her.

"Shani," May says, still frowning. Which is enough to get my heart racing again. "I'm sorry you didn't tell me, too." Her eyebrows knit even tighter, so that there's a pool of wrinkles between them.

And then she starts crying. "I *told* you I hadn't done anything yet," she says through tears. "Like, *anything*. We could've figured it out together. Or not at all." She puts a hand to her forehead. *"Fuck."*

"I'm sorry," I tell her. "I'm *so* sorry."

"Don't apologize." She sniffles. "Well, I mean, do. But not for what happened to you."

And now *I'm* crying, which means that we're part of the wide-berth, weeping-in-the-cafeteria club.

"Can I say something?" she asks after we've both done our best to get the tears under control.

"Of course."

"I told my roommate about you." I tilt my head at her, confused, but she continues: "I'm not that close with her. I'm not that close with anyone at school, really. But last week she texted me asking how my winter break was going, and the story came spilling out. And then I had to tell her it all ended. She even *called* me after that, which she'd never done before, and we had this whole long conversation and she cursed you out and I laughed and cried and it was really, really nice." She takes a sip of coffee, blowing on it even though it can't be more than lukewarm. "I guess the point of the story is that I usually keep stuff in. It took a full five years of having a crush on my friend before I told her. Nadia, is her name, the friend I had a crush on. Since you seem to think stories need names."

She smiles a little after she says this, and I'm so encouraged by the tiny facial expression that I beam at her.

But then her smile fades, and she doesn't add anything else.

"That's a really long time to have a crush on someone," I say. I want her to keep talking.

"Yeah, I know. And I probably wouldn't have told her, ever, if it hadn't started to take over my whole life. There wasn't a second of the day where I wasn't thinking about her." She takes a breath. "And that's what you did to me. In, like, a month. I don't want to say you're all I think about but . . .

"When I left the other day, after Beatrice screamed and all of that happened, I felt ten times worse than I did after Nadia rejected me. I was walking home from your place, and every ounce of me was thinking about you. I couldn't figure out what I did wrong." She wipes her eyes and says, "*Fuck*," one more time for good measure.

I put my head in my hands, then look up. "Please let me say sorry again, okay? Because I'm so, so, *so* sorry. And you didn't do anything wrong—you did everything *right*."

I try to breathe. "I'm sorry that I didn't tell you why I was hurting." I want to keep going, to apologize until the word *sorry* is two disjointed syllables with no meaning, but I stop when I see the expression on May's face.

"You know I even told my mom about you?" she asks. "I tell her everything, anyway. But when I was home in Ithaca I told her about you, too."

"Was that how you came out to her?" I ask.

"No, she knew about Nadia, so she knows."

And because we're getting everything out into the open, I say, "I saw my mom the other day. She came down to DC after all the shit went down. I came out to her then."

May swallows the large sip of coffee she had in her mouth and her eyes grow wide. "You weren't out to your mom?"

"No," I say. "It never came up." Which is a lie, so I correct myself. "Well, I never told her. I thought I'd wait until I was in a serious relationship with a girl. I was thinking Sadie would be *it*. But obviously she wasn't."

"You told her about me?" May asks, incredulous.

My armpits are suddenly very damp. "No," I say. "Because I realized it was silly that I'd been waiting to be with someone to tell my mom, when being gay is such a big part of my life. Not just the dating-girls part. All of it, you know? And it started to feel like I was lying to her. So I told her, with no person attached to the news."

Her face is a shade of red that it hadn't been a moment ago. "So, you didn't tell her about me?" she asks, and I can't tell what she hopes the answer will be.

"No," I say. "Because, you know. Things weren't going too well."

"No," she agrees. "They weren't."

And that's when I decide to tell her about the idea I had while we were riding to the hospital. It was just a daydream then, but now it feels like something that could plausibly happen. Something we both might *want* to happen.

"May?"

"Yes?"

I take a breath. "What if we start over?"

She tilts her head. "What?"

"Okay, so, I think that, even though we said we wanted to go slow, things ended up going pretty fast. Right?"

"Um, yeah?"

"So what if we start again? I know the break is ending, but we have a couple of days. We can go back to when we both had a crush on each other but we hadn't kissed yet. And maybe, since we're starting over, we never will. But we can *actually* go slow this time. At a pace we're both comfortable with, so that neither of us gets hurt. Obviously, I understand if you don't want to but—"

"No," May says quickly. "I like that idea." She stares into the distance for a moment, deep in concentration. I don't breathe. "And since we're starting over, maybe we didn't meet because you almost ran me over with your car." She smiles.

"Or maybe we still did," I say, smiling too.

"In my head, the new way we met is that I saw you flirting with a child barista at a coffee shop and I thought you were so cute that I was jealous of the kid so I dueled him for your honor."

"Shut up," I say, grinning. Then, silence. "Can I say it one more time? I'm so sorry, May."

"For what?" She raises her eyebrows. "If we're starting over . . ."

"I'm still allowed to be sorry!"

"Well, I won't hear it."

"Fine," I say.

"Fine," she says.

We're both grinning like fools, the happiest people in the hospital café, a previously unknown category of cafeteria-dwellers.

After that, we talk for another minute about the new fictional way we met each other—May insists she had a Wild West–style saloon brawl with Luke to win me over—and then we buy a coffee for Lauren.

But as we're walking to the elevator, I hear a sound coming from May. At first, I think she's crying again, and I'm panicked because I have no idea why. But then I look over, and she's laughing.

"What are you doing?"

"The conversation we had before," she says, taking a breath to quell the giddy excitement, "was so unbelievably gay."

"What?"

"We just processed our feelings"—she tries to take another breath—"for like a full half hour. I've never felt more like a lesbian in my entire life," she says, "and I pined for one girl for five years."

And I start laughing too, because fuck it. It's funny. Relationships are funny. They're messy and scary and horrible sometimes, yes. But funny all the same.

May and I don't hold hands or anything as we enter the elevator. We don't touch at all. But, in a weird way, it feels even more like the start of something than our first kiss. It feels right.

When we get to Beatrice's room, two more people have arrived—

"George!" I say, happy to see him, even if it's under weird circumstances. Tasha must be done with her meeting, because she's here too. I wave to her, and she lifts her hand from where it's placed on a still shell-shocked Lauren's shoulder.

"Hello there!" George says in his gruff voice. "I was just thanking Lauren here for taking care of Ma. I suppose I owe a thank-you to you, too?"

The answer to that is a resounding no, but Lauren graciously says, "Shani and May made sure we got here right after the ambulance so Beatrice wouldn't be alone."

"Well, thank you both, then," George says to me and May.

"Did the doctor come by again?"

"She sure has." Beatrice rolls her eyes. "That woman thinks I'm senile. Joke's on her, because my mind's just fine! Would be better after a touch of Baileys, though."

"Ma, absolutely not," George says. "I don't want you drinking. Isn't that what got you off-balance in the first place? Were you drunk when you fell?"

Beatrice makes a sound like "pssh" and reaches out to slap her son. "What put me off balance is being ninety-six years old, is what. The Baileys only helps."

"Beatrice doesn't need surgery," Lauren interjects, "but they're keeping her overnight to monitor her just in case."

"That's great," I tell Beatrice. And I do feel relieved, but there's something else, too. The past few days have been a marathon of getting shit off my chest, and to really do that there's one more thing I need to say. "Could I talk to you?" I walk over to the side of her bed.

"Doll, you can talk to me about anything."

I glance around the room. "Maybe alone? It'll only take a minute."

"Of course," George says, and he leads Lauren and Tasha into the hallway. May raises her eyebrows at me, and I try to communicate that it's fine, that she doesn't need to stay. But she does anyway.

"So, you know how I told you I had a boyfriend?" I ask

Beatrice, warming her up.

"Sure, angel. But I've never seen him around. Is he invisible?" She laughs, then winces.

"Not far off," I say. "He doesn't exist."

"Whatever suits your fancy, doll."

"No," I say, trying again. "What I mean is that there never was a boyfriend. And there won't ever *be* a boyfriend. I'm a lesbian." I turn to May, who gives me an encouraging smile.

After a few seconds, Beatrice grins. "You sent them out of the room for that?" She swats at me playfully. "You think I haven't seen you sneak around with this angel?" She points to May, whose eyes go wide. "Doll, I *adore* lesbians. They've always offered me the best advice about men." I smile and shake my head, feeling relieved. Then Beatrice says to May, "Treat her well," which makes me want to fall into a sinkhole and give Beatrice a huge hug, simultaneously.

May seems startled, but I shrug like, *It's Beatrice, what are you gonna do?*

Then May says, "I will," and I stifle both laughter and tears.

After a few awkward seconds, May opens the door so Lauren, Tasha, and George can come back in. We all move to stand around Beatrice's bed, a grab bag of human existence.

I gaze at everyone, at George and Lauren and Tasha and

Beatrice and May (but mostly May), and a thought pops into my head: I'm no longer dreading going back to school.

It's not like anything's changed with Sadie but . . . I don't know. I like the idea of these people all existing simultaneously, of them being in the world with me. Just knowing they're out there, somewhere, makes me feel better.

"Stop staring at me like I'm dying," Beatrice says to us after a minute. "You can do that when I'm dead!"

She barks with joy, and I try to memorize the sound, to capture it in my head.

And because apparently our favorite activity is gay staring, when I glance over at May, she's looking right back at me.

You're So Gay

It's my second-to-last time waking up in Beatrice's bed. A month ago, this fact would've delighted me, seeing as it's a certified-haunted sex bed. But now I feel a bit nostalgic. I think I've been giving the bed too hard of a time.

I reluctantly get dressed for my last day of lab and head for the Metro. May hasn't texted, but I'm trying not to worry about that. It's been less than a day.

But there's still that terrible part of my brain that's shouting about how something's horribly wrong and the world is on fire and I need to avoid all human connection.

I try to quiet the internal screaming by making one very important stop before my commute.

"Shani!" Luke calls out when I enter The Big Blue Dog.

"Hey, Luke," I say, walking over to the counter. "What's up?"

He looks shocked that I both said his name and asked him a question, but after a moment of awe he says, "Good, good," then adds, "I mean, nothing much. That's what I meant—not that I'm *not* good." A Cheshire-cat smile creeps onto his face. "Actually, I'm amazing, now that you're here."

Aaand there it is.

"So glad to hear it," I say, not wanting to crush his spirit just yet. "Can I get a coffee?"

"You don't want a 'Shani'?" he asks, opening the fridge and pulling out a jar of maraschino cherries.

"No." *Please, for the love of all that is holy, no.* "Thanks, though."

He looks dejected but pours a cup of drip coffee. "On the house," he says. "But you already knew that."

I grab the cup and cradle it in my hands. "I just stopped by because I wanted to let you know that today's gonna be my last day working in DC for a while, so it'll probably be my last time coming in for coffee."

"What?" he asks, and much to my dismay, his eyes go all red and watery.

He turns, grabs a towel, and half-heartedly wipes the nozzle of the espresso machine.

Oh no.

I try to think of something comforting to say, but I figure he probably doesn't want me to draw attention to the fact that he's crying. So as a compromise, I just stand there awkwardly.

"Anything you want," he says after a minute, his eyes still red. "Anything at all. Do you want another drink? I'll make you a second one. Or a Danish? I can get you a Danish, too." He pulls the bottom of his apron up to wipe his eyes, which can't be sanitary.

"No, Luke, it's fine. But thanks so much for all the coffee." And I mean it. It's been good to have him and his bizarre devotion to me as a constant over the past month.

"I didn't think you'd be leaving so soon," he says, fidgeting. "There's something I want to tell you, too."

Fuuuuuuuuck.

"Okay," I say, too cheerily, my voice too high.

"I wanted you to know"—he takes a deep breath—"I actually, um, like you. Like, I have feelings for you in a more-than-friends way." He looks down. "Yeah."

And since my new thing is coming out to every human being I've ever met, I say, "That's really sweet, Luke, but I'm gay."

A beat. Then the tears—a stream of them, dribbling down his face.

"It's okay," I say, trying to comfort him over my sexuality. "If it makes you feel any better, I'm also, like, way too old for you."

"I'll wait," he says, sniffling. "I don't care how old you are."

"But I'm gay," I say again, slightly less comforting this time. "I'm, like, very much a lesbian."

He looks up at me with puppy-dog eyes. "Are you sure?"

I think of all the people I've ever liked.

I think of May.

"Yes," I tell him. "I'm sorry, but yes."

He sucks up all the snot he's produced from crying over me. After a moment, he asks: "But really, do you want a Danish?"

I smile at him. "Sure, Luke. I'll take a Danish."

"Last day," Mandira says when I walk into lab with a belly full of coming-out pastry and get settled at my bench. "How are you feeling?"

"Sad," I tell her truthfully.

Even though I was kind of a shitty employee for most of my internship, I don't want to leave. I still want to prove myself to Dr. Graham, to the fossilized fish, and especially to Mandira. I need to prove that I have what it takes to be a paleoichthyologist.

"Aw," Mandira says. "I'm sad, too." Then she adds, "Though it's certainly been an interesting few weeks. I can't say we've had any other intern who was willing to dig through trash for a fossil."

"I'd do it again."

"Well, let's hope you don't have to."

Dr. Graham emerges from his closet, holding a toothbrush and a fossil in very Dr. Graham-ish fashion.

"It's Shani's last day," Mandira tells him.

"I see." He spins the toothbrush in his hand. "Well, I've enjoyed having you here," he says in a sterile way, but my heart's still warmed by the statement.

"Thanks," I tell him. "I've enjoyed being here."

After that pleasant Dr. Graham interaction, I spend an hour or so cleaning fossilized fish scales and not throwing precious specimens in the garbage.

"Starbucks?" Mandira asks. "My treat."

"Absolutely."

We head out, and as we're walking, she says, "So, I got you a little parting gift." She holds out a paper bag stuffed with blue tissue paper.

"You really didn't have to."

"I know," she says, "but open it anyway."

I peer inside the bag. "Is this . . . ?"

"Take it out," she says.

We're stopped on the sidewalk, and I move over to let haggard tourists by as I pull the gift out of the bag.

It's a teeny-tiny novelty trash can, complete with a shiny red lid and a little foot pedal.

"For old time's sake," Mandira says, and I laugh. "You can put anything other than fossils in there."

"I'll never use it," I say. "I'll just stare at it and think fondly of the lab. Thank you."

"You're very welcome."

We keep walking, and as we get on line at Starbucks she adds, "You know, if you wanted to come back for the summer, we'd love to have you. I spoke to Dr. Graham about it the other day."

I stare at her, incredulous. "Really?"

"Sure," she says. "I believe in you. And you have the passion, even if you get distracted sometimes."

"All the time," I correct her.

"That's not true," she says. "Have a little faith in yourself. The past week or so has been great on that front. You've been putting in the work, and it shows."

My heart pounds. I have to tell her the real reason my work ethic's improved. "So, you know how you said you were proud of how I've been balancing dating and work better?" She nods. Anxiety bubbles up in my chest. Deep breath. Honesty. "It's actually because, well, May and I were sort of broken up." Mandira seems surprised when I say this, but I keep going. "We weren't dating, and that's why I was doing better. It sucks, but that's why."

And to my relief, all Mandira says is, "Are you okay?"

I nod. "Yeah, things are better now. And I really like her but . . . I don't know. I still kind of feel like I shouldn't be dating anyone."

"You should do what feels most comfortable, but if you

want to date her you totally should."

Now it's my turn to look surprised. But before I can ask a follow-up question, we get to the front of the line and she orders coffees for us and a venti hazelnut hot chocolate with whipped cream and strawberry syrup for Dr. Graham.

"Why don't you try bringing her into this part of your life?" Mandira asks as she shakes a packet of sugar and dumps the contents into her coffee. "You can tell her about fish evolution, and then she can tell you about whatever she loves."

"Weather," I say. "She loves weather."

"There you go." She puts the lid back on her coffee and takes a sip. "It's fun to date someone who's a huge nerd if you're also a huge nerd. Like, my girlfriend's a freak for infrastructure. She knows more about the DC sewer system than practically anyone else." Mandira grins. "I love her so much."

We walk outside into the brisk but pleasant winter day, me holding a coffee and a trash can, Mandira holding her coffee and the hot chocolate abomination she ordered for Dr. Graham.

I turn to Mandira and watch as she sips her coffee, effortlessly cool. A person I can't help but aspire to be.

"I also wanted to say that I'm sorry," I tell her after a minute of silence. "For putting all my relationship drama onto you. I just knew that you'd understand." I sigh. "But I know that it was really, really unprofessional."

"Shani, no," she says. "These past few weeks have been so fun, even if we haven't got the *most* work done. And honestly, I feel like *I've* been a little preachy about relationship stuff and—" I try to interject but she stops me and says, "No, I have. But seriously, I've never had someone who felt like a mentee before. There aren't that many aspiring paleoichthyologists, and there are even fewer who are queer. We gotta stick together."

I beam at her. She said I was her mentee. Mandira's my mentor.

And since she's my mentor, I figure I should tell her about what happened at the hospital yesterday, and how May hasn't texted me since.

When I'm done with the story, Mandira looks over at me. "I'm only saying this because I've been there, but there's a slight chance that you *might* be overthinking it." She frowns sympathetically. "Have you thought of maybe—and I know this sounds wild—texting her?"

I snort, but it's a good point. "You think I should?"

"Absolutely."

When we get back to lab, before I sit at the bench, I follow Mandira's advice and send May a text.

ME: do you maybe wanna hang out later?

since i'm leaving tomorrow

Seconds later, an answer:

MAY: definitely

I take a breath, feeling better already.

"I texted her," I tell Mandira, putting my phone away. "Thanks for telling me to do it."

"What's a mentor for?"

I'm walking back to Beatrice's house when Taylor's name pops up on my screen. I answer the FaceTime right away.

"Hey," I say, moving my phone directly beneath my face so I can still see the sidewalk. Only Taylor gets to see me from this angle. It's a best-friend angle.

"WOW AM I LOOKING AT THE FACE OF SOMEONE WHO'S DONE WITH HER INTERNSHIP?"

I smile. "So weird that you could see it on my face."

"I'm very perceptive." Taylor smiles too, and I see that she has her going-out makeup on. It looks good.

"Of course."

"How's Beatrice?"

"Better, I think. She might even be home from the hospital now."

"So glad to hear it," she says. "Is your mom picking you up today?"

“Tomorrow morning,” I tell her as I turn on my flashlight. It’s dark and there are no more Christmas lights to illuminate the sidewalk.

It’s funny how Christmas is a months-long season, but once the calendar flips to January so many people immediately dump anything and everything related to the holiday.

I wouldn’t admit this to anyone, but I sort of miss it. The festivity, the warmth. Maybe it’s not the *worst* season in the entire world. I guess I could transfer all my hatred to Valentine’s Day. Like, why is everything pink and red come January first? Love is *not* in the air!

“I can’t wait to see you for like thirty seconds before you head back up to school.”

“I had you penciled in for a full minute.”

“That’s so good of you.” Taylor snorts, then her face gets slightly more serious as she asks, “Are you ready to go back?”

“I think so.”

“Like, Sadie ready?”

“Honestly? Yeah.”

Taylor raises her eyebrows. “Really?”

I shrug. “I’m scared of running into her but not, like, shit-my-pants scared.”

“I’d be pretty worried if you were shit-your-pants scared.”

“Fair.” I take a breath, and Taylor doesn’t ask any

follow-up questions for a minute. She knows when I need to let my thoughts run wild.

Because, yeah, it's going to suck ass if I end up running into Sadie—which I'm assuming I will—but it won't be the end of the world.

When I left Binghamton a month ago, the thought of going back to school and not being Sadie's girlfriend was the most horrifying thing imaginable, even with what happened.

But now . . . I don't know.

I'm ready to go back and be *Shani*. To be the girl who loves fish a little too much. To make friends, to do college right.

And I'll have May. Not as my entire life but as part of it. Maybe she'll even be an equal part to the fish and Taylor and my mom and new friends and whatever else.

Taylor's face is still there when I'm ready to talk again.

"Are you going out?" I ask her. "Or is the makeup just . . ."

She smiles and pulls the camera out farther, to show a cute jean-jacket/black-dress combo.

"Who with?"

She brings her phone back to her face, then looks down and smiles. "Teddy."

"Oh my god," I say. "So that's, like, a thing?"

She smiles even bigger, confirming that it is, in fact, a thing. "I guess so. He's back in Queens for the rest of winter break and . . . yeah."

"Well," I say, steeling myself, "you look hot."

"Obviously," she says, then adds, "Thanks, Shan."

She knows how hard it was for me to say that, but I'm glad I did.

Because she looks hot! And from here on out, I want to tell her. I want to do a better job of being her friend.

After that, we talk about nothing in particular for a few minutes, and it's unbelievably nice.

"I'll see you tomorrow," I tell her when I get to Beatrice's door.

"Can't wait," she says. "Love you."

I stick my tongue out at her, though I don't know if she can see it through the dark on my side of the screen, so I add, "Love you, too."

When I open the door, there's a commotion. "Beatrice?"

"Doll!"

I head into the living room, and sure enough, there's Beatrice, lounging on the couch. George is sitting in a large cushioned chair, and Lauren's reading a book on the floor, her back propped up against the couch where Beatrice is resting.

"Hey," Tasha says, smiling at me as she comes out of the kitchen with a glass of water. She hands it to Beatrice.

"Hey," I say, smiling back. "How's it going here?" I kneel beside Beatrice. "Are you okay? How are you feeling? When did you get back?" I have a lot of questions, but mostly I'm relieved to see her in her own home and not a hospital bed.

She lifts her tiny arms with their huge skin flaps and superhuman strength and pulls me in for a hug.

"Careful, Mom," George says.

"It's my hip that's hurt, not my arms," she says. "And I'm fine, doll."

George shakes his head and sighs. "Since the three of you are in the same place"—he gestures to me, Lauren, and Tasha—"I have something to say. My mom might not be able to have you girls living with her much longer. She's fragile right now."

Beatrice swings her arm to whack him. "Oh, shut up, doll. Fragile, my ass. I'll take them as long as they'll have me."

She grabs on to my arm, and I put my hand over hers.

"Um, I'm actually leaving tomorrow," I say. "My internship is over."

"Tomorrow? That soon?" She rubs her free hand over the blanket to smooth it out.

"I know, I can't believe it."

"Remind me again how long you've been here, angel? A year?"

I can't tell if she's being serious, so I laugh and say, "A month."

"That's it? It feels like forever."

"It does."

But it also feels like two days. Time is wild.

"Well, no matter," she says. "You'll always have a home here."

I smile with my lips pressed together and wipe away the tears that have somehow formed in my eyes. "Thank you," I say, my voice thick.

"Now go be young," Beatrice says with a wink. "It's only your last night in DC once—but don't do anything I wouldn't do."

"Absolutely."

My plans for tonight are simple: I'm going to see May.

I was *this* close to spending my last night in DC stewing, alone in my bedroom, waiting for her to text. But then I texted first. And she texted back. It's magic, really. Witchcraft.

Before I go, I nudge Lauren's foot, and she glances up from her book. "Thanks," I say. She gives me a questioning look. "For the dog walking job, I mean."

This earns me a smile. "Yeah, that's not what I thought would happen when I asked you to fill in for me." She closes the book. "So, you and Greg's daughter, huh?"

I nod. "Me and Greg's daughter." Then I add, "I know you get weird vibes from her or whatever, but she's really nice once you get to know her, and like—"

"No, no. Yeah, I know. I'm sorry for saying that. I didn't know anything was happening between you two."

"You wouldn't have known."

"I probably could've guessed." I laugh a little, and Lauren says, "But she's been, like, way more chill since I got back from Houston. I think you've been a good influence on her. She smiles now, for starters."

I smile when I hear that. "Yeah?"

"Oh, for sure," she says. "I'm really glad I offered you the job. I offered it to Tasha, too, but apparently she hates dogs—"

"I don't hate dogs," Tasha calls from the kitchen. "I hate being outside in the cold."

"You're from Russia," Lauren calls back.

"Not all Russians like the cold," Tasha says, standing in the doorway now.

It's clearly a conversation they've had before because Tasha shakes her head and grins, and Lauren beams back at her and sticks her tongue out, and then we're all laughing for no real reason, even George, who just moments before tried to kick us out of the house. Though, to be fair, he was protecting his mom.

I'm sure I would do the same.

I go upstairs, pack the red-lidded novelty trash can in my suitcase, grab the gift I got for May after work the other day, then head back down.

I don't even try to sneak out. I wave and say, "bye," to everyone in the living room, like the decent human I'm trying to be.

When I get to May's house, I ring the doorbell, but no one answers, so I text her, heart pounding.

ME: I'm outside

I look into their window, past the still-lit electric menorah.

I see May first. She's sitting at the kitchen table with Greg, and they're both smiling at something. The house is bathed in warm yellow light.

I don't want to bother them by ringing again. I told May I'd pop by but didn't specify a time.

They're eating dinner—soup, maybe, though I can't really tell from here. It feels like more of an intrusion than when I overheard their fight.

I give them another minute, then five, then ten. I don't want to mess up whatever's happening. I bounce in place so that I don't freeze.

And then I ring again.

This time, Raphael barks, and there's movement inside.

When the door opens, it's Greg who answers. "Hello," he says.

"Hi."

He doesn't move out of the doorframe. And then: "You're here to see May, I think?"

I try to hide my surprise. "Yeah."

He nods. "I'll get her."

When the door opens again, it's May, in her pajama bottoms and coat and red beanie.

“Hey,” she says, slightly breathless.

“Hey,” I say back, and I can’t help but smile a tiny bit.

She sits down on the porch steps, and I sit next to her. Close but not touching. Atoms apart.

“So, you and your dad?”

“We’re okay,” she says. “A little better, I think.”

“Good,” I say, staring straight ahead. “Good.”

A beat.

My face gets hot as I ask, “Does he, um—does he know about me?”

She nods slowly and takes her time before she says, “He knows about you, yeah. I told him.”

I can’t help but smile at that.

“Cool.”

“I think so.” She turns to face me. “Okay, why are we being so weird around each other?”

“Well, we haven’t even been on our first date yet,” I say, sticking with our starting-over plan. “Maybe things are supposed to be a little awkward.”

We look down at our feet, left, right, up—anywhere but each other.

And then, before I think better of it: “Can I kiss you?”

“Fuck yes.”

She slides into me, hard, and our hips bump. “Ow,” I say, laughing. She puts a hand on the back of my neck.

I turn toward her, and she turns to me. Our knees knock

and my neck hurts, but it doesn't matter because we're kissing and she's warm and I sink into her and it feels *right.*

"Is this okay?" she asks into my forehead, her thumb rubbing the soft skin where my ear meets my neck.

I nod, and lift my head so that our noses bump.

She pushes me back. "No, really. Is this okay? I want to make sure."

I try to hold in laughter, but it's hard. "Yes. It's so totally okay."

"And you'll let me know when it's not?"

I pull her into me, so that we're facing each other and one of her legs is resting on top of mine. We're almost falling off the stairs, but it's fine. It's *incredible.*

I touch her waist gently with both of my hands. "I'll let you know. I promise."

She nods and kisses my neck and my forehead, and then we're in the most awkward position possible, our limbs fully tangled. I try to figure out how to move, how to disconnect our bodies, but May does it first by removing her leg from my knees. Then she pulls my head down onto her lap.

She rubs the loose curls off my forehead with her hand, and I close my eyes.

"Are you sure you're gonna be okay?" she asks.

I turn so that I'm facing up, looking at her bushy hair silhouetted by the porch lights. "Definitely." I pull her down to me so that I can kiss her. Our noses knock against each other and our mouths almost miss. They don't quite fit from this angle. It's imperfect, but it's not the end of the world. It's not the end of us. "Thanks for checking in."

"Obviously," she says. "But you have to talk to me, too. Okay? Whatever we do, you have to talk to me."

I nod, and we stay there for another minute, her rubbing my forehead, me resting in her lap.

"What's gonna happen?" she asks. "After you leave? When we're back in New York?"

I sit up. "Total honesty, right?"

"Right," she agrees.

"I guess I don't know." Now that I'm not touching May, I hug myself for warmth. "Because I'm trying to do better, to *be* better for the people in my life, and I know that also means you. It means you more than anyone else, probably. And even if we're starting over, you still mean so, so much to me. But I care about you too much to jump into something and then have everything get messed up and I guess I'm worried that I don't even know who I am on my own, but at the same time I want to know who I am with you. I just don't know. I really don't—"

"Shani," May says, which thankfully shuts me up. "It's okay." She pulls me toward her again and I contort myself so that my head's on her shoulder. It feels nice once it's there. "I was just asking because I wanted to know where you're at with all this. Would it help if I tell you how *I'm* feeling?" I nod into her jacket. "Okay. So, I guess what I'm feeling is that I want to wait until you're ready. Not just to have sex"—I cringe at the word, which probably isn't a great sign for my level of readiness—"but for us. For you and me. I know it's not a guarantee, that there will be a you and me, but if and when you're ready . . ."

May trails off, and I sit up to look at her. "What?"

She laughs. "Ithaca and Binghamton are only an hour apart, right?"

I shove her. "You were the one saying that was practically to the moon and back before!"

"Well, I changed my mind."

We sit pressed against each other, facing forward.

After a minute, she says, "So, it's only been a few weeks—"

"Yeah, a pretty fucking eventful few weeks," I say.

"Can you let me finish? I'm trying to tell you something." I snort, but when she looks over at me her face is serious. "It's only been a few weeks, and this is so dumb, and I know we haven't even been on our first date yet"—I grin at her playing along with my starting-over game—"but I think I—what I want to say is that I—"

"May, I love you, too."

Her face breaks into the biggest smile, and then mine does, too, and we're kissing again and her arms are around my neck and my hands are on her waist and I want to live here, on the porch, in this perfect in-between where we don't need to have anything defined, but we know exactly how we feel. Where we've fallen in love after only a month of knowing each other.

We're once again lesbian stereotypes, but they're stereotypes for a reason. I want to live my life being irrationally hopeful. Loving people and fish and cities with my whole heart.

After a few more minutes of kissing, I start to feel the cold, so I stand up and May follows.

She crosses her arms. "You didn't let me finish saying it."

"I knew what you were gonna say."

"That was a bold assumption."

"Was I wrong?"

She bites her lips and rolls her eyes. "No." She leans forward to kiss my nose. "Fuck, you're cold." I laugh, and she does too. "I love you, Shani."

I kiss her nose back, because it's there and it's perfect and I have to. "You're so gay."

She laughs. "Correct."

And we kiss one more time to prove it.

"I have a gift for you," I tell her as I grab it from her porch steps. "Another one, I mean."

"Okay, now it's almost *too* much," she says. "You're basically Santa. Are you gonna go caroling next or . . . ?"

"Yeah," I tell her, pushing the gift into her hands. "I'll sing, 'God Rest Ye Merry Gentlemen,' or some shit."

May takes the gift but doesn't stop looking up at me, mouth tauntingly close to mine. "Let's hear a sample. We could do a little caroling role-play."

I raise my eyebrows and don't even try to hide the way my cheeks flush. "I didn't know you were into that."

"There's a lot of things you don't know about me."

That statement doesn't fill me with the dread it might have a few weeks ago. Instead, I'm just excited to learn more about her. To discover everything about this girl who I already love.

I pull us back down to the steps and nod at the gift, another museum gift shop poster, curled into the same tight tube as the last one. "Open it."

May rolls her eyes but unfurls it. When she does, she stares for a moment, not saying anything.

"It's just that you left the other one in my bed," I start, worried she doesn't like it. "And then we had that fight, and I wanted to get you something different because things are different between us now and—"

Instead of responding, May knocks me over onto the cold wood of the porch and kisses every square inch of my face.

"I love it," she says. "And I love you."

I beam at her, and we both admire the poster. It's a print of a Hockney painting called "Domestic Scene, Los Angeles," and that's exactly what it is. In it, two men are showering together: One is covered by the spray of water from the showerhead, and the other is standing behind him, tenderly rubbing his back.

"Hockney really said 'gay rights,'" May says as she rolls the poster back up and puts the rubber band back on.

"Oh yeah," I add. "He said, 'Gays are freaks for showering together.'"

May laughs and leans into me. "It's true."

I kiss the top of her head, remembering how gently she rubbed my eyes with the washcloth that day. How warm and comfortable it was, even then.

After a minute of porch-cuddling, May nods toward her brightly lit house. "I should probably get back to dinner."

"Yeah." I stand up and brush the dirt off my pants. "Okay."

She starts walking in, but before she does, I say, "Wait, May?" She turns around. "When my mom comes to pick me up tomorrow—do you wanna meet her?"

The next morning, I once again run outside in PJs and sneakers.

"No trouble getting here?" I ask when my mom opens the passenger door to let me into the warm car for a hug.

"I only hit five or ten girls," she says after she lets go. "Fifteen, tops."

"Very funny."

We get out of the car and go inside. Beatrice is staying on the couch until her hip's better, and she's still asleep when my mom and I slip through the front door.

"Should I wake her up so you can say hi?" I whisper to my mom as we stand at the bottom of the stairs.

"No, no, let her sleep," she says. "I'll say hi once we have your stuff in the car."

But right before we get to my room, a voice carries through the house: "Dolls?"

"Well, I guess we're saying hi now," my mom says to me, before she starts back downstairs. "Auntie Bea?"

"Angel!"

So now I'm running downstairs, too, and my mom turns on all the lights and kneels next to the couch to give Beatrice a hug.

"I hope she didn't give you much trouble," my mom says, pointing her thumb back at me.

"That doll?" Beatrice smiles at me and waves me downstairs with her strong, jiggly arms. "She's been a perfect angel." My mom snorts, and I roll my eyes. "We've been taking care of each other, haven't we, doll?"

"We have," I say, sitting on the end of the couch that Beatrice's feet don't quite reach.

Beatrice winks at me.

I wink back.

Then I let my mom and Beatrice catch up for a while as I get dressed and bring my stuff down to the Subaru.

It takes too many trips to move everything, and I'm

shoving the last of my bags into the car when my mom comes outside and asks, "Do you have anything else in your room?"

"I think this is pretty much it," I say as I try and fail to get my giant suitcase into the back seat.

"Put it in the trunk. Here—" She lifts the suitcase over her head and throws it in. It's a feat of superhuman strength that I cannot even begin to comprehend. "So, a quick goodbye to Beatrice and then we hit the road?"

I look down at my feet. "Um, so, there's one more stop I need to make—*we* need to make, actually. If that's okay?"

"Yeah, sure," she says, wiping a bead of suitcase-induced sweat off her forehead. "Where?"

"Just a house down the street." My mom gives me a funny look—which, like, fair—and I remember my whole trying-to-be-honest thing, so I add, "There's a bit more to it than that, but I'll tell you in a minute, okay?"

"Is everything all right?"

"Yup," I say, but my voice cracks. I clear my throat and add, in a lower register, "Yes."

I send May a text, keeping my phone close to my chest.

ME: we're on our way

May texts back immediately:

MAY: hell yeah

I smile down at my phone, and we start walking, though I stay a few steps ahead of my mom.

Oh boy.

This is happening.

Deep breaths, Shani.

(Deep breaths are not happening.)

I stop abruptly and turn around, and my mom almost trips over me.

"Sorry!"

She looks slightly annoyed. "What's going on, Shani?"

"So, um . . . ," I start. I'm not sure how to finish the thought, but I'm determined to do it all the same. "You know that girl who we, uh, kind of hit with the car when you dropped me off?"

"Oh boy, do I," she says. "I haven't stopped thinking about her."

Same.

I guess that makes it a bit easier. At least May's been taking up space in my mom's brain too. *Definitely* not in the same way. But still.

"So, I'm kind of . . . dating her?"

My mom's eyes go wide, then she laughs and hugs me, though for what I don't know. "How on earth did that happen?"

I'm so relieved that it's a physical feeling. Even though I already came out to my mom, I didn't know how she'd handle this.

"I walked her dad's dog," I explain, then I tell her about the portrait gallery, about getting snowed in, about exploring the museums together.

"That's really sweet, Shan."

We've been standing in the spot where I stopped short, but now I wish we were walking so she couldn't see the tears dripping down my cheeks. I reach the heel of my hand up and rub my face, hard.

"Are we going there so you can say goodbye?" my mom asks.

"No," I say. "Well, yeah. But we're mostly going so you can meet her. I want you to meet her."

And without missing a beat, my mom smiles and asks, "So, what's her name?"

"It's May."

A beat this time. "Jewish?"

"Mom." I roll my eyes. "Yes. Not that it matters."

"No, you're right, it doesn't. I just wanted to know. You had a great-aunt May, you know."

"Mom, stop."

I turn around and walk ahead of her again, rolling my eyes one more time for good measure. But then I smile, too. Because this type of fighting doesn't feel raw and potent like the fights we were getting into at the start of break. It feels like the kind of argument anyone might have with their Jewish mother.

When we get to May's house, I feel nervous in a different way than yesterday. My mom doesn't say anything, but she's waiting expectantly by the door.

Even though it's way too early, I ring the bell. May told me Greg would be at the station, anyway.

The door opens a crack, and a corgi-shaped missile comes scampering onto the porch.

"Who's this little guy?" my mom asks, bending to pet Raphael, who's bouncing with excitement.

"That's Raphael," I tell her.

I look up, and there's May, leaning against the doorframe, shaking her head, and stifling a laugh.

"Mom," I say, and she turns away from Raphael. I nod toward May.

"Sorry, sorry," my mom says to me. She stands up and brushes herself off.

I grab Loaf Boy and tuck him under my arm so that he doesn't run away. "Mom, May," I say. "May, Mom."

May gives a little wave, and my mom smiles and says, "*Hi, May,*" with wiggly eyebrows and a *meaningful* look in my direction.

I put my head in my hands. "Oh my god, Mom."

"Can I just say?" My mom turns to May as I lift my head. "I'm so, so sorry about the whole car thing. Are you all right?"

May laughs. "I'm fine, yeah. No lasting damage."

"Well, that's a relief!"

"Do you want to come in?" May asks as she opens the door the rest of the way.

Raphael squirms out of my hands, so I set him down, and all four of us head into the warm house.

May brings us to the kitchen, where the TV is showing Greg on the morning news.

"Thank goodness it'll be sunny today," my mom says, looking at the five-day forecast. "I can't handle another drive in the snow."

I point at the TV, to Greg. "That's May's dad."

My mom pulls her reading glasses out from her jacket pocket and moves closer to the small TV. "Very nice," she says, nodding approvingly.

After that, it's slightly awkward, but Raphael runs between us begging for pats, which helps break the ice. My mom asks May about where she goes to school and what she's thinking about majoring in (atmospheric science, of course). It's stilted and a little cringey, but it feels wonderfully normal.

During a lull in the conversation, Raphael somehow jumps from the kitchen floor directly onto my mom's lap. I'm not sure how the front part of his body sends messages to the back, but it does, and he plops his heavy body onto her. She pets him, and I know she'll be distracted for a while.

I kick May's leg under the table and say to my mom, "We'll be back down in a few minutes, okay?"

My mom nods. "Sounds good." She scratches between Raphael's shoulder blades. "Take your time."

May and I run upstairs, and when we get to her room, she shuts the door and we're just standing there for a moment. Then I close the space between us and rest my forehead on her shoulder and she pulls me in. I wrap myself around her and we hug for a long, long time.

And then everything from the past four weeks—all the dates we went on, the mistakes I've made, the fights we've had, all of it—comes up and out and my throat feels tight and I'm crying—sobbing, really—and making choked, ugly sounds.

All I can think to say is, "I'm gonna miss you."

May hugs me tighter, sniffling. "I'm gonna miss you, too. So, so much." She leads me to the edge of her bed, and we sit down. She leans her head on my shoulder, and I wrap my arm around her waist. "But I'm just in Ithaca. We'll see each other. And you can visit me whenever you want. Any time, really."

I smile weakly. "And you could always come to Binghamton."

"Ew, why, never." She grins, and I hit her arm. Then she adds, "Kidding. Super kidding. Of course, I'll come to Binghamton. Whenever you'll have me."

I nod. I needed to hear her say that. Because I know that, during this coming semester, I'll have a life outside of the girl I'm with, outside of May.

But I'm so glad she'll be in it.

"I don't wanna leave," I say, wrapping myself around her again. We fall back onto her bed.

"Well, this isn't goodbye. It's 'I'll run you over with my car again later.'"

I push her away, laughing, then bury my face into the comforter. "Stop, oh my god."

She lifts my chin. "Never."

We kiss, and I flatten myself against her, breathe her in.

And even though I could stay here and kiss and talk and cuddle and simply exist with May forever, I know we can't leave my mom downstairs with Raphael for too long.

"One more minute," May says, pulling me down when I try to sit up.

We press our foreheads together, and I close my eyes. I rub my thumb over her waist, and she strokes the back of my neck. One minute turns to two turns to three, and once again it feels like the Earth was created just for us.

"All right," May says finally, jumping off the bed. "Up and at 'em." She reaches out her hand.

With no hesitation, I grab it.

When we get downstairs, Raphael's napping in my mom's lap, and she's looking at something on her phone, reading glasses perched precariously at the end of her nose.

She takes the glasses off when May and I walk into the

kitchen. "Ready to go, Shan?"

"Let me just say goodbye to Raphael." I kneel next to my mom and tap the pup between his ears to wake him up. He yawns and stretches his tiny corgi legs, and I smile and give him a scratch under his chin.

He jumps off my mom's lap and I pick up my long baby and hold him out in front of me as I kiss him on the top of his head. "Bye, Raph," I say.

Raphael pants in response. I tuck him under my arm.

To my surprise, May comes over and kisses Raphael, too. Then she immediately wipes her mouth.

"Ew." She makes a face. "It's weird that people kiss dogs, right?" But she keeps her hand on his head, petting him and not recoiling. He leans into her touch.

And even though my mom is standing right there, I half answer May's question by kissing her. It's just a peck, but I know she knows what I mean.

She whispers in my ear, "I love you, Shani."

My face gets hot, and I can tell my mom is purposefully staring at her phone to give us privacy.

I whisper back, "I love you, May."

And Raphael howls to seal the deal.

"She seems like a sweet girl," my mom says as we head back toward Queens on the highway at a speed that seems to be pissing off every other driver on the road. But inside the car, things are good. Great, even.

Right before we left, Beatrice had said the same thing about May (though she called her an angel). "And don't forget what I said about the Staten Island ferry," Beatrice had said. "It's the most romantic place in the entire state of New York. No beau required." She barked, and I hugged her as hard as I could without jostling her hip.

"She is," I tell my mom, because it's true, even though *sweet* isn't the first word that comes to mind.

Maybe brave, or beautiful, or stubborn. She's more headstrong than an ox.

And I love her so fucking much.

On the car ride down to DC, it felt like everything in my life was irrevocably damaged: my passion for fish, my dating life, my relationship with my mom.

But now, somehow, it's not.

My mom and I talk about my class schedule for next semester—lots of bio, a bit of geology, and maybe a karate class for my physical activity requirement. I figure it can't hurt to punch and kick and scream for an hour or two every week.

Then my mind wanders, and I think about the juvenile coelacanths that Mandira and Dr. Graham found. They were buried, dormant, stuck underground for millions of years, only to be fondled and admired by the likes of me.

Maybe it's okay not to know exactly what I want. To feel lost. Maybe I still have a million years to go before I'm unearthed. But I know that someday I will be, and it'll be a breakthrough. A miracle.

"Can I say something?" my mom asks.

"You already did."

"Ha ha." She glances over at me, smiling, and she veers so far into another lane that she just stays there. "I'm sad you weren't with me for the holidays—"

"Jeez, Mom, I know."

"Let me finish." She takes a breath. "I'm sad you weren't with me for the holidays, *but* I'm glad you did this internship. I think it was good for you to get away." She looks at me again, not for quite as long, but long enough for a Prius to honk at us. "And I'm proud of you for doing it."

"Thanks," I say. "I'm glad I did it, too."

We drive in a comfortable silence for a while. The road clears, and the Subaru takes us home.

"And you're welcome," she says, looking over at me, eyebrows raised, "for hitting May with the car."

Acknowledgments

It's not an exaggeration to say that I've been thinking about these acknowledgments for years. When I was writing this book, lonely and heartbroken on a weeks-long train journey, I imagined what spiteful words I would write to the person who broke my heart.

Now that seems irrelevant. My life is filled with joy and love, and, even though I began writing this story as a wounded kid fresh out of college, I'm somehow barreling toward my mid-twenties living an entirely different life. (I know, I know.)

I'm typing this in a sunny apartment that I share with my cat, who is sleeping soundly next to me; with my girlfriend, who cooks elaborate meals and reminds me how much she loves me; with art lining the walls drawn by friends who are my family.

I wanted to start these acknowledgments with spite, but not anymore.

All I want to do now is wrap my arms around the version of myself who wrote this book. If you feel any piece of what I felt, of what Shani's feeling in this book, know that one day it will pass. It might take months or years or longer, but something bright and wonderful will take its place.

Now onto the actual thank-yous.

First, to my editor, Stephanie Guerdan. I cannot imagine what the process of revising this book would've been like without you, and I'm grateful for the notes and the memes. And to the HarperCollins union! Everyone go follow them on IG—Harper is the only unionized Big Four publisher (wild!).

To my agent, Jim McCarthy—by the time this book comes out, we will have been working together for three years, which seems unreal (time? I don't know her). Thank you for suggesting that I add more corgi to the book; you always know just what to say.

To Natalie Shaw, who captured Shani and May even better than I could've imagined. The sapphic yearning on this sweet, sweet cover is unparalleled.

To everyone at HarperTeen—Chris Kwon, Shannon Cox, Sean Cavanaugh, Jon Howard, Robin Roy, Rosanne Lauer, Lauren Levite. Thank you for supporting my book behind the scenes. I hope you know how much your work means to me. And thank you for being so diligent about corgi size.

Why do I feel like I'm already being played off at the Oscars? No, this speech is not stopping any time soon. Okay, here we go.

To my eternal alpha reader, my lab adviser, empathy adviser, Russian adviser, and Capricorn adviser (I've kept a note of all your titles since 2019), Lena Kogan. Thank you for letting me sleep on your dorm floor, cry while you made me matzah brei, and for literally everything. This book has always been for you.

To my mom, sorry I sort of came out to you on a car ride home from a comedy podcast taping. Not my best work. I love you to the moon and back.

To the people who read the book while it was an ever-changing Google doc that I would send to you at frantic hours of the night: Louisa, Zareen, Gruber, Sal, Sabrina, Lylia, Lena (I think that's all of you? I'm literally just looking at the sharing permissions on the doc, but if I forgot you, I'm sorry). Thanks for reading my words when they were just summaries of scientific papers about coelacanths.

Thank you to Sally for listening to me read this book aloud more times than I can count, and for always picking up the phone. Sorry for all the times I've had to end our calls abruptly to poop.

To my writer pals who make being in this industry much more fun: Camryn Garrett, Helena Greer, Christina Li, Racquel Marie (could never forget that *c*), Emma Ohland, Angela Velez, and Joelle Wellington.

Thank you to the early readers who said such nice things and do such incredible work to make this industry better for everyone: Dahlia Adler, Aashna Avachat, Jennifer Dugan, Gabby Noone, Becca Podos, Kelly Quindlen, Rachel Lynn Solomon, and Misa Sugiura. Thank you also to Olympic medalist Erica Sullivan for blurbing my book. I'm still reeling!!

Thank you to the members of the Women Want Me, Fish Fear Me team for your support and chaos on the Discord!! I'm honored that you and so many people supported this book before you even read it.

I've kept a list of people to thank in my acknowledgments for two years, so we're still going. Let's do this rapid-fire: to Youtuber Mike's Mic for "It's Christmas, Let's Go Home," to MUNA for the song "Winterbreak," to David Hockney for color and light, to Politics and Prose (congrats on being DC's first unionized bookstore!!!) for being the inspiration for the bookstore in this book, to Sophia for being my teen on the ground/allowing me to borrow your corgi. To Laura, who I found on Craigslist and who inspired so much of Beatrice. Thank you for letting me sleep in your primary bedroom and for trying to feed me 30-year-old freezer-burned cheesecake.

To Dr. Josh Drew for teaching me about fish. And to Dr. Paul Hertz for teaching me evolutionary biology and hiring me to be your TA even though I killed all my brassica. I hope you're enjoying your retirement—you made more of an impact on me than you could know.

Thank you also to my coworkers at QABC for your support. Being an indie bookseller in addition to being an author has given me so much perspective and joy. Thank you especially to Torrin and Kaye for reading the book early, and for Tegan for everything you do for kid lit.

Thank you to Mateo for the ferry ride where you reminded me about Michelle Obama taking away our vending machines. Gracias a Monica y Victor por hacerme sentir bienvenida.

Finally, thank you to all the people who let me stay with them while I wrote this book.

First of all, my Grandma Phyl and Don. Those two weeks I spent with you writing and doing the crossword and going to see *Little Women* are two of my favorite weeks to look back on. I love you.

To Zaidie, thank you for the vegan food and the endless support. Thank you for giving me forecasts about the publishing industry.

To Sabrina, for the pomodoros and the commiseration and the amazing notes.

To Lousia, stream "LA Winter."

To Deb, thanks for letting me read your graphic novels (the ones you own and the one you wrote).

To Vy, for your hot water bottle and your endless kindness.

And to Daniela, where it all began, where I finally

understood the emotion that Shani would feel while she was sleeping in someone's house in a different room when all she wants to do is hold them close—I'm glad I get to do that now. Love you more than words, love our little guy, love our life.

(Thank you, Flan!! I love you, my son!!!!!! It's past your bedtime! Go to sleep!!!!)

Finally: this book was written on the unceded ancestral lands of the Duwamish people. If you live on these lands, I would encourage you to pay Real Rent, which calls on people who live in Seattle to make rent payments to the Duwamish tribe. Additionally, the Duwamish tribe is currently fighting for recognition and the Treaty rights that go with that. You can sign their petition at standwiththeduwamish.org.